John Dickson Carr and The Murder Room

>>> This title is part of The Murder Room, our series dedicated to making available out-of-print or hard-to-find titles by classic crime writers.

Crime fiction has always held up a mirror to society. The Victorians were fascinated by sensational murder and the emerging science of detection; now we are obsessed with the forensic detail of violent death. And no other genre has so captivated and enthralled readers.

Vast troves of classic crime writing have for a long time been unavailable to all but the most dedicated frequenters of second-hand bookshops. The advent of digital publishing means that we are now able to bring you the backlists of a huge range of titles by classic and contemporary crime writers, some of which have been out of print for decades.

From the genteel amateur private eyes of the Golden Age and the femmes fatales of pulp fiction, to the morally ambiguous hard-boiled detectives of mid twentieth-century America and their descendants who walk our twenty-first century streets, The Murder Room has it all. >>>

The Murder Room
Where Criminal Minds Meet

themurderroom.com

T0371398

John Dickson Carr (1906–1977)

John Dickson Carr, the master of the locked-room mystery, was born in Uniontown, Pennsylvania, the son of a US Congressman. He studied law in Paris before settling in England where he married an Englishwoman, and he spent most of his writing career living in Great Britain. Widely regarded as one of the greatest Golden Age mystery writers, his work featured apparently impossible crimes often with seemingly supernatural elements. He modelled his affable and eccentric series detective Gideon Fell on G. K. Chesterton, and wrote a number of novels and short stories, including his series featuring Henry Merrivale, under the pseudonym Carter Dickson. He was one of only two Americans admitted to the British Detection club, and was highly praised by other mystery writers. Dorothy L. Sayers said of him that 'he can create atmosphere with an adjective, alarm with allusion, or delight with a rollicking absurdity'. In 1950 he was awarded the first of two prestigious Edgar Awards by the Mystery Writers of America, and was presented with their Grand Master Award in 1963. He died in Greenville, South Carolina in 1977.

(Titles in bold are published in The Murder Room)

Poison in Jest (1932)
The Burning Court (1937)
The Emperor's Snuff Box (1942)
The Nine Wrong Answers (1952)
Patrick Butler for the Defense (1956)
Most Secret (1964)

Henri Bencolin

It Walks by Night (1930)
Castle Skull (1931)
The Lost Gallows (1931)
The Waxworks Murder (1932) *aka* The Corpse in the
    Waxworks
The Four False Weapons, Being the Return of Bencolin (1938)

Dr Gideon Fell

Hag's Nook (1933)
The Mad Hatter Mystery (1933)
The Blind Barber (1934)
The Eight of Swords (1934)
Death-Watch (1934)
The Hollow Man (1935) *aka* The Three Coffins
The Arabian Nights Murder (1936)
To Wake the Dead (1938)
The Crooked Hinge (1938)
The Problem of the Green Capsule (1939) *aka* The Black
    Spectacles
The Problem of the Wire Cage (1939)
The Man Who Could Not Shudder (1940)
The Case of the Constant Suicides (1941)
Death Turns the Tables (1941) *aka* The Seat of the
    Scornful (1942)
Till Death Do Us Part (1944)
He Who Whispers (1946)

The Sleeping Sphinx (1947)
Below Suspicion (1949)
The Dead Man's Knock (1958)
In Spite of Thunder (1960)
The House at Satan's Elbow (1965)
Panic in Box C (1966)
Dark of the Moon (1968)

Historical mysteries

The Bride of Newgate (1950)
The Devil in Velvet (1951)
Captain Cut-Throat (1955)
Fire, Burn! (1957)
Scandal at High Chimneys: A Victorian Melodrama (1959)
The Witch of the Low Tide: An Edwardian Melodrama (1961)
The Demoniacs (1962)
Papa La-Bas (1968)
The Ghosts' High Noon (1970)
Deadly Hall (1971)
The Hungry Goblin: A Victorian Detective Novel (1972)

Short story collections

Dr Fell, Detective, and Other Stories (1947)
The Third Bullet and Other Stories of Detection (1954)
The Exploits of Sherlock Holmes (with Adrian Conan
     Doyle) (1954)
The Men Who Explained Miracles (1963)

The Door to Doom and Other Detections (1980) (includes
    radio plays)
The Dead Sleep Lightly (1983) (radio plays)
Fell and Foul Play (1991)
Merrivale, March and Murder (1991)

Writing as Carter Dickson

The Bowstring Murders (1934)
Drop to His Death (with John Rhode) (1939) *aka* Fatal
    Descent

Sir Henry Merrivale

The Plague Court Murders (1934)
The White Priory Murders (1934)
The Red Widow Murders (1935)
The Unicorn Murders (1935)
The Punch and Judy Murders (1936) *aka* The Magic
    Lantern Murders
The Ten Teacups (1937) *aka* The Peacock Feather Murders
The Judas Window (1938) *aka* The Crossbow Murder
Death in Five Boxes (1938)
The Reader is Warned (1939)
And So To Murder (1940)
Murder in the Submarine Zone (1940) *aka* Nine – and Death
    Makes Ten, also published as Murder in the Atlantic
Seeing is Believing (1941) *aka* Cross of Murder
The Gilded Man (1942) *aka* Death and the Gilded Man

She Died a Lady (1943)

He Wouldn't Kill Patience (1944)

The Curse of the Bronze Lamp (1945) *aka* Lord of the
    Sorcerers (1946)

My Late Wives (1946)

The Skeleton in the Clock (1948)

A Graveyard to Let (1949)

Night at the Mocking Window (1950)

Behind the Crimson Blind (1952)

The Cavalier's Cup (1953)

Historical mystery

Fear is the Same (1956)

Short story collections

The Department of Queer Complaints (1940)

The Man Who Could
Not Shudder

John Dickson Carr

An Orion book

Copyright © John Dickson Carr 1940, 1967

The right of John Dickson Carr to be identified as the author of this
work has been asserted in accordance with the Copyright, Designs and
Patents Act 1988.

This edition published by
The Orion Publishing Group Ltd
Orion House
5 Upper St Martin's Lane
London WC2H 9EA

An Hachette UK company
A CIP catalogue record for this book is available from the British Library

ISBN 978 1 4719 0521 6

www.orionbooks.co.uk

I

"A haunted house?" said the art critic.

"Yes, and very badly haunted," said a voice we could not identify.

"How do you know?"

"I don't know," retorted the editor of the *Fleet Street Magazine*. "All I know is that it's on the market. Here it is advertised in the *Times*."

"But does it say it's haunted?" persisted the art critic, who is a Scot and cautious.

"Not in the advertisement, dammit. It's under 'Essex.' It says, 'Longwood, picturesque Jacobean manor house, thoroughly modernized in 1920. Company's electricity, gas, and water. Main drainage. Lounge hall, 4 rec., 8 bed. (h. & c.), 2 bath., modern off., etc.' Do you think that if they had a ghost they'd put in, 'gho., guaranteed to haun.?' "

"Where is the place?"

" 'Thirty-five miles from London, four miles from

Southend-on-Sea.' "

"Southend. Oi " said the actor.

"What's the matter with Southend?" truculently demanded a novelist, who keeps a cabin cruiser there. "Finest air in the world at Southend. Finest—"

"Yes, I know. Ozone. Awful stuff. And it's got the longest pier in the world, as you were about to say."

This conversation took place round the bar at the Congo Club, in a crush so great that you could not move your elbow without spilling somebody's drink. It took place on the afternoon of Saturday, March 13th, 1937, among a group of people whose names (with one exception) you need not bother to remember, because they do not appear in the rest of the story.

But the exception is notable.

Near the bar hatch opening into the lounge, there is a big white-marble mantelpiece with a mirror behind it. I have a very vivid memory of Martin Clarke leaning his elbow on this mantelpiece, a pewter tankard in his hand, and pricking up his ears like a dog. The fire crackled and popped just behind his legs, and must have been uncomfortably hot; but he did not move.

Under Clarke's thin white hair, flat-brushed and brittle looking, the pink scalp was beginning to show. But the rest of his face was of a deep, ingrained tan which no English winter could rub out. It showed up his light eyes, extraordinary eyes. Though he must have been over sixty at this time, his face was as mobile as a boy's. The wrinkles round eyes and mouth were amusement wrinkles or curiosity wrin-

2

kles, if they can be called that. He jumped at the very mention of a haunted house. In the mirror behind him you could see the back of his scalp stir. But he was too polite to butt into the conversation at a club where he was a stranger.

We very nearly drifted away from the subject, at that. The conversation began to degenerate into a violent argument about Southend. The source of the actor's grouse against that town, it appeared, was that he had once gone to an amusement fair there, and somebody sold him oysters at four for sixpence, and they disagreed with him.

"Anyway," said the art critic, "I don't believe it."

"You don't believe it?" said the actor. "You come with me and I can show you the stall where I bought 'em. Vile things. Tasted of iodine. They—"

"I wasn't talking about oysters," said the art critic. "Confound your oysters. I was talking about ghosts. Who says this house is haunted."

"*I* say so," declared the voice we had been trying to identify.

Hoots of derision went out in ripples and spilled drinks on the edge of the crowd. This was because of the speaker. He was a young man, with a traditionally solemn face, who writes humorous articles. But he appeared to be serious.

"All right, you bourgeois," snapped the young man, waving a pink gin at us. "Go on. Laugh. But it's true. Longwood House is known to have been very badly haunted for several hundred years."

"How do you know that? From personal experience?"

"No, but—"

"There; you see?" interrupted the art critic, with triumph. "It's always the same. Everybody has heard of a haunted house, until you try to pin 'em down. It's like the Indian ropetrick."

"I suppose you'll deny," said the youngster hotly, "that a man was killed there as late as 1920?"

This looked more like business.

"Killed? You mean murdered?"

"I don't know whether he was murdered. I don't know what did happen to him. All I know is that it was the most mysterious business I ever heard of, and if you can find a reasonable explanation of it you'll do better than the police have been able to do for seventeen years."

"What happened?"

Our informant seemed gratified at the interest he had aroused.

"I don't remember the name of the fellow who died," he went on, "but he was a butler. An old man of over eighty. A chandelier fell on him."

"Stop a bit," muttered the editor, peering at his newspaper. "I think I do remember something about it, at that."

"Ah!"

"No, go on: what happened?"

Somebody bought our informant another pink gin, and he drank it earnestly.

"In 1920," he said, "one of the last surviving members of the Longwood family decided to open up the house again. It had been vacant for lord knows how many years, after some nasty business that had

4

driven the family out once before."

"What business?"

"I don't know," said our informant, beginning to feel badgered and to make gestures. "I'm telling you what happened in 1920. The house was in a pretty bad state of repair, so the owner had it modernized and moved in.

"The source of all the disturbance (I can tell you this, straight from the horse's mouth) was in one of two rooms. One was the dining-room, and the other was a room on the ground floor that the owner used as a study. Now, the dining-room has got a ceiling fifteen feet high. There's a heavy oak beam down the middle of the ceiling, and from this beam hangs (or used to hang) the main chandelier. It was one of the old-fashioned kind that they stuck candles into, and weighed a ton. It was supported by six chains hung from a central hook screwed into the oak beam. Is that clear?"

He was beginning to enjoy himself, seeing that he had caught our attention.

"Hold on," interrupted a black-and-white artist with a nasty suspicious mind. "How do you happen to know all this?"

"Ah!" said our informant, holding up his glass mysteriously. "Now listen, and drink it in. One night—I don't remember the exact date, but you can look it up in the newspaper files—the butler was going round to lock up the house. It was about eleven o'clock. This butler, as I say, was a frail old man of over eighty. The family were all upstairs, getting ready to go to bed. And they heard a scream."

"I knew they would," said the novelist gloomily.
"Don't you believe me?"

"Never mind; go on."

"They also heard a crash that rattled their teeth,
and sounded as though the house were falling. They
ran downstairs to the dining-room. The hook sup-
porting the chandelier had been torn loose from the
oak beam. The chandelier had fallen on this servant,
crushing his head and killing him instantly. They
found him under the wreckage, together with a chair
on which he had been standing."

"Standing on a chair?" interposed the editor.
"Why?"

"Wait! — Now," continued our informant, pale with
earnestness, "look at what happened. The chandelier
couldn't have fallen by itself. A builder testified that
it had been there for a good many years, but that it
was still solid. And, if you're thinking of murder,
nobody could have *made* it fall. That's to say, there
was no possibility of jiggery-pokery by which somebody could have made it fall from upstairs or anywhere else. It was simply on a big hook set in a solid
beam, where nobody could tamper with it. There was
only one thing that could have happened, and the
evidence proved it did happen.

"The butler's fingerprints — both hands — were
found on the lower part of the chandelier. Now, he
was tall. But, if he stood on a chair under it, and
stretched up his hands, his fingers still would not
reach within three or four inches of the chandelier.

"What he must have done was this. He must have
climbed on the chair, and then jumped up into the air

6

and caught the lower part of the chandelier. Then (this can't be doubted, from the condition of the hole in the beam) he must have swung energetically back and forth, like a man on a trapeze, until his weight pulled the whole thing out of the ceiling, and . . ."

"*Wow!*" said the art critic.

Such a yell of laughter went up from beside the bar that even men in far corners of the lounge turned round to look.

It was not alone the intense seriousness of our informant's face. But the picture of a frail old man of over eighty, swinging joyously back and forth on the chandelier like Donald Duck, was not one which could be considered without emotion of some kind.

Our informant changed color.

"Don't you believe me?" he demanded.

"No," we said as one man.

"Then why don't you look it up? Go on—I dare you! Look it up!"

The editor called for silence.

"But look here, old man," he protested, in the kindly and consoling tone you might employ toward the feeble-minded. "Was this butler potty?"

"No."

"Then why should he have done anything like that?"

"Ah!" said our informant, finishing his drink with a richly sinister air, and whacking down the glass on the bar counter. "That's the whole problem, if anybody here would do me the courtesy of considering it. There you are. That's what he did. But *why* did he do it?"

This sobered us somewhat. But it cannot be denied that we were all getting a trifle excited.

"Nuts," said the art critic.

"It's not nuts. It's gospel truth. The condition of the wood in the hole from which that hook had been torn (the coroner admitted this at the inquest) proved conclusively that the butler must have swung back and forth on it before it fell."

"But why?"

"That's what I'm asking you."

"And anyway," the novelist pointed out, "That's got nothing to do with the argument. Where's your ghost? It doesn't prove a house is haunted just because an aged retainer jumps up and starts swinging on the chandelier, does it?"

Our informant drew himself up.

"I happen to know," he declared, emphasizing the last word, "that the house is haunted. I know somebody who spent several nights there, and saw for himself."

"Who?"

"My father."

There was an awkward silence, after which somebody coughed. You cannot, in decency, come out flat and tell a fellow that his old man is a liar.

"Your father saw a ghost at Longwood House?"

"No. But a chair jumped at him."

"What?"

"A damned great wooden chair," cried our informant, thrusting out two thin-veined hands as though to show the dimensions of something, "of the kind they used to have in the old days. It jumped at him."

Seeing the skepticism in the faces round about, his voice grew shrill. "I know it's true, I tell you. He told me so himself. I suppose you think that's funny too? What would you do if a damned great wooden chair came right off the wall and jumped at you?"

"Stand and defend myself to the death," said the black-and-white artist. "Or look for the strings that were tied to the chair," he added. "Yoicks! Let me out of here. I've had enough."

"There weren't any strings tied to it," our informant bawled after him. "The light was on. My father—"

"Sh-h, now! Take it easy. What's yours?"

"Pink gin. But—"

The talk, dexterously steered, rounded the dangerous corner of Longwood House. And presently we went in to lunch.

Throughout this debate my guest, Martin Clarke, said not a word. He remained by the fire, for the most part looking reflectively into his pewter tankard, and swirling round its contents. He did not meet my eye, I suspect, because a friendly question would have made him explode into speech; and he would have been delivering an excited monologue for the rest of the afternoon.

For myself, the effect of the young humorist's story remained and rankled as something vaguely unpleasant. Perhaps I had taken the wrong sherry before lunch. I don't know. But, when you came to consider it, the suggestion underlying that tale of the agile butler was anything but comic. The narrator (I say this with all due respect to him) has a funny face; and we laughed less because of the story itself than because it came from him.

Assuming that our legs were not being pulled, and assuming he had got the facts right, it wasn't funny at all. An old man of eighty loses his head, and jumps up to catch at a chandelier – why? Because something is after him?

Clarke did not refer to the matter until we were leaving the club. Throughout lunch he was silent, though he chuckled several times, and once he lifted another pewter tankard to pledge my health. We were going down the steps, into a bright windy March day which tossed the trees in Carlton House Terrace, when he spoke.

"Do you know the name of a good architect?" he said.

Now, one of my best pals is a good but impoverished young architect. I recommended him with enthusiasm. Clarke got out a little pocketbook and wrote down the name.

"Andrew Hunter, New Stone Buildings, Chancery Lane. Ah, yes." At mention of the street, he brightened. "Well, if my investigations are satisfactory, I shall call on Mr. Hunter soon."

"Are you thinking of building a house?"

Clarke replaced the pocketbook, folded his silk scarf neatly into the opening of his overcoat, settled his neat bowler hat more firmly, and struggled along head down against the wind.

"I am thinking of buying one," he smiled. "But after all, Mr. Morrison, I am a business man. I do not buy pigs in pokes. Much as I am interested in ghosts, I am still more interested in making sure that the roof does not leak and that the drains are in order. They will doubtless ask a stiff price, so I must be prepared. Admirable! Admirable! Admirable!"

A fortnight later he bought Longwood House. But there, dimly shadowed, as Tess said afterwards, was the beginning of the terror.

II

I was having tea with Tess when Clarke came in to tell us the news.

Tess (who has since, I am bursting with pride to say, become my wife) was sitting by the fire in the living-room at my flat. The warmth of the fire was grateful: April had come in treacherously, with squalls of rain.

At this time Tess was a buyer for a fashionable dress shop. Despite the murky weather, she kept that look of sleekness and trimness which came as much from a sleekness and trimness of body as from the effect of her clothes. Her hands were clasped round her knees as she sat on the edge of the deep chair by the tea table. The firelight tinted her face, showing the worried gleam of hazel eyes under honest un-plucked brows, and putting a sheen on her rich black hair.

"This new friend of yours," she said. "This Mr.

Clarke."

"He's not exactly a friend of mine. He's a friend of Johnny Vanderver. Johnny wrote and asked me to look after him when he came to London —"

Tess threw back her head and laughed.

"Bob," she said, "you are the most horribly conscientious man I know. Why do you put yourself out for all these people?"

"Clarke's an interesting chap."

Tess nodded, stirred her shoulders, and looked sideways at the fire. Her face, never quite sure of itself despite her practicality and straightforwardness, grew clouded.

"I know he is," she admitted. "He's very nice. I like him tremendously. Only —"

"Only what?"

She looked me in the eyes.

"Bob, I don't think I trust him. He's up to some kind of game."

"Clarke?"

"Clarke."

"Look here!" I said; and, in that snug afternoon, I felt unwarrantably stirred up. "You mean you think he's some kind of crook?"

"No, not that, exactly. I mean, I don't believe he's a confidence man who'd try to sell you fake gold shares, or anything like that. Only . . . oh, I may be all wrong! I probably am."

"I think you are."

"But what do you know about him, Bob? Who is he?"

"So far as I can gather, he's a Yorkshireman who

13

has spent most of his life in southern Italy. He had some sort of business there; he prospered and prospered, and finally he decided to retire to England for good. He's got about twenty hobbies, and an insatiable curiosity about life in general. At the moment he's 'doing' London with a thoroughness beyond any guide book. In particular—"

"Yes," said Tess. "Museums."

I could agree with this in some detail, for I was beginning to feel something of an authority on museums. Clarke missed nothing, but his particular enthusiasm was museums. The man was nuts on museums. Not only for big show places like the Victoria and Albert, or the Royal United Service, but also for exhibitions I had never even heard of before. Even if you know the byways of the town, do you know the London Museum in St. James's? Or the Guildhall Museum? Or the Soane Museum in Lincoln's Inn Fields? Or the Dickens Museum in Doughty Street? Or the manuscript museum of the Public Records Office in Chancery Lane?

In these places Clarke was as excited as a schoolboy. We wandered through a half-lighted world, a world of charts and musty clothes. We pored over Keats's death mask and the signature of Guy Fawkes. In dim basements we studied models of old London. We worked out, from decaying shirts and breeches, the height and weight of Charles the First.

I don't mean that I was forever in Clarke's company. He knew two other people—a Mr. and Mrs. Logan, Mr. Logan being something in the wholesale grocery trade—who entertained him royally. But whenever he tracked down a new museum, he came rushing round and got me to go with him. It seemed a harmless enough hobby.

"Oh, harmless!" said Tess, pouring tea. "I admit that!" She lifted her eyes. "But, Bob. Which is the museum where they have all the Hogarth engravings?"

"The Soane. Hold on! Didn't you go with us to that one?"

"I did," answered Tess, without expression. The white china teapot gleamed as she manipulated it. "Did you notice the expression on his face when he was looking at those pictures?"

"Not particularly."

"The picture of the hanging, for instance?"

"No."

But discomfort touched that chimney corner, palpably and uneasily. The steam of the hot tea drifted up past Tess's face as she poured. She handed me the cup.

"Look here," I said; "what are you getting at?"

"Oh, I'm being a silly fool! All the same, what's this talk about his trying to buy a house that's supposed to be haunted?"

"He's trying, right enough. He'll get it if he can get it cheaply enough."

"But why? I mean, why does he want it?"

And here, I confess, I felt a trifle guilty. I had not told Tess about Clarke's great scheme, the scheme for which I was feeling almost as enthusiastic as he was.

"Well, it's like this. Among other things, he wants to give a ghost party."

"A ghost party?"

"Damn it, Tess, it'll be the psychological experiment of the age! It'll be material for me! It'll be . . . See here. This is how we do it. Clarke invites down to the country, for a housewarming, say six guests. Each guest is carefully chosen as being a different emotional type. Do you see? We invite, for instance, the hard-headed business man who doesn't believe in any ruddy nonsense. We invite the artistic type, all imagination and nerves. We invite the scientific type. We invite the lawyer or the legal type, who believes in nothing but evidence. And so on. For several days we expose these people to the influence of Longwood House; and see how it takes each of 'em in turn.

"There is no deception, of course. Each guest is warned beforehand what to expect, and comes at his own wish and of his own free will. It's a psychological experiment, including the experiment on ourselves. For all I know, I myself may be the first to bolt. But as a week-end game for a dull month—wow!"

Tess smiled.

"And did you think I would object, Bob?"

"Object?"

"I mean, by the way you're arguing? You're standing up and shouting as though you were trying to convince a jury."

"Sorry. But—"

"I think it would be terribly interesting," said Tess. She beckoned to me, and I went over to sit down on the arm of her chair. She put her head against my shoulder, so that for the moment I could not see her face. "And you want me to come?"

"Of course. Clarke particularly wants it. Mind you, this may not lead to anything, because Clarke may not get the house. That's why I haven't mentioned it before."

Tess pressed her head closer. Rain squalls stung the windows at dusk, and the warmth of the fire was good.

"Bob, I don't know what to think. I mean—you don't think we're likely to *see* anything, do you?" She forced out the words, still without looking round. "I don't mind funny noises, creaks and taps and that sort of thing. But, honestly, if I actually *saw* something in a house, I don't think I could bear it. That's what's so odd. Do you think the house is haunted? I didn't know you believed in ghosts."

"I don't. That's just the point."

"Well, then?"

"But you don't like it, Tess. And that's enough. If you don't like it, it's off."

"You mean that?"

"Darling, of course I mean it." She pressed her warm body closer into the crook of my arm. "But it's no good saying I don't think there's something awfully queer about it. Mr. Clarke sent Andy Hunter down to have a look at the house, didn't he? What does Andy have to say about it?"

"I don't know. I haven't seen Andy since."

"And that," said Tess, suddenly disengaging herself and getting to her feet as the doorbell began to buzz and clamor through the flat, "is Mr. Clarke's ring now. Bob, I've got a feeling—"

Mr. B. Martin Clarke, beaming all over his face,

brought life and enthusiasm into the flat. To dull people like myself and Tess, content as a rule with our commonplace existence (she with her dress-buying and I as a hack writer) there was stimulus in Clarke's sheer zest for things.

He shook out his wet overcoat in the entry, and hung it up. He carefully hung up his bowler hat. He passed his hand across his flat whitish hair, to make sure no brittle strand was out of place. He straightened the jacket of his neat tobacco-brown suit: he affected such suits, and must have had half a dozen of them, though their shade seldom varied. Then he came bustling in to the fire, holding out his wet hands to the blaze.

"I've got it," he announced triumphantly.

There was a clatter on the tea tray. Tess righted the milk jug.

"Congratulations," I said. "You remember Miss Fraser?"

"I do indeed remember Miss Fraser," smiled Clarke, taking Tess's hand and pressing it. He had an old-fashioned courtesy of manner, mixed with just the right informality of manner to show that he was no desiccated dodderer, but knew a thing or two himself.

"That is why I chose a Saturday afternoon," he went on. "Because I hoped I should find you two together. First, I have to report the great news that I am the new owner of Longwood House. It's mine. Mine! By Jove, I can't believe it!"

The infectious enthusiasm of his manner was as overpowering as it is difficult to describe. For a moment I thought he was going to dance a jig on the hearthrug.

"Second, the time has come and the hour has struck. I have been bottling myself up long enough. But now I can tell you. Miss Fraser, I have a proposition to put before you — both of you."

"I know," said Tess. "The ghost party. Tea?"

Clarke did not seem too well pleased.

"You know about it?"

"Yes; Bob has just been telling me. Tea?"

"And — er — what do you think of my idea?"

"I should love it," said Tess.

Clarke's enthusiasm boiled and bubbled again. "Miss Fraser," he said in a low, fervent voice, "you don't know what a load you have taken off my mind." It was curious: he seemed almost dazzled with relief. He went over to press her hand again, and pat her on the shoulder. "I depended on you and Morrison, above all people, to help me. If you had let me down I should have sulked and chewed nails." He looked at me, and spoke more quietly. "Morrison, the house *is* haunted."

"You're sure of that?"

Clarke's face assumed an air of desperate seriousness.

"I make no rash statements," he said. "I will withdraw the word supernatural, if you like. I only say that there are certain manifestions which may be natural or supernatural, but which puzzle me. I quote Samuel Wesley: 'Wit, perhaps, might find many interpretations; but wisdom none.' I only say that the house is infested and polluted most damnably. We are in for a rare time."

"Tea?" asked Tess patiently.

"We are—tea? Admirable, admirable, admirable!"

He took the cup from her rather absently. Sitting down on the couch that faced the fire, he put forward one foot and balanced the cup and saucer on his knee.

"The difficulty," he went on, stirring the tea so rapidly that it slopped over, "is to dig out the past history of the house. We must have exact details. I have tried making friends with the local parson, who should know if anybody does. The padre is inclined to be suspicious. I think he wishes the house had been allowed to rot. But a few generous contributions to home charities (tactfully made, of course!) should help. When the docket of wickedness is fully spread before us, then the time for our party will be ripe."

He gulped tea, slopping it on his chin; then, as though ashamed of himself, Clarke put down the cup and spoke more quietly.

"All that remains, for the moment, is to choose the guests for our party—"

I exchanged a glance with Tess.

"Yes. What guests?"

"Ah, that is where I shall have to enlist your help. In all this broad city I know only four persons: you two, and my friends Mr. and Mrs. Logan." Clarke looked thoughtful. "That, however, is all to the good. Apart from any considerations of friendship," he smiled, "I should want you four in any case. You represent exactly the sort of—er—"

"Guinea pigs?"

"My friend!" said Clarke, hurt. Thick contrition oozed from his voice and from his intricate gesture. "No, no, no. But as types we are all ideal. Miss Fraser, for instance, represents the practical business woman."

Tess made a face.

"Whereas you, my friend, are the literary man."

"Hold on!" I said, with a sudden dark suspicion growing to annoyance. "You haven't cast *me* as the type that's all imagination and nerves, have you?"

"To a certain extent. You don't mind?"

I suppose I shouldn't have minded; and yet all of a sudden it annoyed me like hell. Nobody likes to be told a thing like this, more especially when it is not true. What really irritated me was any suggestion of the "artistic," which is the word in the dictionary that I detest most. The thought that I might for all this time have figured in Clarke's thoughts for this rôle made me want to get up and kick him, hard, in the seat of the pants. And — with that slippery intuition of his — he saw it.

"On the strength," I said, "of being a magazine hack?"

"On the strength," said Clarke, "of a powerful imagination. My dear sir, don't misunderstand. You are confusing imagination with weakness. You are confusing nerve with nerves. No. The part of the 'nervy' person must be allotted to someone else."

"To whom?" Tess asked quickly.

"To Mrs. Logan. You don't know the Logans?"

We shook our heads.

"Mrs. Logan is Welsh," said Clarke. "Or at least so

I should judge from her Christian name, which is
Gwyneth. She is much younger than her husband;
extremely attractive physically; and not, I should
have thought, of the temperament to enjoy this. But
she seems keen to go. And in any case"—here a
curious smile spread across Clarke's face, showing
teeth as white and strong as a dog's—"I think her
husband will persuade her to go. Logan himself you
will like. He is the modern business man of the most
hard-headed and skeptical type. A charming couple.
Charming!"

Tess regarded him with a look I could not decipher.

"Then that's five of us, including yourself," she
suggested. "How many others do you want?"

Clarke spread out his hands.

"I should prefer to have not more than seven. As
for the persons, I leave that up to you. If you could
suggest, for instance, someone of strongly scientific
mind?"

"Andy Hunter."

"Who?"

"Andy Hunter," I said. "The architect you sent
down to look at the house. You must have met him."

Clarke hesitated. He seemed not to leap at this
suggestion.

"Yes, it is certainly worth considering. A very
pleasant young man. I daresay he would do."

"Then that leaves you with one more person to
complete it," said Tess, though Clarke opened his
mouth as though to protest. "And, I say! If you want
to do the thing up right, isn't there one type you've
passed over? What about a spiritualist?"

"I had thought of that, Miss Fraser. And I say very definitely: no. This is to be a representative group of ordinary, skeptical human beings. If I were to invite a professional spiritualist, we should hear much talk of auras and 'conditions' and similar tommyrot. We should be surrounded by a difficult theatricalism from the beginning. And that is precisely what we want to avoid. Do you agree?"

"Then," I put in, "what about a detective?"

There was a slight pause, while Clarke's eyes slid sideways.

"A detective?"

"Yes. After all, these phenomena are open to investigation, aren't they?"

"I don't think I understand."

"Well, you see, some of us don't believe in ghosts. You say that inexplicable things happen in the house. I imagine we're at liberty to investigate them exactly like any other mystery? Then why not have a professional detective on the premises? I know a C.I.D. inspector—his name is Elliot, and he's a very good fellow—whom we might be able to get if we tried."

Clarke pondered this.

"I think not," he decided politely. "In my estimation, that would be going as unnecessarily far in one direction as inviting a spiritualist would be going in the other. It would be asking for superfluous trouble. I am definitely against it. Of course, if you insist?"

It was on the tip of my tongue to insist, and I know Tess felt the same. I have since wondered what would have happened if we had insisted: whether black murder would have fallen among us just the same.

But Tess diverted us, by whacking both arms of her chair and sitting up with an air of inspiration.

"Julian Enderby!" she exclaimed.

Clarke spoke quickly. "And who is Julian Enderby?"

"That is, if he'd come," mused Tess. "He's not very good at what you might call 'playing.' But he's a solicitor. If you want somebody of the legal type, who'll consider evidence and nothing but evidence, I should think Julian would do wonderfully."

I had to agree with this, though it was an infernal nuisance how the name of Julian Enderby seemed to crop up forever between Tess and me. Enderby was all right, and doubtless a good enough chap. But he was an old admirer of Tess's; and somehow we seemed to have got entangled with him as though with a revolving door.

Clarke looked thoughtful. "Admirable!" he said. "That is just the sort of person we want. If, as you say, we can get him. You will — er — communicate with Mr. Enderby?"

"Bob will. Won't you, Bob?"

"Then we are seven," beamed Clarke. "As for our final consideration, the date of this house-warming . . ."

Tess's face clouded. "Yes, and that's the trouble. Please don't think I'm trying to be a spoilsport, Mr. Clarke. But I could be much more keen about a week end in the country if it weren't such foul weather. Just look at those windows! Do you think this is quite the right time of year for it?"

Clarke stared at her.

"My dear young lady," he protested, "you don't think I want to do this *now*?"

"Don't you?"

"Certainly not. That house has been vacant for upwards of seventeen years. It will take more than a month to put it in anything like a decent state of repair. No, no, no. I was merely, like a crafty host, planning ahead. Let us see." He drew out a pocket diary and leafed through the pages.

"What would you say to a Whitsuntide party? Whitsunday, this year, falls on May 17th. Suppose we made our party from Friday the 14th to Tuesday the 18th? Could you manage time away from business for that?"

"Yes. I — I suppose I could."

Clarke laughed. "You're not nervous, Miss Fraser? Come, come, come! Don't tell me you're nervous. Eh?"

"Yes, I am, a bit. And I think you know it. I only want to ask one thing, though. Are we going to see anything?"

"See anything?"

"You know what I mean. You say you've been there, and seen or heard 'manifestations.' What kind of manifestations? What happens there, exactly? I was telling Bob a while ago that I wouldn't so much mind a lot of noises, like mice or a creaky shutter; because I used to hear that sort of thing at home. But are we going to see anything?"

"I hope so, Miss Fraser."

"What, for instance?"

Again rain gusts spattered the windows, and ran

across the roof tops. We could listen in comfort to the low growl of the chimney, drawing strength from these lighted boxes which stretch round in the ordered streets of a town. May 17th then seemed a remote date, a disappointingly remote date. I remember feeling a twinge of impatience at the remoteness of it: so much work to be done, so many dreary weeks to plod through, so many busses and tubes and thundering in our ears, before we should find romantic adventure in a house by the Essex coast. Why the devil couldn't it happen next day?

Why the devil should it ever have happened?

III

"There she is," said Andy Hunter. "There's our home for the next four days."

He stopped the car. Tess and I stood up in the back of the car to get our first view of Longwood House.

The house faced south. Therefore the pink sunset lay toward our left and slightly in front of it, a burning bush of a sky which kindled every detail of the façade. The house stood on a very slight rise amid flattish ground, separated from the main road only by a little rough-stone wall which you could have jumped over, and set back fifty yards from the road without so much as a bush or a tree in front of it. But there were trees behind it, a low horizon shading from green to smoky purple toward the coast.

Tess, I remember, let out an involuntary gasp of admiration.

Longwood House was of two stories only. It was very long and low-built on the side facing the road, with a little wing projecting at the east which gave it a shape thus: ⌐_____┐ It had a low-pitched shingled roof, and was built of heavy black timbering picked out with rows of white plaster designs like fleur-de-lis. The pink sunset flamed on that rich woodwork, like an armorial shield of fleur-de-lis. It flamed on the broad windows, with mullions dividing each window into four lights of oblong panes; on the little arched hood over the main doorway; on the hexagonal bay windows at the junction of the two wings; on the stacks of twin and triple chimneys rising in silhouette against the darkening northern sky.

It was as ripe with age as an old oak. Yet it showed as trim as the driveway, of finely crushed gravel, which entered at a point higher up than the house and curved round in a broad sweep all along that black-and-white front.

Tess stared at it.

"Why, it's beautiful!" she cried.

Andy Hunter took the pipe out of his mouth and craned round at her.

"Well, what did you expect?" he demanded.

"I don't know. A dank old ruin, rather."

"Dank old ruin be blowed!" said Andy indignantly. "What do you think I've been doing here for the past six weeks?"

People sometimes laugh at Andy for his slow and solemn mind; his sedate and solemn behavior; his habit of considering an idea for minutes before speaking, like a man walking round and inspecting a house. That is because they do not know him.

All surface details—the long lanky figure, the minor public-school tie, the pipe—abet this impression. He sat with his head back, the pipe held out in

28

front of him, and an expression of annoyance on his swarthy face. I remember being at a dance once, at which Andy, then aged twenty, was squiring a romantic young lady aged eighteen. I remember passing a balcony where the two were talking on a romantic summer night: the young lady remarking on a fine yellow moon, and Andy proceeding to give her a long scientific explanation as to why it was yellow.

He had a very similar expression now. But again it would be misleading, just as it misled those who thought he had no imagination.

"It doesn't even look as though there could be anything wrong with it," said Tess. She paused. Then, with a solemnity matching Andy's own, she reached out and tweaked his nose.

"Here, dash it all!"

"And when I say 'anything wrong with it,' " continued Tess, "don't pretend to misunderstand. You know perfectly well I don't mean anything wrong with the roof or the drains. Don't you?"

"Sit down," said Andy. "I'm going to start the car."

"Don't you?"

The fading sunset light was full on Andy's face as he blinked round. It seemed to me that his eyes under thick eyebrows that almost met in the middle, moved away; they assumed a kind of bursting stolidity. He sniffed. His lips barely opened when he said:

"Rubbish."

"Andy, you've been down here day after day. Give us a fair answer! Mr. Clarke says that all sorts of things happen in the house. Have you ever seen anything?"

"No."

29

"Or heard anything?"

Andy let in the clutch. The car coughed, and moved up from the main road into the gravel driveway, so that Tess had to sit down.

The house, ancient and faintly sinister, began to grow upon us. The black-and-white armorial shield grew so distinct that we could pick out flaws in the timbering, a crack or two in the plaster, and a garden hose lying coiled beside the front door. The flower beds were raw and not yet planted, but the lawns had been shaven to that putting-green smoothness which seems to have lighter stripes in it. It was a clear, warm, windless evening. Many of the windows at Longwood House had been set open.

And now the weeks had passed, and it was the middle of May. Warmth and greenery closed us in. It was, as Tess said, a fine and noble-looking house. But I had taken the trouble to look up its history, wondering why Clarke seemed to have found so much difficulty in tracking down the details of that history. After all, nobody with any journalistic sense bothers about the stories of the local parson when there are such publications as the *Reports of the Historical Monuments Commission*. Whether or not Clarke had got the details, I had.

"Is the place much changed?" I asked Andy.

"Changed?"

He stopped the car before the front door. There seemed to be a great hush when the motor died. Our voices rose loudly in the warm evening air; and it was so quiet that we could hear, behind one of the open windows on the ground floor, the faint ticking of a typewriter.

"Changed when it was remodeled in 1920," I explained.

"Why do you want to know that?"

"The *Historical Monuments Commission* say that they tore out a lot of paneling then, and put in some new fireplaces. I suppose you've put up a new chandelier in the dining-room?"

Andy snorted.

"There's nothing they loved better than spoiling paneling," he said, with a true architect's worship of oak panels. "They did more than that. They put . . . hullo! Who's that?"

He had turned round, to indicate something, toward the windows of a room on the ground floor. It was from this room that we could hear the ticking of the typewriter; and, with a closer look, you could see the typewriter itself on a table close to the window. The typewriter noise broke off as Andy turned.

A man's face appeared at one of the open lights of the window. It was an aggressive face, with an unhealthy complexion like a boiled egg, and a broad nose. It glared at us for a moment, and then was withdrawn. The four panes of the broad window were shut with a slam, one after the other; then the typewriter noise recommenced.

"Temperamental sort of bloke," said Andy. "Damn bad manners, if you ask me. Who is he?"

"That," observed Tess thoughtfully, "must be the hospitable Mr. Archibald Bentley Logan, of the wholesale grocery trade. It's nobody I ever met, anyway. Have you met the Logans, Andy?"

Andy's brow was like a thundercloud.

"No," he said. "But, whoever he is, it's still damn

31

bad manners. Just can't bear to be interrupted in his typing, I suppose."

"Unless it was a ghost, of course," smiled Tess. "You know how it always is in the stories. You meet some perfectly ordinary-looking person, who chats about the weather; and at the end of the story you find he died the night before. If—"

We all laughed at this. But, whatever opinions we might have given, they were cut short by the arrival of our host. Clarke came bouncing out of the front door, a sturdy and stocky figure in country tweeds, rubbing his hands together like an innkeeper.

"So you got here safely, eh?" he said, somewhat superfluously. He shook hands with each of us in turn. "Your bags? Good! Hand 'em out. Er—Mr. Hunter. Better leave the car where it is, for the moment, and I'll have it taken round to the garage. Oh, yes, we have a garage."

" 'Taken round to the garage,' " repeated Tess. "You didn't find any difficulty about servants, then?"

"Eh, my dear?"

Tess was smiling in the twilight: a nervous, flickering little mask of a smile. "You see I'm practical," she said. "That bothered me, rather. I wondered how you would deal with the servant problem, if the house has such a reputation. You didn't have any trouble?"

"No trouble at all, my dear," Clarke assured her affably. "That is to say, I have only two servants who sleep in. But the excellent Mrs. Winch and her niece will look after us admirably. They know all about the house, and they don't care a rap."

"Don't care a rap," said Andy. He took the pipe out of his mouth and gave one of his rare, startling little laughs.

"What on earth – ?" said Tess.

"Don't you see it?" demanded Andy, with great earnestness. "Don't care a rap. Joke. Ha ha ha."

We all laughed again, though it was the least funny thing that even Andy had ever said. And it occurred to me that we were all laughing too much, including Clarke. But this did not last.

"Are we all here?" I asked; and Clarke's amusement stopped.

"No. I regret to say that there has been a slight hitch. Logan and his wife are here, yes. But Mr. Enderby has telegraphed to say that he will be detained, and will be unable to join us until to-morrow." Clarke's voice, usually a pleasant and silky baritone, had a faint note of shrillness in it. "A nuisance, because I had hoped to have us all here for the first night. However, it cannot be helped. Come in, come in come in! I must show you my treasure house."

He bowed us ahead of him.

The front door, as we had noted, was shaded by a peaked hood with wooden sides: rather as though you entered through a kind of deep sentry box. At the back of it an iron-studded door stood wide open, giving a glimpse of a big dusky hall paved with dull reddish tiles.

The last light was almost gone. Tess went first. I followed, carrying her suitcase and mine; but, so that she should not stumble in the dark box, I stood to one side to give her the benefit of whatever afterglow remained. Andy was behind me with his own suitcase, and Clarke in the rear. Clarke was just drawing

33

Andy's attention to the steeple of Prittleton church, just visible above the trees toward the west, when Tess, in the dark entry, screamed.

Then she screamed again.

There are small sounds which can re-create with unbearable vividness every detail of a past scene. Most distinctly I remember the thump when I dropped the two suitcases I was carrying. Even today it is impossible to hear a sound like that, metal cleats striking the floor, without remembering how we first crossed the threshold of Longwood House.

I remember the faces of Andy and of Clarke, colorless and startled, framed in the outer opening of the sentry box. I remember Tess within a step of the house door; the outline of her rakish fashionable hat, with the half-veil, in darkness; and the tense feeling of her rounded shoulders. Beyond those two outcries, she had controlled herself. Her voice was light and high-pitched, but calm.

"Something caught my ankle," she said.

"Where?"

"Here. Where I'm standing."

Clarke slipped smoothly past us. You had a sense of smooth hands, deprecating. "But, my dear young lady," he protested, "that is impossible. There's nobody here, as you can see for yourself. You must have tripped over something. Probably the door mat."

"No," said Tess. "It had fingers."

Clarke walked up one step, through the doorway, and into the hall. He touched a switch and put on the electric light.

It was a big square hall, with walls of white plaster against which the throat of the fireplace stood out dark with soot by contrast. An oak settle stood sideways before the chimney piece, and a black oak staircase, not large but graceful and finely carved, ascended along the rear of the right-hand wall. The dark red tiles of the floor, though uneven with age, had been scrubbed until they had almost eased to be dull. There was a spinning wheel (a museum piece) in one corner, and a grandfather clock in the other.

But most of all you were conscious of the atmosphere you breathed: an odor peculiar to such houses. It is not unpleasant. It is compounded of a faint dampness, the smell of the polish used on oak, and the smell of the old wood itself; it is reminiscent of a schoolroom, the more so as this particular hall was lighted by only one electric bulb hanging from the central beam.

"You see?" said Clarke, as light streamed out into the entry. "There's nothing here."

Tess did not reply. She came into the hall.

"You imagined it, Miss Fraser."

"You must have imagined it, old girl," agreed Andy. Yet his face (he needs to shave twice a day) seemed less swarthy under its early-evening stubble. "Look, here's the door mat." He kicked it out of the way in the entry.

"I didn't imagine it," said Tess. "Something with fingers caught hold of my ankle. It was nasty."

"But, my dear young lady," protested Clarke, "you are looking at me as though you thought I were trying to play some joke on you!"

Tess's tense expression relaxed and lightened into a smile. She was fighting this.

"I'm sorry, Mr. Clarke. I *won't* be a spoilsport.

35

And, after all, what did anybody expect? That's what we're here for, isn't it? I seem to have got the first pinch of the haunting, that's all."

"But—"

"There was something there, Mr. Clarke. I felt it."

Two doors opened into the hall, one at the left and one at the right. We looked toward the door at the left, because a light had been switched on there. And a woman, who could be nobody but Gwyneth Logan, came out and joined us.

Now I am not going to pretend that I was deeply impressed by my first sight of Mrs. Logan. Whatever powers of fascination or beguilement she possessed, they were not immediately apparent. Or perhaps the moment was too confused. I had a vague picture of a woman of medium height, twenty-eight or twenty-nine years old, with a good though not striking figure. You first noticed her hair: which was light brown, of great softness and smoothness, parted in the middle and drawn back over her ears. She had one hand on the doorpost, plucking at it. She wore a dress of plain dark green, with tan stockings and shoes. Her manner was reserved and rather shy.

"I thought I heard someone call out," she said, as though to explain her presence. She had a soft, low voice, hardly seeming to open her lips when she spoke. "I—I was with my husband."

Clarke's cheerful heartiness blew away bogles.

"Ah, there we are!" he said, bustling across to her and hauling her out of the doorway. "I want you to meet the rest of our party, and be friends at once. Gwyneth, I want you to meet Miss Fraser. Mr. Morrison. Mr. Hunter. This is Mrs. Logan."

"How do you do?" smiled Gwyneth. "I've been so wanting to meet you, Miss Fraser. I'm your chaperon, you know. You must be tired after that drive. Won't you all come in and have a drink before you go upstairs?"

"Thanks," said Tess. "I should like a drink *very* much."

The room at the left of the hall, it appeared, was the drawing-room. It was very long and spacious, with two of the big windows opening on the front driveway. Evidently as a concession to modernity, it had been furnished with rich but subdued heaviness: fitted carpet, deep chairs upholstered in wine-colored velvet, fat-bowled Chinese lamps on the side tables. The light of these lamps vied with the afterglow in the sky outside many-paned windows, just as the past still vied with the present. For the walls were oak-paneled, and reflections of the lamplight shone down their length as in so many small gloomy mirrors. The chimney piece — between the two front windows — was of raw and smoky stone, having cut in its hood the date 1605.

From beyond a closed door at the far end of the room, we could again hear the ticking of a typewriter.

"My husband," smiled Gwyneth Logan, nodding toward it. "He can't get away from business, poor old boy. He promised he would take a complete holiday. But he no sooner got here than he thought of half a dozen letters he must write or die. Martin" — she looked at Clarke — "has been good enough to turn the study over to him, lock, stock, and barrel."

"Lock, stock, and barrel is good," agreed Clarke, chuckling for a reason I did not understand; and it

37

seemed to me that Gwyneth started and flushed slightly. There were curious undercurrents here, as palpable as draughts.

"Anyway, we simply must rout him out now," she went on in a rush. "He—er—knows you're here. He saw you drive in."

"Yes. And didn't seem too pleased about it," said Andy.

"Oh, you mustn't mind that. That's only his manner. Mr. . . .?"

"Hunter."

"Hunter, of course! Martin has told us so much about you." She nodded toward a cabinet of bottles in one corner. "Would you mind?"

As Andy went over obediently to pour out the drinks, a maidservant slipped into the room, and, at a nod from Clarke, began to draw the curtains. They were curtains of heavy velvet; they ran with a soft swish and rustle on their metal rods, winking back the lamplight.

"And now, as the ghost observed in the anecdote, we're all locked in for the night," said Clarke.

The maid, a stolid-looking but not unattractive girl of sixteen, glanced over her shoulder.

"Will that be all, sir? I've taken the bags upstairs."

"That will be all, thanks, Sonia."

"Dinner at eight, sir?"

"Dinner at eight, Sonia."

Clarke took out his watch, consulted it, and replaced it with a small satisfied pat. He stood with his back to the big stone fireplace; the whole room seemed to smell of stone.

"Now," he went on seriously, "we are ready for

whatever may happen. It is fully dark. Nothing ever happens here, it appears, until after dark."

"It happened to Tess," I said.

Andy's voice struck in sharply. I seem to remember small bits of sentences, flying and clashing jerkily. "What'll you have to drink, Tess?"

"Gin-and-it, please."

Andy brought her a gin-and-it, and a sherry and bitters for Mrs. Logan.

"Mr. Clarke?"

"Whisky, by all means. Whisky," continued Clarke, "was a luxury very rare in Italy. They call it 'veekeey'; and as a rule it is abominable stuff. It would be interesting to compile a list of the various pronunciations into which the name of that world-wide article is tortured."

"What happened to Miss Fraser?" asked Gwyneth Logan.

Now Mrs. Logan was sitting between Tess and me, on a broad velvet-covered sofa. And it began to dawn on me that she was a very attractive and even troubling sort of woman. Perhaps it was the mere unintentional closeness of the contact. Gwyneth Logan was one of those women whose arms you cannot brush without intense awareness of their physical presence.

"I tripped over a door mat," said Tess flatly. Tess had removed her hat, and was turning it over on her lap. She also eyed Gwyneth Logan. "At least, that's what they tell me. What really happened was that something with fingers — "

"Whisky for you as usual, Bob?" interrupted Andy. "Right. And for me." The syphon hissed. "What do

39

you think of the decorations? Not bad, eh? All Mr. Clark's work." Then Andy's voice grew loud, an unusual thing, so that it could have been heard in the next room. "Get him to show you the collection of guns."

IV

"Something with fingers?" prompted Gwyneth Logan. But Andy's remark had completely diverted Tess's attention. Tess flung her head round.

"Guns?" she said.

Clarke chuckled. "You needn't be alarmed, Miss Fraser. To be exact, it is a collection of pistols. But the newest of them has not been fired since the Battle of Waterloo, and the whole lot together could not harm a fly."

He extended his glass toward the closed door, from behind which we could still hear the tapping of the typewriter.

"Would you like to see them? They belonged to the last surviving member of the Longwood family, when he left her. I found them packed away in a chest in the attic, between many layers of newspaper. Presumably they go with the house: at least, the executors made no trouble about my keeping them. I put them back where the last Longwood left them. Come along. Logan has been there long enough at his infernal typing."

Gwyneth, clearly, would have liked to hear more about what happened to Tess. You could almost feel it burn from her. She must have had remarkable self-control under that shy and rather nervous manner. Yet her lips were emotional: intensely so, like her wide-spaced blue eyes.

"Oh, well, then we'll go and look at the pistols," she said indulgently. "Only I claim the right to talk to Miss Fraser afterwards. Bentley! I say, Bent-ley!"

None of us, perhaps, expected too hearty a welcome from Mr. Archibald Bentley Logan when his wife opened the door. But we got one nevertheless.

"Coming, my dear," said a brisk voice. Mr. Logan was engaged in licking the flap of an envelope. "Just finished. That's the lot. Hah!" He put the envelope on the table, smoothed it, smote it with his fist, and drew a deep breath. "Seven letters in an hour. Not bad, eh? These our fellow guests. Good!"

The room in which he sat was built on a pattern much the same as the drawing-room, though a trifle smaller, and formed the end of the west wing. It also had two broad windows facing the main driveway, with the fireplace between them.

But you made out details with difficulty, since the only light burning was a darkish-shaded drop lamp over the typewriter table. This table stood against the nearer window, between the fireplace and the east wall. It was a heavy, long table, its narrow end against the window and projecting out into the room. The typewriter had been drawn close to the window; the rest of that smooth walnut table, with the glow of the drop lamp shining down on it, was cluttered with notepaper, envelopes, stamp sheets, pens, and two or three bottles of ink.

"Morrison?" inquired Mr. Logan, rising magnificently to shake hands as introductions were performed. "Heard a lot about you, sir. Hunter? Heard a lot about *you*. And this must be the little lady," he overwhelmed Tess, "who's taken Clarke's fancy so much. Come down to shiver in the haunted house, eh?"

Logan had an enormous portentousness of manner. Though not an unduly tall man, he was very broad and bulky, and his mirth was Gargantuan: it snorted through his nostrils. He gave the impression of being as big as the room. Seen at close range, he appeared much less unpleasant than he had seemed before; he had a hard, shrewd face, sly rather than kindly, but with kindliness too; I rather liked the look of him. He was almost bald. A walrus mustache would have suited him, but instead he had a furry patch of grayish mustache which looked as though it had grown there by accident. He wore a hard white collar with a blue shirt, and was attempting without success to lick an inkstain from his finger.

"Haunted or not," he declared, desisting from his attacks on the ink, "it's a good buy. A damned good buy. Eh, Clarke?"

"I flatter myself so," said our host.

"A good buy," repeated Logan portentously, reaching out and whacking the mantelpiece as though to assure us of its solidity. "And d'ye know what he paid for it? I'll tell you. A thousand pounds freehold. Not a penny more. Eh?"

"Well —" said Clarke.

Logan wagged his head.

"Eh, lad, but that's business!" he declared, with a gleam of admiration in his eye. "Freehold, mind. And seven and a quarter acres to boot. Extra expenses? Say three, four hundred for repairs. Do it up right. And what do you get? *This*." He whacked the mantelpiece again. "Clarke, you're hot stuff. I'd never have thought it of you. As for any depreciation in value caused by ghosts . . ."

He grinned at me, and I grinned back at him.

"Meaning," I said, "that you're prepared to give the raspberry to any ghost you happen to see on the premises?"

But to my surprise he grew very serious, and held up his hand in protest.

"Not at all," he said. "I'm a modern man."

"A modern man?"

"Exactly. I don't scoff. No, indeed. These things can't be taken too seriously." He gave a portentous nod of his head, rebuking us. "I had the right kind of bringing-up; my parents were honest, sensible, religious people; and what's believing in an afterlife *but* believing in ghosts? Or, if it's not ghosts, it's something. Maybe a scientific force. How do we know? Maybe we'll discover it. That's progress. No, indeed," said Logan, not without pride, "I don't scoff. I'm a modern man: I can believe anything."

"Very succinctly put," observed Clarke.

"Though, mind you," the other amended, giving us a broad wink, "as for scaring — well, that's different.

I'd like to see the johnny-on-the-ghost that could scare *me*."

"A dangerous remark, sir."

"Maybe, maybe."

"Your position, then, is that you believe in ghosts but defy them to scare you?"

"Damme, I believe it is," said Logan, snorting through his nostrils with surprise. He laughed aloud. Catching his wife's eye, he went over and put his big arm round her shoulders.

"Eh, Gwinnie?" he said. "I'll tell you what I am. Lawk, I haven't thought of this for years! D'you remember the tale they used to read to us, about the boy who couldn't shudder? Well, I'm the man who can't shudder, by cripes! And d'you remember what happened to the boy in the tale? He grew up and got married. And his wife threw a pail of water over him; and *that* made him shudder all right. Eh, Gwinnie?"

Gwyneth laughed dutifully, and with evident delight. Of all the pairs in the world you would have said to be ill-matched, these two would appear to be it. Yet she appeared to regard him with genuine devotion: to hang on his every word.

He gave her a quick glance.

"Eh, Gwinnie?"

"That is a woman's practical mind," observed Clarke, with a smile. "But if you are anxious to get the opportunity to shudder, you may have it here. This is one of the—er—alleged haunted rooms."

"This?" demanded Logan, surprised.

"This," smiled Clarke. "Let's have some light."

He went over to the door and touched a main

45

switch.

Logan's instinct seemed right. Illuminated now by a lamp hanging from the central beam across the ceiling, the study neither looked nor *felt* haunted. It was a comfortable room. There were bright rag rugs on the floor, and low bookshelves built along the west wall. In one corner stood a tall cabinet, with a sailing-ship model on top of it: not one of the atrocities you see in department stores, but a noble three-masted square-rigger beautifully fashioned to the very peak of her topgallant royals.

In addition to the two south windows, there was a big north window with a radio-gramophone under it. Three or four cane-bottomed chairs supplemented a center table piled with magazines. The walls were of white plaster, set off by the black woodwork; they had no ornament except (incongruously) a gold-and-enamel triptych which presumably Clarke had brought from Italy. The chimney piece between the south windows was a massive affair, of red brick. It stretched almost to the ceiling. On its face, over the opening of the fireplace, the collection of pistols had been hung up one above the other, like rungs in a ladder.

Clarke indicated the collection of pistols. They had been polished, so far as was possible; and their metalwork winked under the light against the dark red brick.

"Here you are, Miss Fraser," he said. "At the top," he pointed, "a late sixteenth-century wheel lock. Notice the fine design: even weapons had beauty in those days. At the bottom, a Napoleonic cavalry pistol. Between them"—he brushed his hand up over the horizontal row—"three centuries of gun-making are represented."

Tess hesitated.

"Do they," she said, "do they shoot?"

"Hardly. Feel the weight of one of these." He lifted down the cavalry pistol from its three wooden pegs. Then his eye twinkled. "Why do you ask that, Miss Fraser."

"I was thinking of somebody getting killed," said Tess.

We turned to stare at her.

It had slipped out. Knowing Tess, I knew that: she blurted it out before she could stop herself. But it had an effect none the less. There was a change in the atmosphere as palpable as a chilling or darkening of the room, all the worse because its source could not be identified. Tess tried to recover herself.

"I mean," she said desperately, "I—I was thinking of a story."

"Story?" echoed Gwyneth Logan.

Tess must have been an admirable liar in her business affairs. In one second, as explanation, she had plucked out of the air something I had told her long ago.

"Yes. In a story, don't you see? There was an old-fashioned gun hung up on the wall. It was loaded, and had a percussion cap. The sun came through a window, shone through a water bottle on a table, and made a burning glass of it. The burning-glass ray exploded the cap of the gun; and it went off."

Again something alien and sinister touched our

circle, though Clarke laughed.

"We have no percussion caps, I'm afraid," he said dryly. "Or much sun either." But I did not like the look of his eye. "Now note this one!" He bustled again. "A lighter pistol, once the property of the Bow Street runners: note the crown and broad arrow. This next one —"

"Wouldn't give twopence for the lot," stated Mr. Archibald Bentley Logan, with flat candor. "But that ship model, now!"

"Ah, that?" said Clarke, turning round. "You like it?"

"We-el . . . not bad, not bad. Wouldn't like to sell it, would you?"

"I'm afraid not."

"Come, now!" urged Logan, squaring himself and giving Clarke a peculiar leering look, which intimated that he was ready to be confidential. "What'll you take for it? Fair offer? Not that it'd be much good to me, mind!" Here he eyed the ship with growing disparagement. "But I just happen to fancy it; and what I fancy, I fancy. Eh, Gwinnie? Come on, now! Whatsay? A quid? Two quid? Three, even? Fair offer!"

"I am sorry. It is not for sale."

Logan snorted through his nostrils with amusement. He was genuinely interested now.

"Nonsense," he said. "Anything's for sale. Including —" Logan stopped. His tone changed. "I'll tell you what I'll do," he confided, disengaging his arm from his wife's shoulder to take a notecase out of his pocket. "I'll give you five pounds for it. Five pounds on the nail. Whatsay?"

"Bentley, my dear—" said Gwyneth.

Logan suddenly chuckled. But his expression was very shrewd.

"Gwinnie wants to apologize for me again. She's always apologizing. Old boor who should know better, eh?" His eye grew more shrewd. "My dear, I *do* know better. But, damme, can't you take a joke? Can't you enjoy a game? This is business. It's the best game in the world."

"We're already playing a game, my dear," said Gwyneth, with surprising smoothness. "Anyway, if you must do this, why not pick up something really pretty? That gold-and-enamel thing hanging on the wall, for instance." She pointed. "What is it, Martin?"

Clarke looked. I caught the flash of a smile at the back of his eyes.

"It's a triptych, Gwyneth."

Her forehead clouded. "I'm afraid that doesn't mean very much to me. Am I dreadfully ignorant?"

"An altarpiece panel. It has two wings or leaves, which fold together in front when it is closed: it's closed now. When you open it out, the three leaves show a religious picture, often very handsome."

"Oh? May we see it?"

At the eagerness in her voice, Clarke's face was convulsed; there is no other term for it. But he restrained her gently as she stepped forward.

"Presently. I think it would interest you." Here he looked her in the eyes. "But we mustn't gobble all the good things at once; and, I suggest, it's time we went up to dress for dinner. After all," he beamed at us, "these good people will want to see their rooms."

Andy Hunter spoke suddenly. "I say: what did happen here?"

He snapped out the words with vehemence, opening and shutting his hands. As nobody replied, Andy continued with the same doggedness:

"We've heard a lot. Spooks and curses and whatnot. But what actually happened? Who were this Longwood family, and what did they do? That's what I'd like to know."

"Second the motion," murmured Tess.

"To give a whole history of the Longwood family," answered Clarke, again consulting his watch, "would take all evening. Their chief characteristic seems to have been inquisitiveness. We first hear of them in the year 1605, when one of them was concerned in the Gunpowder Plot. They then had an uneventful history—squires, parsons, lawyers—until 1745, when another got mixed up in the '45 Rebellion. But it was not until 1820 that any real devilry seems to have attached to them or to this house. The head of the house in that year was one Norbert Longwood. This was his study."

"Who was he?" demanded Andy.

"A doctor. A savant, a member of the Royal Society, a friend of certain medical bigwigs whose names escape me."

"Their names," I said, as Clarke turned round sharply, "were Arago, Boisgiraud, and Sir Humphrey Davy."

"So? And how did you happen to know that?"

"Looked it up," I explained. "They all seem to have been writing pamphlets at each other about that time. What medical discovery they were about I don't know. But what happened? Have you anything else to add?"

"No," admitted Clarke. "Dr. Norbert Longwood is as elusive nowadays as he seems to have been then. All we do know is that he died horribly in this room in the autumn of 1820. The servants were so afraid of witchcraft that his body lay for two days in this room without being touched. That is why he is said to pluck at the ankles of people who pass, and try to get his fingers round them."

I reached out and put my arm round Tess.

"The room has been altered since then," Clarke went on hastily. "At that time it was dark oak and bookshelves and doctor's drugs. Now it's as cheerful a place, I submit, as you would well want to see. The later Longwoods wanted to cleanse it. Finally, there is that story of the chandelier falling on the butler in the dining-room seventeen years ago."

Clarke seemed possessed with an odd excitement. He struck his clenched fist into the palm of his other hand.

"It's all too muddled. Fact has somehow got mixed up with legend, and I'm wondering whether it is not too late to separate them. That always happens. If you know anything about such stories, you can predict it. There is always some common-or-garden variety of incident, unreliable because you find it in a hundred ghost stories, which invariably gets tangled up with the original facts; and people go on repeating it. For instance! When you came into the house, did you notice a big grandfather clock out in the hall?"

We nodded.

Clarke shrugged his shoulders.

"Enter legend," he said. "The clock is supposed to have stopped at the time of Norbert Longwood's death, and have refused to function since. That's nonsense. First, because the clockmaker at Prittleton tells me there's nothing wrong he couldn't put right in a few days. Second, and more important, because that same tedious story recurs over and over again in similar accounts. You understand what I mean?"

Tess persisted. "Yes," she said, "but has anything ever been *seen*?"

"It has."

"What?"

"Norbert Longwood," replied Clarke. "After his death."

He paused for a moment.

"It's a brief story, if not a pleasant one. Try to forget it, if you can. But I want to tell it to you because to me it seems to carry absolute conviction. Its details ring true, as opposed to the obviously bogus story of the stopped clock.

"About six months after Norbert's death, he was seen in this room by a cousin of the family. This cousin, by the way, had not been here at the time of Norbert's death. The account comes from his diary. It occurred on the night of the 16th March, 1821.

"He came into this room at about a quarter past eleven, thinking the place empty. To his surprise he saw a man in a black broadcloth coat sitting by the fire, back turned to the door. The cousin was about to speak when this man got up and turned round. The cousin recognized Norbert Longwood. Norbert was solid, and, but for his pallor, looked alive; he wore a frilled linen shirt front and black D'Orsay side whiskers. But what struck the cousin as worst of all — something he did not understand — was that on Norbert's face there was a long red scratch, as though made by the point of a pin, extending from the outer corner of the eye down almost to the jaw.

"The room smelt moldy, too.

"This cousin turned and ran. At the breakfast table next morning he said, as casually as he could, that he thought he had seen Norbert. He told his story to the rest of the family. There was no comment until he mentioned the scratch. Then Norbert's sister (Emma, her name was) seems to have fainted. Afterwards she told them all what she had never told anybody before. When she was laying out Norbert's body for burial, she had accidentally scratched the face of the dead, with the pin of her brooch, while bending over it. She had hurried covered the scratch with powder; and had never mentioned the matter since. That's all."

Clarke dusted his hands, dismissing the story.

"And you ask us to forget it," muttered Tess. "Oh, my God!"

"Yes, that's a pretty story to frighten women with, isn't it?" demanded Logan. Surprisingly, his voice was shrill and accusing. "Go on with it! What are you giving us?"

"The story," explained Clarke, surprised. "I do not vouch for it. I only quote it."

Andy did not say anything. But he took out his pipe and began to fill it.

On Gwyneth Logan the story seemed to have least effect of all. Her clear blue eyes regarded the fireplace thoughtfully, and the chairs round it. She nodded.

"Yes," she agreed, "my aunt Jennifer once told me you had to be careful with things like that. She did something very much like that when my uncle died. And, speaking of that"—evidently supremely unconscious, she seized the opportunity to turn round and appeal to us—"don't you think it's time for all of *us* to go and dress for dinner?"

V

At one o'clock in the morning, I had to admit that I was getting the wind up.

Not that anything had happened, mind. It was waiting for something to happen.

The plan of Longwood House was spread out in my mind like a map. We had explored all of it, before and after dinner. The east side of the house on the ground floor — across the main hall from drawing-room and study — consisted of dining-room (with kitchen and servants' offices behind), library, and billiard-room. This billiard-room comprised the little wing which was built off from the right side of the

house, thus:  . And from the billiard-

room windows you could see out along the whole front, a splendor of black-and-white fleur-de-lis as the moon rose.

Upstairs, the bedrooms were small. My own room was at the rear, facing north. It had been hung with bright curtains; it was swept and garnished; an electric bulb hung from the ceiling; and there were bedside books on the mantelshelf. The trouble was turning out that light and trying to go to sleep.

At one o'clock I got up, turned on the light for the third time, and put on my slippers and dressing gown.

We had taken the wrong amount to drink at dinner. I don't mean that we had taken too much: on the contrary, it was just enough to scratch the nerves to wakefulness. Vivid images crowded after it. Gwyneth Logan, suddenly beautiful in a low-cut black gown; the candlelight at the dinner table softening her hair and eyes and shoulders; a packet of superfemininity suggesting sheer nakedness. Then Bentley Logan, his shift front bulging like dough in an oven, telling stories and barking with laughter at the candle flames. The rattle of a coffee cup; a careless, wrong word; a business discussion, with undertones; and the distinct impression that, when we had all parted for the night, Clarke had pressed something into Gwyneth's hand.

It was impossible to sort out these impressions now. But it would have been easier if Clarke had not told that story about the corpse with the scratched face. I kept seeing the infernal thing in corners, when the light was out.

There was a quality of *emptiness* about that darkness and quiet. You remembered the wall of darkness built up for a mile around on every side. When the light switch was pressed, you were built into it, as into a catacomb bricked up. There was a faint lightness about the walls: an unpleasant hump to the furniture:

a suggestive sound to the faint breeze making a window curtain jump at the corner of your eye.

You turned this side and that in the bed. The darkness got heavier. You told yourself not to be an ass, and that others were sleeping peacefully.

But were they? Wasn't it possible to hear their hearts beat, and see their open eyes? — or was it only something over there in the corner, which you couldn't see because your back was turned? I am trying to be honest about this and it was the peopled weight of the darkness, lurking there to do as it liked, which drove me out of bed and flung me at the light switch again.

I put on my slippers and dressing gown. I lit a cigarette, was annoyed at the absence of an ash tray, wondered what to use for an ash tray, and compromised (as we usually do) by dropping the burned match into the soap dish.

In the raw reaction of seeing light, nerves crawled. I would have given five pounds for a strong whisky and soda, to send me to sleep. There was no reason why I should not go downstairs and get myself one, except that it would be an admission of weakness if anybody saw me, and it seems the height of something-or-other to creep out and take whisky in another man's house in the middle of the night.

No: no whisky. Reading might do it. The cigarette smoke rose up blue, tasting thin and bitter. I was going over to the mantel to get a book when I heard, from somewhere down in the house, a heavy thud as though a sofa had been lifted and dropped.

Then silence.

Though that noise was not loud, the whole house seemed to vibrate to it: the tingle of the window frames, the jar of the electric bulb, the fancied shift of a plaster ceiling, for the thud had been in my chest as well.

And here I made a discovery. In the shock of that noise, I think I discovered what is at the root of all the psychology of fear. The hot-and-cold feeling I experienced was one of pure relief. Something had happened: it could be investigated. It was no longer a question of lying supine, between starchy sheets, without shoes or the moral armor of a dressing gown, waiting in the dark for something to come to you. You could go to it. You could face it. And it was thereby shorn of half its terrors. We are frightened of ghosts because, in the literal sense, we take them lying down.

In the drawer of the dressing table was an electric torch, carefully brought along for just such an expedition as this. I got it out, switched it on, and went out into the hall: closing the bedroom door behind me.

This was what I had imagined myself doing. But going down those stairs was no pleasant experience.

The thud seemed to have roused nobody else. I could not remember the position of the hall light switch, and did not look for it. No creak came from the stairs, no sound from my felt slippers. In the lower hall I snapped on the torch again. Its beam brushed uneven red tiles, brushed the grandfather clock, turned left to the door of the dining-room and right to the door of the drawing-room.

From somewhere on the right — in the direction of the drawing-room — there was a noise. Turning off the torch again, I blundered into the drawing-room.

"Oh!" said a voice.

I groped forward until I bumped into a fat velvet-covered chair, and leaned across this to touch the china bowl of a lamp. I turned on this lamp, and met Gwyneth Logan just coming out of the door to the study.

She was some distance away from me, her hand on the doorknob. She wore a flowered silk dressing robe, rich-colored against the dark door, over a lace night-gown imperfectly caught at the breast. Her brown hair, masses of it, had been loosened round her shoulders. Her poise was that of one ready for flight. Her nostrils were dilated and her face crimson. With one hand — in which she seemed to be holding some very tiny object — she automatically pulled together dressing robe and nightgown; with the other she closed the door.

"Oh!" she whispered again.

Embarrassment (why?) flowed over both of us.

"I thought I heard a noise," was my own remark, loudly spoken in the old room.

"It must have been me," said Gwyneth, laboriously. "I was down here."

"Yes."

"I was — " Both of us had been stopped, floundering for words, when she broke off from another reason. Her words, spoken through her nostrils, were pinched for breath. Her eyes moved past my shoulder.

I heard Bentley Logan breathe before I turned round and saw him. He lumbered in from the main hall, kicking the door wide; but it did not strike the wall and so it made no sound. He wore an old purple dressing gown, too short for him in the sleeves.

"So you're the man," he said.

And he was carrying a .45 army revolver, his thumb pulling back the hammer to cock, so that it was practically a hair-trigger.

"So you're the man," he repeated in a high voice.

Now you may think that this situation had begun to resemble a French farce. But it hadn't. It wasn't funny at all. Logan's face looked not so much impassioned as dry and sick. The grayish tufts of hair were ruffled at either side of his bald head; the patch of mustache worked, as though the man were either going to sneeze or weep. If you have ever seen such emotions stripped raw, you will jump back from what you see. For there was power here too; it was going to burst, and everything else with it. His eyes blinked to adjust themselves to the light.

"Don't you lie to me," he said. "It's been going on for four months."

"Bentley!" urged Gwyneth, not quite at a scream.

"My wife," he said. "Four months."

"Sh-h! I tell you—"

"My wife," said Logan. "Museums! Sneaking out and going to the—" he tasted the words with hatred, and then mimicked. "the Victoria and Albert Museum. Whoring *there*. My old mother would have—"

I went past him and shut the door to the hall. This was not a very sensible thing to do, for his thumb was still fumbling over the hammer of the revolver. But I was afraid he would rouse the house, and that would be worse.

Tess, for instance.

"My dear," said Gwyneth, pretty steadily, "you're being s-silly, and I hate you. I don't know what you're talking about. I tell you, I never saw Mr. Morrison before to-day!"

She almost wept over this. Its sincerity was so patent, there was so much in the last statement of a woman who feels herself wronged, that it would have impressed me. But I was surprised that it impressed Logan. Perhaps it didn't, or perhaps he had another reason.

"No, Gwinnie?" he asked—softly, all of a sudden.

"No!"

"Then what are you doing down here?"

She moved away from the study door too quickly, letting go the knob as though it burned her. He interpreted that.

"So you were in there. What were you doing in there? And what's that you've got in your hand?"

"I won't tell you."

"Let me see what you've got in your hand, Gwinnie. Come on. Let me see."

"I won't!"

"Look here," I said, sliding in front of him. "Keep your voice down and stop acting like a lunatic. She's done nothing."

This stopped him for the moment. Perhaps, in his heart of hearts, he was half afraid to go for his wife. The man had regained his wits: he was merely fighting mad, looking for an excuse to go for anybody. There were big purple veins in his temples, and you could see the blood go up in them as in sluggish thermometers.

"You keep out of this, my lad," he said, twitching his head round, and twitching it back as I got in front of him. "Maybe you're concerned in this, and maybe not. But Gwinnie's concerned in it. *I'm* concerned in it. I'll settle it how I choose. Are you going to get out of my way?"

"No."

Logan nodded. He carefully dropped the revolver, still cocked, into the pocket of his dressing gown. He nodded again. Then, breathing sweat and whisky, he came for me bald-headed.

But neither of us ever landed a blow. Gwyneth flung back her arm, clumsily, and threw at him the tiny object she had been concealing in her hand. It struck the lapel of his dressing gown and fell on the carpet: where Logan seemed to stumble over it, like a bull stumbling over a pebble. He stood still, a big lump of a fist poised in the air, and stared down at it.

It was a small key.

Nothing more than that. Much too small for a door key, it was more like the key to a jewel box or to a diminutive clock.

We heard Logan breathe. "What's this thing?" he

demanded, pulled up by pure incongruity. "What is it?"

"It's a key," said Gwyneth.

"I know that. The key to what?"

"I'm not going to tell you," answered Gwyneth.

He seemed to have forgotten me. He bent over and picked up the key, a man out of his senses. He turned over the key in his big palm. His voice grew almost pleading.

"Don't tease me, Gwinnie," he said. "I'm that daft I don't know what I'm saying, most. But don't tease me. I forgive you. I know you've been seeing this fellow for four months, whoever he is. But, whatever you've done, it's all right if you'll just come back to me and act sensible. Just tell me: who were you with?" He pointed to the door of the study. "Who's in that room?"

"There's nobody in that room," returned Gwyneth.

She opened the door to reach inside and switch on the light.

"Look and see, darling," she invited.

Muttering something to me (I could almost swear it was an apology), Logan blundered past. She stood aside for him. She was obviously afraid of him, with a shrinking and physical terror. But, though the color remained in her cheeks, and she drew the dressing robe closer about her body, she put her hand on his arm.

"Listen, my dear," she urged in her soft voice. "Before you look, let me have a word. I know it isn't your fault. I know you don't sleep well at nights . . ."

It was the wrong approach. He turned on her.

"And *I* know," he said, "you gave me double my usual sleeping dose to-night."

She shut her eyes, patiently. "If you will think that, my dear, you must. But please, before you go storming the house down and frightening people with that horrible revolver, listen to what happened. You're an awfully silly boy sometimes." She opened her eyes. "You know I've never met Mr. Morrison before; now don't you?"

(He did know it. How, I couldn't say.)

"Well, then!" she cried, shaking his arm. "I was waked up by a noise like a bump. A loud noise. I came down to see what it was. That is, I mightn't have had the courage to come *clear* down, you see. Only on the stairs I met Mr. Morrison, and he offered to come with me. He'd heard it too. So we had a look round but we couldn't find out what made the noise, and indeed I still don't know what it was. Now there's the plain, silly truth."

I had to admire her.

Gwyneth Logan told this string of whoppers with candid blue eyes opened to their widest, with no flicker of an eyelash or lessening of their chiding appeal. She leaned closer. Her mouth had a pout of accusation.

"I'm *not* going to tell you about the key," she went on, shaking her head firmly. "I'm going to punish you. But oh, dear, you're not jealous of a key, are you? Do you see anything wrong with that? As for the rest, though, it's perfecty true." The blue eyes swept round. "Isn't it, Mr. Morrison?"

(Well, what are you to do when a woman puts you in a position like this?)

"Quite true," I lied—and regretted it.

For the hearing of this conversation was not confined to the three of us. With a subconscious fear of interruption, I had been glancing from time to time toward the door to the main hall. I had not actually seen it open, even to the foot-wide extent it stood now. But two things became plain. First, there was a light on in the main hall. Second, somebody's right hand was placed against the doorpost, as though the left hand had extended to open the door.

That right hand was familiar, down to the turn of the fingers and the gleam of the pink nails. It belonged to Tess. I could imagine her as clearly as though she were in front of us.

The fingers hesitated, tightened hard round the doorpost, and then were withdrawn. The door closed with a soft click which disturbed neither of the Logans.

"Now look!" said Gwyneth, stepping aside. "See if I've been up to any bold, bad wickedness. There's nobody in the study."

She was right.

Logan went to look. He even made sure that all the windows were locked on the inside. He was not merely troubled, as I was, by the puzzle of a key without any lock. Unless the woman were a sheer romantic liar—and, often, the dreamy expression of her eyes made this seem probable—that key must have some meaning. But there was no lock in the room.

Nor any person, nor even any ghost. Bare lights shone down on the rugs of the floor on the brick mantelpiece with its glistening tier of pistols; on typewriter table; on cane-bottomed chairs, bookshelves, the radio-gramophone, the triptych, and the noble ship model.

Logan was still half-demented, not himself. He kept his face turned away from us. His shabby flannel dressing gown was hunched up round his shoulders, and his leather slippers creaked from fireplace to table. He undoubtedly had taken a double ration of sleeping drug that night. He could not fight it. While Gwyneth came over to pat him reassuringly, her bright brown hair as rich as fleece round her shoulders, Logan suddenly plumped down in a chair and pressed his hands over his eyes.

The tragedy occurred just after breakfast next morning.

VI

I came down to breakfast with a headache and a bad taste in my mouth.

Though it had gone nine-thirty, nobody else seemed to be stirring. It was a damp, overcast morning, unnaturally warm for so early in the year. The downstairs hall smelt of it, a dusky place. That morning's post, together with the *Times* and the *Daily Telegraph*, had been piled on the oak settle before the fireplace.

There was a telegram for me. It had been handed in the evening before, but anybody in the country who expects to get telegrams delivered after five o'clock in the afternoon is guilty of wishful thinking. And it was from Julian Enderby, our one missing guest. It said that Enderby expected to arrive in the morning, and asked me to convey his regards to Tess.

I left it on the settle, taking the *Times* and the *Telegraph* instead. In the dining-room, Andy Hunter was having breakfast alone.

"Morning," grunted Andy without enthusiasm.

"Morning. Sleep well?"

"Like a top," said Andy defiantly.

"Didn't see or hear anything unusual during the night?"

"Not a thing."

But he did not look as though he had slept well. His swarthy, scrubbed face had shadows under the eyes. With his knife and fork he poked and prodded at the bacon, pushing it about his plate as though he were playing some game with it.

I put the newspapers on the table and went to the sideboard, where I helped myself to eggs and bacon, and poured out coffee whose fragrant steam was good for a headache. A pull at the coffee was strengthening.

"Anybody else up yet?"

"Logan's up," said Andy.

"Logan?" This was startling. "How is he?"

"Full of beans. Finished breakfast at nine, and out now for his morning walk. Back punctually at ten — nothing like a schedule — to answer his correspondence. Got six letters this morning. God! Imagine it. Six!" Andy hesitated. He carefully put down his knife and fork on the plate in the position that indicated he had finished. Then he picked up another fork and began to play with it. "I say, Bob."

"Yes?"

"Mrs. Logan," said Andy, concentrating fiercely on drawing a design with the fork.

"What about her?"

"Dashed fine-looking woman, isn't she?"

I dropped my own knife and fork.

The dining-room at Longwood house had a vast height of ceiling in comparison with the other rooms. Two steps led down into it, and the bedrooms above had been squeezed to seven-foot ceilings, in order to provide that height. Long, spacious, glowing with paneling as black as a cat's fur, it had the usual two big windows looking out on the front driveway. At the east end was a door leading into the library. And from the central beam hung the iron chains of that weight of a chandelier which had once fallen on and crushed an agile butler.

All the lights of the windows stood open. There was a breeze through them, with a smell of earth and grass in it. As Andy spoke, I noticed that the chandelier swung and trembled slightly. I remembered hearing my grandfather once say that the finely poised chandeliers in old houses, no matter how heavy, were apt to swing in the faintest draughts.

If the dining table had been pushed a couple of feet to the left, Andy's head would have been just under that chandelier. But this was only an impression, flashing and gone. I stared at him for another reason. I groaned at him:

"Not you too?"

"What do you mean, not me too?"

"Don't tell me *you've* gone and fallen for Mrs. Logan?"

Andy was shocked. "Good Lord, no. She's married," he said simply. "Besides, I only met her yesterday."

"Well, so did I. But that didn't prevent her husband from accusing me of being her lover."

Now I hadn't meant to say this. I was under no pledge of secrecy, but still I did not mean to mention it. It slipped out. On the other hand, if I couldn't confide in Andy I couldn't confide in anybody.

"Have you got sunstroke?" he inquired. "What are you talking about?"

"The beautiful Gwyneth has a boy friend. Or at least Logan thinks she has. I can't make out whether she's a plain, disinterested, romantic liar, making mysteries where there are no mysteries; or whether she's capable of making trouble. She and her boy friend seem to be in the habit of meeting at the Victoria and Albert Museum — yes, I said the Victoria and Albert Museum! — which, of all places of rendezvous in the world, would seem to be the worst. Logan doesn't know who the man is. But he's ready to go for anybody."

I continued to eat bacon and eggs, while Andy sat up straight.

"Rot. I don't believe it."

"Suit yourself. But Logan —"

"Logan's a swine," said Andy.

"Why? Has she been telling you so?"

If my shot had not been a direct hit, at least it was close enough to draw blood. Andy put down the fork.

"No. Not exactly. But you can see for yourself, can't you? Look here: finish your breakfast, and let's go and have a hundred-up in the billiard-room. I want to talk to you."

"About the Logans?"

"Not about the Logans," returned Andy, putting the tips of his spatulate fingers on the edge of the table, and pressing hard with both hands. "About other things. About a thing or two I happen to know in connection with — this house."

I finished in a hurry. This was something like it. I

also wanted to talk to him, about an incomprehensible key and Gwyneth Logan's incomprehensible errand in the study.

We went through into the library, a big place stuffed with ponderous books, and then turned right into the billiard-room. This billiard-room, as has been indicated, formed the little wing which projected out at right angles from the main body of the house.

Though care had been taken to make the woodwork look old, the billiard-room was obviously a modern addition. Its biggest windows faced west: that is to say, by standing at one of them you could look straight along the whole front facade of the house. And, after a decent show of taking the cover off the billiard table, and taking cues off the wall with concentration, Andy and I gravitated to one window.

The sun was trying to struggle out. It made the shingled roof look black and shabby; it caught patches and gleams from the fleur-de-lis design of black and white. Green striped with darker green, the smooth lawn sloped up to the gravel driveway curving parallel to the front, with unplanted flower beds at its edges. But they were being planted. A gardener, exaggerating the crick in his back as gardeners will, had wheeled up a barrow full of geranium plants. He was turning over the earth by the drive outside the study windows, and puddling it with the garden hose preparatory to bedding the geraniums.

A pastoral scene. It was very warm.

"Oh, hell!" said Andy suddenly.

He reached out with his billiard cue and poked

open several panes of our window, with such violence that I thought he was going to poke a hole in the glass.

"I said I didn't see or hear anything last night," he went on. "Lie number one. I did."

"Well?"

"Something happened in the study," said Andy. "I know, because my bedroom is just above it. Did you hear anything?"

Warm scents entered. We were both looking across toward the broad windows of the study at the other end of the house. The sun was strengthening, the day was brightening: you could see into that room.

"At about one o'clock in the morning," I said, "there was a kind of bump or thud as though a sofa had been lifted and dropped."

Andy took this literally.

"Not a sofa, old boy. A kind of—" he struggled, "piece of wood. Big piece of wood, it sounded like. It made a devil of a noise in the room below me."

(So Gwyneth had been up to something in the study.)

"What did you do?"

"Nothing, old boy. None of my business."

Now there was clearly more on Andy's mind than this. But for a moment, our attention was diverted. Bentley Logan, evidently returning from his morning walk, appeared in the driveway outside. He came round the opposite end of the house, and strolled along the drive toward the front door.

Of the hysterical and half-drugged man of last night, no trace remained. Logan's step was jaunty. He wore a cap, with a yellow pullover and flannel trousers; and he was smoking a cigar. He exchanged a word with the gardener in passing, affably. Then he went indoors to write his letters.

At almost the same time—from the main road, far down on our left—a motorcar pulled in. It was a sleek motorcar, reflecting back the sun. But it approached at a modest, decorous speed. It swung round before the house and stopped trimly. Out of it stepped a man of something under middle height, dressed in brown with sober elegance, and just beginning to be stout. He removed his gloves. He also removed his hat to mop his forehead with a handkerchief, and we saw the flat fair hair neatly brushed and parted.

Andy spoke with unusual harshness.

"Who's that?"

"Our one remaining guest. Julian Enderby."

"Enderby."

"The solicitor. He's a very clever fellow. Also a friend of Tess's."

"Don't like his looks," said Andy, with that flat forthrightness which takes you between the eyes.

"Oh, Enderby's all right."

"Don't like his looks," said Andy.

He seemed, in fact, more exercised by Enderby's arrival than the presence of a casual stranger would warrant. He watched Julian go up to the front door and disappear under its sentry-box hood.

"Come on," I said. "What's lie number two?"

"Eh?"

"You told me a while ago that saying you heard or saw nothing unusual during the night was lie number one. Let's hear lie number two."

"There isn't any," snapped Andy. "Look, there's the old blighter again.

This time he did not refer to Enderby, but to Logan. From our vantage point we could see more or less clearly into the nearer window of the study. It was an oblique view. We saw the typewriter table, and the typewriter. We saw a part of the brick mantelpiece. We saw the side and back of Logan's yellow pullover as he edged in to take the chair behind the table.

This we saw over the way — thirty yards off, say — behind faintly sun-misted glass.

The gardener continued to bed his geraniums.

Murder was within a step of us.

"You're a secretive devil," I said to Andy, "even when there's no reason for it. *What do you know?*"

Andy made his decision. Propping his cue against the wall, he took out pipe and pouch, and with sinewy fingers began to stuff tobacco into the pipe. He turned round from the window, and I crowded after him.

"It's about this 'haunted' house," Andy began; but he never got the opportunity to finish.

First, there was the crash of the revolver shot.

Second, there was the behavior of Bentley Logan. Andy had his back to the window, and could not see into that little corner of death behind the typewriter table. But I saw it. Logan, a bulky man, was kicked backwards as though he had run into a wall on a motor-bike going full tilt. His yellow-clad arms flew out; and he disappeared backwards from the window.

The noise of the .45 (Logan's own .45) continued to fill our eardrums even after the shot. Behind the house, a dog began to bark wildly. The stooping gardener jerked upright, so that the spray of the garden hose hissed across the driveway and then splashed up on a window.

These details I remember before Andy dragged at my arm, and we began to run. We ran through the library, which was empty. We ran through the dining-room, where Tess sat at the breakfast table, staring. We ran across the hall, also empty. We ran through the drawing-room, in which the maid, Sonia, was dusting. It was Andy who opened the door of the study.

The bullet had struck Logan in the center of the forehead, passing clean through and shattering the back of the head: for there was much blood behind though little in the front. You could see the dark stuff in the white wall where the bullet had finally lodged. Its impact had knocked him back against the wall. He lay beside the window in a position partly turned toward us, in his yellow pullover and flannel trousers, with a big stomach on him. His eyes were half open. You did not even need to touch him to know that he was dead.

Then something moved, and we saw Gwyneth.

Andy said something to her: I don't know what, and it is doubtful whether she heard either.

Gwyneth stood some eight or ten feet away from him, by the far corner of the mantelpiece. Had she been holding the revolver, she could have fired straight across the front of the mantelpiece and killed Logan where he lay. The revolver itself, glistening all except its black handle, was lying at her feet on the hearthstone.

But she did not bend down to touch it. Her arms

were crossed on her breast, the fingers gripping her own shoulders. As her eyes moved round first to us, then to the dead man and back once more to us, she started to rock herself back and forth. She was so frightened that her attempts to speak produced only little moaning noises.

I heard Andy's voice. "Steady," he said. "*Steady!* What happened?"

Gwyneth seemed to wake up, and conquer her mouth. Her first words were curious.

"I didn't do it. They did it."

"Who did it?"

"The room did it," answered Gwyneth.

Then I understood the expression of her mouth and eyes. It was not caused by the shock of seeing her husband die a violent death, or by grief or remorse or guilt or any of those emotions we usually know. The cause of that expression was superstitious terror.

Mind you, this was at just past ten o-clock on a warm May morning, with the sun beginning to climb on mullioned windows. It was no bogle trap for a winter night. But I know that I shivered. For the first time, the room felt physically cold; it was as though something had snapped its jaws. The old bones of the house were apparent now. Something upreared outside the window, and peered in with its nose pressed flat against the glass: it was only the gardener, but this could not have come with more ugly effect if it had been Norbert Longwood returning to see what had happened.

"You're not going to believe me," insisted Gwyneth, with a powerful strength of sanity. "Nobody will believe me. I don't believe it myself. But I saw it."

Behind us there was a noise of running feet. I glanced back, to see Tess in the doorway, and Julian Enderby with her.

"You saw what?" roared Andy, with the same insistence. He waved his hands at her. "*What* happened?"

Gwyneth moistened her lips. Without a word Tess ran to her, and put her arm round Gwyneth's shoulder. Gwyneth shivered as though she could not bear to be touched, but she went on trying to explain.

"This g-gun," she said, kicking at the .45 revolver so that it slithered across the hearthstone and slid off on the floor. "That gun there. It was hanging on the wall."

"Nonsense," said Tess. "That's —" She checked herself.

"It was hanging on the wall," persisted Gwyneth. "Look."

Flinging her shoulder loose from Tess, she pointed to the brick mantelpiece.

There was the tier of ancient pistols, hung up just as they had been the night before. But with one exception. Last night there had been twelve pistols, each set about three inches above the next. Only eleven remained now. In the place which had been occupied by a Napoleonic cavalry pistol, there was now a blank space where you could see the three wooden pegs which had held up the weapon.

"Do you see that blank space?" insisted Gwyneth. "Do you?"

"Well?"

"This" — again she kicked in the direction of the .45 revolver — "this was hanging up in that space. I tell you it was! I saw it. It came off the wall, and it hung in the air for a second, and then it shot my husband."

There was a silence.

This was because we did not clearly realize quite what she had said. The sense of the words did not penetrate.

"I tell you it's true," screamed Gwyneth. "There was nobody holding the gun. It came off the wall by itself, and hung in the air, and shot my husband."

A precise, pleasant, common-sense voice slid through and took charge of proceedings.

"The lady is hysterical," interposed Julian Enderby. "Take her into the other room, Tess."

Gwyneth backed away. She avoided all of us, retreating toward the low bookshelves at the other side of the room.

"I'm not hysterical, and I'm not mad," she went on. "I saw it with my own eyes. I was here, waiting for my husband when he came in. I knew he would come here to write letters when he got back from his morning walk. I wanted to – to tell him something. I was hiding."

"Hiding?" repeated Tess. "Why?"

Gwyneth disregarded this. She ran to the far side of the mantelpiece, whose big bay would have hidden her from the sight of anyone entering the room. She peered round the side of the mantelpiece in grotesque mimicry, looking across to the place where Logan lay sprawled behind the typewriter table on the other side.

"He came in," Gwyneth said, and gulped. "He had a bunch of letters in his hand. He was whistling to himself. I wanted to surprise him. I looked out, but I didn't speak.

"He walked over to the typewriter table, and got in behind it, and put the letters down. The typewriter wasn't as close to the window as he usually keeps it: to get more light, you see. He picked up the typewriter, to move it over and set it closer to the window. Just as he picked up the typewriter, I saw what I'm telling you. It *moved*. The gun *moved* up off the wall, just as if somebody was holding it, and came out in the air. There was an awful noise, and a hole came in Archie's face. He went back, all flapping-like and horrible; the revolver dropped down on the floor by my foot."

She put her hands over her eyes, convulsively, and dug the fingernails into her forehead; it was as though she saw or felt a bullet hole in her own forehead.

"The room killed him," she insisted. "The room killed him."

VII

Thirty minutes later, Julian Enderby came softly into the study — where I was waiting alone, except for the dead man.

Julian carried a bed sheet, which he unfolded and draped over Logan's body. I admired his unhurried precision. He was a good-looking devil, except that his face had become a trifle plump; his fair hair was flat and burnished in the sun. A great ladies' man was Julian, and nobody had ever seen grime under his fingernails even at the end of a long day's work. If some people thought him a little too close-mouthed, a little too frantically sharp over small matters of pounds, shillings, and pence, still he had a real strain of good-nature.

Also, he was obviously nervous.

"Hello, Bob," he said. "I've telephoned the police. This is a bad business."

My assent was given in the form of a grunt. I sat down beside the center table and began to turn over the pages of a magazine.

"It's bad," Julian repeated, sitting down opposite. "They invite me down for a week-end party; and it turns into a murder case. That never does any good. No, it doesn't."

He reflected on this. Then he looked across the table. We speak of people "throwing a glance," and that is how he looked: as though he expected me to catch something. His face was distinct in strong sunshine, the chin up, and little wrinkles round his eyes as fine as though drawn with a pin.

"Who is this woman?" he asked.

"Mrs. Logan?"

"Yes. Is she—" He tapped his forehead.

"She's not certifiable, anyway."

He seemed to find this an odd answer, for his eyes remained fixed and wide open. But he dismissed it. "I didn't want to come here," he complained. "It struck me as a foolish sort of party. And as for these Logans, they say the husband was—socially impossible."

"He was a damned decent fellow."

"Well, you needn't be so hot about it!" protested Julian, staring.

I was remembering one small thing, which would always color my memory of the dead man. I was remembering that Logan, with a loaded revolver in his hand and half-demented from thinking he had met his wife's lover, still had dropped that gun into his pocket to come at me with his fists. The murderer had had no such scruples.

"Sorry, Julian. But Logan was all right. This murder, as I see it . . ."

"I don't want to hear about it!" he interrupted

hurriedly. "The less I know, Bob, the less I have to tell. And I advise you to look sharp in the same way. All the same, it is an extraordinary business."

He could not help himself. That dry, tortuous brain of his was already weighing and measuring evidence. He jumped up from his chair.

"Let us consider the factors involved," he continued, clearing his throat, and beginning to pace up and down in front of the fireplace. He peered at the revolver on the floor, but he did not touch it. "You have no authority, imprimis, for saying that this is murder. I say"—he forestalled me firmly—"you have no *authority*. The three possibilities are (a) suicide, (b) accident, or (c) murder. On the other hand, suicide does not appear very probable."

"It wasn't suicide. Hang it, I saw the fellow through the window!"

Julian frowned. He cocked his head with great reserve, and some pompousness, while I explained.

"Yes, that is fairly convincing," he admitted. "Let us continue. Our second possibility, accident, does not seem very probable either. A gun does not go off by accident, and then land on the floor a dozen feet from its victim." He pointed. "Secondly, you say that that blank space on the wall among the old weapons was formerly occupied by a Napoleonic cavalry pistol: which suggests arrangement of some sort."

"Arrangement!" I said. "Arrangement!"

Julian paid no attention.

"To continue," he resumed, with a sidelong glance. "I have been speaking to—er—Mrs. Logan. She persists in this extraordinary story that the revolver got up off the wall, and shot her husband of its own

82

accord. Now, such a statement is either (a) the truth, (b) a lie, or (c) a delusion. Let us not ridicule this suggestion. No." He was very serious. "Let us examine it, without prejudice."

"Hold on, old son!" I said.

"Much will therefore depend on the sort of person Mrs. Logan is. That is to say, the sort of witness. Is she truthful? Is she mendacious? Is she truthful but unobservant? Is she imaginative? Is she—"

"Hold on, will you?"

Julian stopped, ruffled. I got up from my chair and went to the fireplace. Good ideas come but seldom; you feel that you are carrying a pail of water balanced on your head, and must not be shaken or prodded lest the pail spill over.

I stood on the hearthstone and examined the brickwork of the mantelpiece. The three wooden pegs of that empty space were about on a level with my eyes. A few inches to the left of the first peg, one of the bricks bore a smeared blackish stain. It was almost invisible against the dark red, but plain as print when you found it. Also, it had a distinctive smell.

"Powder marks."

"What?" said Julian.

"Powder marks. Sideways. The revolver was hanging on these pegs, flat against the wall, when it was fired."

We both looked round.

The picture of this crime, clear as a photograph taking form in a hypo bath, began to emerge.

A .45 revolver had been hung up there, with its muzzle pointing toward the left. Bentley Logan, behind the typewriter table, would have been facing that muzzle from a distance of some six feet away. The muzzle would have been just on a level with the center of his forehead.

A voice behind us said:

"Look at the typewriter!"

It was Tess. We hadn't heard her come in, but she was so close behind us that Julian bumped her shoulder when he turned. We followed the direction of her nod, and a little more of the ugly mechanism showed its fangs.

The typewriter table was long and narrow, with its narrow side against the window. Thus its length came out well past the deep bay of the fireplace, as I had noticed last night. It was still covered with scattered papers. But last night the typewriter had been pulled close to the window. *Now* someone had set the typewriter at the other end of the table, dead in line with the front of the fireplace.

"It's been moved," said Tess in an unnatural voice. "Somebody moved it. But Mr. Logan came in here, and saw it — and started to move it back."

I walked behind the table, as though I was Logan about to pick up the typewriter. Standing in front of it, I bent forward. Then was when I realized the full certainty of this murder trap. There is only one way in which anybody ever does pick up a typewriter. That is by standing squarely in front of it, bending down, and catching hold of it underneath with a hand on each side. No mistake could be made. X always marks the spot.

"See?" cried Tess.

Disregarding Julian's frantic howl about finger-prints, she ran and picked up the revolver from the floor. She draped it clumsily across the three empty pegs. When I glanced up from my standing position in front of the typewriter, twelve pistol barrels were pointing straight at me from the front of the chimney piece. But only one of them contained nickel-jacketed ammunition. If the .45 had gone off at that moment, it would have blown the top of my head off.

I ducked back in a hurry, and stumbled over Bentley Logan's foot as he lay under the sheet.

Tess had undergone a revulsion. Her complexion was unhealthy that day, the first time I had ever seen it so. Even her hair, usually black and glossy, looked lifeless. She went to the table and stood with her back to us.

Julian remained calm.

"Interesting," he commented, twirling his neat watch chain. "Most interesting. But, my dear Tess, you shouldn't have touched that gun. Confound it!"

"Oh, who cares?"

"*I* do, my dear. You're quite a detective, Tess."

"I knew there was something wrong about those pistols," Tess retorted simply. "I kept on saying so last night."

(This was true; but she did not turn round, or appeal to me for confirmation. The slope of her shoulders conveyed a hint that she was in no pliant mood.)

"Oh, yes. I told them so," she went on through her teeth. "I knew it was going to be something dreadful. But nobody would pay any attention. And now it's happened."

Julian raised his eyebrows.

"Happened?" he inquired. "I'm not quite sure I

understand. You don't call this conclusive, do you?"

Tess did swing round at this.

"Grant every fact you present," Julian said. "Grant that there's a powder burn on the brick, and that the typewriter has been moved to a different position. Very well. Then just tell me this: *how was that revolver fired?*"

There was a silence.

Tess started to say vaguely, "A string to the trigger, or something like that . . ." But, being an intelligent girl, she checked herself. We could all see the trouble looming. We were fetched up with a bump against a blank wall, a wall as solid and impenetrable as the mantelpiece itself.

"How was that revolver fired?" repeated Julian.

"But—"

"This is none of my business," Julian warned us. He was very emphatic about that. "Still, you promise not to quote me?"

"Oh, go on!"

"A gun may hang on a wall. But it won't go off of its own accord, just when the predestined victim gets in front of it. Hardly. Your first task, therefore, is to discover who fired it and how it was fired.

"I warned Bob a few minutes ago: much, very much, will depend on the testimony of Mrs. Logan. Now Mrs. Logan either lied, or else she told the truth, or else she was the victim of a delusion. She is the sole witness, the only other person in this room at the time of the shooting. If she lied, then it could be argued that she herself simply took down the pistol and shot her husband without any mummery or (ah) hocus-pocus. That is one solution."

I protested against this.

"But, hang it, Mrs. Logan is not lying! The powder burn alone proves that."

"Suppose it were an old powder burn?"

"It isn't: smell it. Which in itself should be good enough contributory evidence. And the rest of it is clear enough. A .45 revolver has a terrific kick. If it were fired while it hung on those hooks, the recoil would make it jump up into the air; and it would land on the hearthstone in just the position we found it."

"Meaning?" asked Julian softly.

"Meaning that, to an imaginative and frightened woman, the gun might very well have seemed to 'come off the wall and shoot her husband' in just the way she said it did."

Julian looked very thoughtful.

Still twirling the end of the watch chain, he began to wander round the room. Color came into his fresh-complexioned face, either from perplexity or from annoyance at being interrupted. His shrewd, light eyes moved from Tess to me.

"What you say," he fretted, "may sound reasonable enough. But it is not reasonable. We return to the same question. The gun was fired—how?"

"I don't know."

"Well, then?"

"There must be some way of explaining it. Lord knows what way. Here's a witness, Mrs. Logan, smack on the scene of the crime; and even *she* doesn't see what fired it! There couldn't have been any threads or strings or similar flummery. Andy Hunter and I arrived in this room not twenty seconds after the shot was fired, and there wouldn't have been time to dispose of any apparatus: even if you could tell me how in blazes it worked. If this business had happened at midnight instead of ten o'clock in the morning, we should all have been shaking in our shoes for fear of ghosts."

"Like Mrs. Logan," murmured Tess.

She was still not looking in my direction. I had a feeling, a kind of vibration in the air, that perhaps my defense of Gwyneth Logan had sounded too strong.

"But there's still no way for the gun to be fired!" Julian almost bawled.

"What about a secret passage?"

An expression of despair went over Julian's face, to be replaced by a humorous twinkle in his eye.

"Now, Bob, we all know how your imagination works. We know you're fond of white ladies and groans on the staircase. We know you'd dearly love a sliding panel. But, whatever else you do, try to stick to facts. A secret passage isn't even relevant: it has nothing to do with the present case."

"Hasn't it? Look at the mantelpiece."

"Well? What about the mantelpiece?"

"It's a new one," I said. "Or a comparatively new one. They didn't build brick mantelpieces like that in the seventeenth century. That one was probably put in when this house was remodeled, just after the war. Suppose it's a trick mantelpiece, with a hollow behind it? Suppose somebody hidden there could in some way reach out and pull the trigger of the revolver without being seen by Mrs. Logan?"

This was beginning to sound so thin that it died in my throat; but, after all, it was a reasonable supposition.

"We've got to have some sort of supposition, my lad. Even you—"

"I have none," said Julian. "I'm not concerned in this, as I keep telling you. Why should I be? I've never even met our host. This is Mr. Clarke . . ."

"By the way," said Tess, "where *is* Mr. Clarke?"

And there she touched on it. Subconsciously, we had all been wondering. Clarke's absence was a tangible thing: you felt the gap. He should have been plunging into the middle of it, bustling everywhere and pressing down on us the weight of that personality which was like the flat of a sword blade. Murder had fallen into the house, and yet Clarke neither appeared nor said a word.

Tess shivered.

"Where is he?" she insisted. "Has anybody seen him this morning?"

"Not I," Julian told her. "I was—er—going to mention that. When I arrived here, I was met at the door by a gray-haired old woman: the housekeeper, I think?"

"Yes. Mrs. Winch."

Julian looked annoyed. "I asked for Mr. Clarke, naturally. I was told that he had got up 'hours ago' and gone 'out back.' I was further gratuitously informed that Mr. Clarke was a poor soul who took nothing for breakfast but a cup of coffee. Presumably 'out back' meant into the garden; so I went there. I was still there when I heard that revolver shot. But I didn't see him."

"And nobody else has seen him," Tess pointed out.

"My dear Tess! You're not suggesting that this gentleman has run away?"

89

"No," said Tess. "But I might suggest worse."

The noise of a motorcar throbbed up the drive and swept past the windows. Since this must be the police, a feeling of adolescent panic spread in this room. We all wanted to get out of here. We had been tampering with the evidence, and the lurid light of fiction showed us that this was bad. But in the doorway to the drawing-room we met Andy Hunter.

"Look here," he began rather breathlessly, addressing me. "There are a couple of blokes outside. They—"

"That will be quite all right," Julian assured him, not without complacence. "It is the police. I took the trouble to phone them, since no one else seemed inclined to do it."

Andy's ignoring of him was so pointed that Julian looked as though he had been struck in the face. "It's no police from hereabouts," Andy said to me. His dark, hairy fingers began to fiddle with the lapels of his sports coat. "One of 'em says his name is Detective-Inspector Elliot, and he's from Scotland Yard."

"Elliot?" cried Tess. "Isn't that the man Bob knows?"

"Yes, it is," I said. "But—"

"And the other," interrupted Andy, "I ruddy well have heard of. It's Gideon Fell."

Julian Enderby began to whistle between his teeth.

"If that's *Dr.* Fell," he emphasized the title, "you couldn't take better advice. Sound man. Very. But this seems just a little too fortuitous to be true." A suspicious frown tightened his pale eyebrows. "The Scotland Yard inspector is going too far. Let's have a few cards on the table. What's he doing here?"

Still ignoring him, Andy turned accusing eyes on me.

"Well, my fine journalist," Andy replied, "you've blown the gaff to the world now. He says you sent for him."

VIII

At the rear of the main hall of Longwood House, a little door took you out into the garden.

On the right was the projection of the kitchens, decorously screened by a laurel hedge. On the left, a tiled porch — roofed over with glass — stretched along the back of the house. It reached almost to the great north window at the back of the study. Iron chairs, painted green and shod with little rollers which made them skid on the tile floor, were scattered about this porch. There was a gaudily striped porch swing, with a canopy.

One of the chairs was occupied by Inspector Elliot, and one by me. The swing (being the only thing big enough for him) accommodated the bulk of Dr. Gideon Fell.

Now this was the spring of the year '37. Andrew Elliot had not yet achieved the great reputation he later attained. In July of the same year he handled the case of the Crooked Hinge, and in the following October he made his name with the Sodbury Cross poisoning case.

But at this time, Elliot, who had been at school

with me, was intensely serious-minded, very ambitious, and ready to be drawn anywhere on a Saturday holiday by a mere hint of crime intended. Yet he was not pleased now. Once he heard what we had to tell him, he looked like a man whose enthusiasm has carried him too far.

"It's murder?"

"It's murder right enough. Take a look in the study and see for yourself."

"And yet you say you didn't send this telegram?" Elliot took a crumpled piece of paper out of his pocket and tossed it at me.

The telegram, marked Southend and dispatched the night before, said:

ANTICIPATE SERIOUS TROUBLE IN GHOST PARTY AT SUPPOSED HAUNTED HOUSE CANNOT COMMUNI-CATE OFFICIALLY WITH POLICE BUT COULD YOU FIND SOME EXCUSE TO SEE ME LONGWOOD HOUSE PRITTLETON ESSEX VITAL. — MORRISON.

"No. I didn't send this telegram, or any telegram. But it seems to have fetched you in a hurry."

"I jumped at the chance," Elliot admitted. "Just now, though, I don't jump anywhere except back to London. This is none of my business. You've rung the local police, have you?"

"Yes; but why not stay? It's going to be a sizzler of a case."

"Because I can't, I tell you! It's none of my business."

"Would you like to hear about it? That couldn't do any harm." I looked at Dr. Fell. "And what about you, sir?"

Dr. Fell inclined his head.

Vast and beaming, wearing a box-pleated cape as big as a tent, he sat in the center of the gaudy swing with his hands folded over his crutch stick. His shovel hat almost touched the canopy overhead. His eyeglasses were set precariously on a pink nose; the black ribbon of these glasses blew wide with each vast puff of breath which rumbled up from under his three chins, and agitated his bandit's mustache. But what you noticed most was the twinkle in his eye. A huge joy of life, a piratical swagger merely to be hearing and seeing and thinking, glowed from him like steam from a furnace. It was like meeting Father Christmas or Old King Cole.

"Sir," intoned Dr. Fell, with Jonson-esque stateliness, "I almost must apologize." He puffed out his cheeks. "It was the haunted house which did the trick. I could not resist the haunted house. I danced fandangos on the inspector's doorstep, with a grace and lightness suggestive of the Three Little Pigs, until he reluctantly invited the old man to accompany him. But murder—" His face clouded. "H'mf. Hah. What kind of murder, Mr. Morrison?"

"An impossible murder."

"So?"

"Yes. A pistol went off of its own accord, without anything to fire it, and killed this chap Logan."

"Ahem," said Dr. Fell. "Inspector, I do not wish to influence you. Heaven forbid. But it occurs to me that it would do no particular *harm* if we were to listen to Mr. Morrison's account. I repeat: it would do no particular HARM. After all, such recitals are often stimulating, and provide an appetite for lunch. Eh?"

Again he broke off. Tess was coming along the porch with a diffidence of manner she did not often show. Once she seemed on the point of turning round in a hurry, and running away. But she held on. She stood in front of them and blurted out:

"Inspector Elliot?"

"Yes, miss?"

"I'm sorry. I sent that telegram."

The little wheels on Elliot's chair creaked as he pushed it back to get up. He was very much the official now: as brisk and noncommittal as a shop assistant behind a counter.

"Oh? And why did you do that, miss?"

"I'm Tess Fraser. I—I knew you were a friend of Bob's. Bob wanted our host to invite you on this week end; but he wouldn't. I phoned the telegram from here last night. I knew if I just sent it care of Scotland Yard you'd be bound to get it."

"Yes, miss. But why did you send it at all?"

Tess's hands pressed tightly against the sides of her dark blue skirt. She was wearing a blue silk blouse with short sleeves, and it rose and fell with the agitation of her breast.

"There's one person dead already," she answered. "And I can prove that this Mr. Clarke is going to try to burn us all to death before we can get away from here."

Then she looked him in the eyes.

From this back porch, with its smooth dark-red tiles, a crazy-paved path led down the long slope of grass to a sunken garden. The sunken garden brimmed with entwined colors, blue, red, and yellow, and a sundial with a metal board occupied the center of it. Toward the west, a line of beech trees showed massive against the sky. The sun had gone.

"*Burn*—" said Elliot, and stopped. "What makes you think that, miss?"

"I want you, please, to take a look in the cellars."

"Well?"

"Every inch of the floor space, in every one of the cellars," replied Tess, "is filled with big drums of petrol covered by straw. This is a wooden house. If you as much as struck a match on the cellar stairs, you'd be burned at the stake before you could move."

The sun had gone.

Elliot directed a startled glance toward me. "Oh? And have you told this to Mr. Morrison?"

"No," said Tess. "Bob prefers to share his secrets with Gwyneth Logan."

"Tess, that's not true!"

She spoke the words as though she had taken a pin and tried to jab out with it. It was accompanied by a flash of hazel eyes. Immediately afterwards she was in tears.

Dr. Fell, whose bulk had hitherto excused him from getting up, now attempted to surge to his feet. His first roll was of such earthquake dimensions that the whole swing creaked and cracked, and the canopy folded together like an accordion. But he contrived, amid many asthmatic wheezes, to struggle upright. His pink face was still pinker with sympathy. And it was to him—instantly and instinctively—that Tess appealed.

"You've got to help us," she urged. "I've heard of

you. I never hoped to get *you* here. But, now that you are here, won't you help?

"This isn't just a case of a woman saying I-told-you-so. But I warned Bob, I told him six weeks ago, that there was something horribly wrong about Clarke. Clarke's sly; and he's — ugh! That isn't all intuition, either. I saw it in his face when he was looking at a picture of a hanging-drawing-and-quartering in the Soane Museum. But Bob simply wouldn't listen: Bob likes everybody. Will you help us?"

"Ma'am," said Dr. Fell, with thunderous earnestness, "ma'am, I should be honored."

"Steady, sir!" warned Elliot.

I took Tess firmly by the arms and pushed her down into a chair. The concentrated contempt with which she had said, "Bob likes everybody" had got me genuinely and blindly mad; it poured with salt scorn; it was doubtless her worst taunt; and both of us made fools of ourselves. She struggled to get loose, giving me a look of tear-stained hatred, but I held harder.

"Let me go! You're hurting me!"

"All right. But we'll talk about Gwyneth Logan later."

"We'll jolly well talk about her now," cried Tess, flinging her head round. "You didn't waste much time, did you? Going down with her to see that — "

"To see what?"

"Never you mind, Bob Morrison. *I* know."

"Well, it's more than *I* know," shouted a bedeviled man who felt the universe conspiring against him. "I didn't go anywhere with her. I found her downstairs.

97

All I did was back her up when she lied to her husband. But what are you talking about? Has it got anything to do with that little key?"

"Of course it has . . . But you didn't know that, naturally?"

"Tess, I swear I didn't!"

"You didn't see Clarke give her the key, just before we went up to bed?"

(True, for a fiver. It was easy enough to remember Clarke slipping something into Gwyneth's hand at the foot of the stairs. I hadn't known it was a key.)

"One moment," said Dr. Fell.

The twinkle had returned to the doctor's eye. He towered over us, chuckling from deep in his stomache. But he grew more serious as he again lowered himself to sit down on the swing.

"You forget," he said, "you forget in your natural enthusiasm that this conversation, however stimulating, is completely unintelligible to the inspector and myself. We have — ahem — " here he got out a big gold watch, which looked like a Dutch man-o'-war, and inspected it, "we have at least half an hour before we shall be obliged to return to town. Is that correct, Inspector?"

"Yes, sir."

"Then might it not be as well to tell the whole story from the beginning?"

"Bob," murmured Tess, staring at me, "I believe you're telling the truth after all!"

"You can be smacking well certain I'm telling the truth."

"Then go on — do as Dr. Fell says! The whole story. *Somebody* should be able to make sense of it."

I sat down on the edge of the low porch, and marshaled facts. I began as far back as that conversation at the Congo Club in March. I described Clarke's purchase of the house, his reactions, his selection of guests. When it came to telling about our arrival here last night, and all the subsequent events, I recounted it in full detail, just as it has been set forth in the preceding narrative. It was a long story, but they did not seem to find it dull.

Dr. Fell was possessed of a mounting excitement. He had long ago lighted a cigar, at which he puffed in the fashion of a child sucking a peppermint stick. He also took out a shabby leather notebook, and wrote with the stump of a pencil. Once he puffed out his cheeks and reared up for Jonson-esque utterance, but checked himself after a glance at Inspector Elliot.

"Archons of Athens!" he muttered, in a hollow voice. "O my sacred hat! I say, Elliot. This won't do."

The inspector nodded. He also appeared absorbed in the story.

"And now," pursued Dr. Fell, making a broad gesture which spilled cigar ash on his waistcoat and notebook, "a question or two. Miss Fraser—h'mf. Hah!"

"Yes?"

"When you first came into this house, something 'with fingers' caught you round the ankle in the entry?"

Tess's face was scarlet, but she nodded.

Setting his eyeglasses more firmly, Dr. Fell looked very hard at her for a moment.

"The incident, you see, has its vague points. For instance, what kind of fingers were they? Was it a big

99

hand or a little hand?"

Tess hesitated. "A little hand, I should say."

"Well, but what did it do? Did it try to pull you down, or anything of the sort?"

"No. It just—just *grabbed*, and then let go."

Again Dr. Fell looked very hard at her, wheezing gently. Afterwards he turned to me. "The mysterious Mr. Clarke," he said, "I find distinctly intriguing. Let us consider the story he told you of this Norbert Longwood, the savant, who died here in 1820. By thunder, I admire Mr. Clarke's nerve!" Again Dr. Fell chuckled. His whole face brightened and beamed with pink transparency. He brushed cigar ash into his waistcoat in an attempt to brush it off. "He told you (I think) that Norbert Longwood was a 'doctor'?"

"Yes."

"And that three of Norbert Longwood's friends or associates in the medical world were named Arago, Boisgiraud, and Sir Humphrey Davy?"

"No, no. *I* said that."

"You said it?"

"Yes; Clarke didn't volunteer any names. In fact, he seemed rather annoyed when I mentioned them."

Dr. Fell spoke thoughtfully. "D'ye know, I find him singularly reticent on many points. One above all. Now, this young man at the Congo Club: the chap who told you that tale of the agile butler swinging on the chandelier. What is his name?"

I gave the name, and the doctor wrote it down. "His address?"

Tess and I glanced at each other, puzzled. Dr. Fell's extraordinary intensity about this point had taken us from a quarter least expected.

"I don't know where he lives. But you could always reach him care of the club."

"Good! H'mf. Now! At about one o'clock in the morning, you say you heard a thud from downstairs. You went to investigate, and found Mrs. Logan coming out of the study, carrying this small key which has caused so much moil and perplexity?"

I nodded. Tess, on the point of speaking, stopped and glanced swiftly at me.

"There you were overtaken by Mr. Logan, who accused you of designs on his wife, but became speedily convinced that he had got the wrong man. However, he said there was some man who had been meeting Mrs. Logan at the Victoria and Albert Museum."

"Bob," flashed Tess, "can tell you all about museums. He's been to enough of them."

"You know damned well," I said, "that we — I mean Clarke and I — never went to any of the big show places. It was all little museums like the Soane and Chancery Lane. Or at least those were the only ones I ever went to. I can't speak for Clarke."

Dr. Fell blinked at Tess.

"Did *you* hear this bump in the middle of the night, Miss Fraser?"

"Yes, I did."

"And go downstairs?"

"Yes."

"And overhear this same argument?"

"Yes, I did," acknowledged Tess, walking her finger along the arm of the porch chair. She looked up.

"Now, this very curious key. Do you know what it means, or what it opens?"

"No, I don't," she returned instantly. "I may have an idea, or be able to guess. But I'm still not sure, and even if I were right —!" She made a fierce, puzzled gesture.

"What about you, Mr. Morrison?" suggested Dr. Fell. "Have you any idea about the key?"

"Yes. That it may be the key to some kind of secret passage," I said. As they all stared at me in surprise, and Dr. Fell with a ghoulish gleam of eagerness and interest, I tried to explain:

"That is, a secret passage behind or communicating with the fireplace. First, it's an obviously modern fireplace. Second, Andy Hunter knows something about this house that the rest of us don't: since he's been the architect in charge, that's only natural. Just before Logan was killed, Andy was on the point of telling me the whole thing. Then the shot was fired; and he turned slightly green and hasn't opened his mouth since. His knowledge isn't guilty knowledge — I know Andy too well to think that — but it's vital to this case."

Though we were some distance away from the front door, we could all hear the rap of the knocker echoing now through that quiet house.

Dr. Fell, occupied with brooding meditations, broke off to peer up at Elliot.

"That, my lad, will probably be the local police," he observed mildly. "We seem to have overstayed our half-hour. Will you go and have a word with them, or shall we creep guiltily out through the rose garden and run away?"

Elliot got up. His pleasant, homely face, with the sandy hair and an ingenuousness which was belied by his hard jaw, wore a look of exasperation.

"I suppose," he said slowly, "I'd better go and see them." Then a burst of candor got past his defenses. "Lord, sir, don't think *I'm* not interested! I'd give a month's pay to look into this business. But it's none of our concern unless they call in the Yard; and even then it's unlikely that I should be assigned to an important case like this."

Tess curiosity was aroused. "I suppose local police forces are a bit reluctant to call in Scotland Yard? Touchy about their own ability?"

Elliot threw back his head and laughed.

"The Chief Constable," he said, "is touchy about his budget. What most people don't seem to know is that when the county police call in a Scotland Yard man, they have to pay for his services. It works out at about thirty bob a day: that's why they're reluctant. However—"

He cleared his throat. He assumed such a casual and dignified air that Dr. Fell blinked at him suspiciously.

"As it happens," he went on, "I have met the local inspector. They nabbed Jimmy Garriety in this district a year ago. I'll go and have a word with the inspector, if you like. Just in passing." He frowned at us. "You others stay here. I'll be back in a minute."

But we needed no instructions to remain where we were. Mr. Martin Clarke, in a Panama hat and a white linen suit, such as you seldom see outside the tropics, had just come up the steps from the sunken garden.

Clarke stopped short when he saw our group. Under the darkening day, with a wind getting up beyond the beech trees, the Panama hat shaded his face. But he carried a light, flexible cane, with which he had been cutting at the grass. His shoulders hunched. He did not speak. If he had said anything, you felt that he would have shouted; and that the shout would have come at you with great and triumphant noise. He took the cane in both hands, and bent it gently backwards and forwards in front of him, as though he held a sword.

IX

"Dr. Fell, I presume?" said Clarke.

They were the first words anybody spoke, and they fell with claptrap violence among us.

He had advanced up the crazy-paved path, outlined against the colors of the garden. He was still bending the cane. The white, strong teeth showed in his tanned face, with many wrinkles round them; and his pale eyes had humor.

"What has happened?" he asked.

"Mr. Logan's dead," answered Tess clearly. "He was shot through the brain with your jumping revolver, and we're all pretty well scared to death."

Clarke did not seem to resent the ferocity of her tone; in fact, it is doubtful if he even noticed it. But I could have sworn that his first expression was one of genuine surprise. This was followed by an inner amusement so huge and distorting that you wondered he did not break the thin cane in his hands. Yet these were only edges, ghosts of looks: in the next second he showed a face of dumbfounded astonishment and concern.

"Good God!" said Clarke, breathing the word. "That is horrible news. That is—" He paused, shading his eyes still further with one hand. "But I don't understand. You mean it was an accident? And you say 'my' revolver. I don't own a revolver."

"The operative word, sir, is 'jumping,'" observed Dr. Fell, getting to his feet with another teeth-jarring creak and crack from the swing. "But I beg your pardon. I must first of all apologize for my own intrusion here—"

"Not at all," said Clarke swiftly.

"—by supplying information," wheezed the doctor. "Mr. Logan was murdered." In five succinct sentences he outlined the situation. "Unfortunately, Mrs. Logan was in the room, and saw the miracle."

"Gwyneth was there," Clarke began with violence. Again he checked himself, hard. "This is even worse than I had thought. Gwyneth!"

"You can't explain it?"

"Explain what?"

"This miracle of self-supporting and self-firing revolver."

Clarke made a gesture of exasperation. "My dear sir, how can I explain it? I hesitate to suggest, in the cold light of day, that this business was supernatural. I don't suggest it. I only suggest that the house is . . ." Again he made a gesture, looking troubled and old. He came up on the porch and sat down. "I will not go in now," he added. "I presume Inspector Elliot is there?"

"Inspector Elliot?"

"Last night," said Clarke musingly, "last night just

before dinner a guest of mine, a very charming young lady, put through a telephone call. I have an extension of the phone in my bedroom; and I happened to pick it up just as the call was going through to the telegraph office. I — er — I did not interfere. The prospect seemed amusing. Inspector Elliot (and you above everyone, Doctor) will always be welcome here. But I confess I don't like to think what you may discover."

Tess was scarlet.

Clarke's amusement changed him. It was not that he showed sharpened claws, or any sign of the poison in his system; there was nothing ugly about the look he turned to us. But he seemed to grow harder, more bland and powerful of manner. It was as though Tess and I were suddenly a couple of school children. Clarke, miles above us, spoke with Dr. Fell as to an equal.

"I hope I can help you," he offered. "I hope you, sir, will be called on to investigate this. Are there any questions you would like to ask me?"

"No," said Dr. Fell.

"No?"

"I mean, sir, that any interference on my part at this time would be both presumptuous and impertinent," intoned Dr. Fell, rapping the ferrule of his stick sharply against the floor. "All the same — Archons of Athens! — what a case!" His ponderous manner collapsed. "I say. This chap Logan. Had you known him for long?"

"For about seven years."

"As long as that?"

"I mean," smiled Clarke, "that I had known him

107

through correspondence. Our businesses were related; and, as you may have heard, he was a powerful letter writer. We struck up quite an acquaintance. But I never actually saw him until a few months ago. He was at Manchester, and I was at Naples."

"So you had business relations?"

"I was a manufacturer of jam," replied Clarke agreeably. He spoke as though being a manufacturer of jam were at once the funniest thing in the world, and at the same time the most distinguished. "Preserves, marmalades, the fine garnishings of the table. From the sun-ripened slopes of Italy to your fireside, breathing sunshine at breakfast. Logan was my wholesale distributor."

"H'mf, yes. Yes. An agreeable partnership, I hope?"

Clarke laughed aloud. "Before he met me," Clarke returned, "he hated my guts."

"So?"

"That changed, of course. It was only one of those senseless feuds which grow, in letters, from misconceptions of the other person. Logan couldn't understand me. He used to get into a lather about it. Man-alive! — why wasn't I, if I called myself a business man, back in the soot of the North, beating my chest and doing things? Why did I want to sink myself in the 'decadent South'? It was wrong. It was immoral. I probably kept a harem and tortured slaves. Anyway, why was I so obviously enjoying myself? That fretted him to a frenzy."

"And were you enjoying yourself?"

"Very much. I had my office in the Strada del

Molo, my house in the Corso Vittorio Emanuela, my villa at Capri . . ."

Clarke leaned back in the chair, relaxed, with a dreamy eye on the ceiling. You could see him against that background, in an aching clarity of sunlight on the harsh colors of Naples, against the bone-white beaches and the silhouettes of olive trees.

"I sometimes wonder why I left it," he declared. "But then I haven't Logan's strength of character. You know what he was. He was the man who could not shudder."

"He shuddered," said Tess, "when that bullet struck him."

"So he must have," agreed Clarke, suddenly jerking upright. "Well, what do you want me to say? *I* don't know what happened. Someone killed poor Logan. Why? Why? Why?"

Throughout this Dr. Fell had never taken his eyes off Clarke. Those eyes, magnified behind the glasses on the broad black ribbon, had a disturbing quality. You felt that at any minute the doctor might rattle off questions like a machine gun; and that he was holding himself in with difficulty. All he said, however was:

"Had Mr. Logan no enemies?"

"None who were here. And yet he must have been killed by somebody here. I am sorry to say it; but it's the truth."

"Killed — how?"

"Ah, there you have me. But haven't you any theory, Dr. Fell? Or you, Morrison?"

"Yes," I said. "The betting is that there's a secret

passage behind the fireplace in the study."

"Oh? And why do you think that?"

"Because of the little key you gave Mrs. Logan last night."

Stillness, the empty quiet of restrained breath, followed that. Clarke pushed his chair a few inches back; and the squeak of the wheels had a piercing quality, like chalk scratching a blackboard. But Clarke's expression remained merely puzzled.

"My dear fellow," he said, "you are harboring illusions. I gave no key to Mrs. Logan, or anybody else."

"Tess saw you. So did I."

"I gave no key to Mrs. Logan, or anybody else."

"It was a little key about an inch long. She used it to open something at one o'clock this morning."

"I gave no key to Mrs. Logan, or anyone else."

"It was—"

"And as for a secret passage," interposed Clarke, changing his tone suavely as the tension began to press and tighten, "we should be able to settle that. I don't know of any such thing. If there is, my architect has been treating me damnably; and I resent it. We must find out. Mr. Hunter! Mr. Hunter!"

I had not noticed Andy lurking inside the back door some distance away, but Clarke (whose eyes followed even the movement of a shadow) had seen him. Andy banged out at us with a defiance which showed he had been listening.

"Bob," he said, "don't be an ass."

"About the secret passage?"

"Yes. There's no such thing." Andy was so desperately in earnest that he became inarticulate. With belated inspiration he took a mass of papers out of the inside pocket of his coat, and began to ruffle them over. He produced, in triumph, a grubby visiting card.

"Read that," he said.

I read it aloud. It bore the name of Bernard Evers, Fellow of the Royal Historical Society, and an address in Clarence Gate. Though it conveyed nothing to me, Clarke nodded with enlightenment.

"Yes, I know it. He's—"

"He's the foremost authority on secret hiding places in England," interrupted Andy, taking the card and shaking it in my face. "Read his book, and you'll find out. He was round here like a shot when he heard the house was being opened up again. He went over the place; I went with him."

Andy conquered the lump in his throat, which seemed to be as big as his own sizeable Adam's apple, and went on with a rush in one of the few subjects that could inspire him with eloquence.

"You see, there's a lot of rubbish talked about secret passages, and hiding holes, and trick doors. Most of it's absolute bilge. Stands to reason. First of all you've got to ask, why should there be such a thing in any given house? What purpose did it serve? That's to say, people in the old days didn't just build such things for fun, you know. They had a reason for doing it.

"And you'll find that in ninety-nine cases out of a hundred it was to hide somebody from searchers. To hide priests, during the persecution of Catholics in

Elizabethan and Jacobean days; to hide Cavaliers, under the Commonwealth; or to hide Stuart adherents at the time of the Jacobite uprisings. To hide them — and then, if possible, to get 'em through and out of the house by a secret exit.

"Well, this house was built in 1605. That was the year of the Gunpowder Plot, when priests were scurrying for cover everywhere. So Mr. Evers thought there might be something here. We went over this house with a microscope. And there's no such thing anywhere. Don't take my word for it! Write to Mr. Evers and ask him. That's all."

Andy cleared his throat. He shuffled the mass of papers in his hand, spilled some of them on the floor, gathered them up, and concluded:

"Bob here is loony on the subject of mantelpieces. The first thing he mentioned, when we got here last night, was mantelpieces. In some old houses, I admit, there has been a hiding hole built *under* the fireplace.* But there's nothing wrong with that one in the study. Every brick is solid; every joint is cemented; and I can get any number of people you like here to prove it."

"But, Andy, it's got to be!"

"Why has it got to be? Just tell me that."

"Because something fired the blasted gun! Other-

*Anyone interested in exploring this fascinating subject is referred to Mr. Granville Squier's monumental work, *Secret Hiding-Places* (Stanley Paul & Co., 1933). With regard to that noble if overworked device, the sliding panel, the author relates that he has found only three genuine sliding panels in the whole of England.

wise we've got the gun rising up supported by a ghostly hand, hanging in the air, and shooting Logan. Do you believe that?"

Our voices themselves were rising up powerfully. Andy did not answer this. His face assumed that mulish expression it always wears when he knows he is right. He leaned against the wall, folding his arms with stately dignity.

"There is," he announced, distinctly articulating each word, "no – blinking – secret – passage. That's what *I* say."

Clarke had been listening with critical amusement.

"I'm glad to hear it," he said. "That is to say, I am glad you've been hiding nothing from me, Mr. Hunter. But in that case, what becomes of Morrison's key?"

"You know perfectly well what becomes of it, Mr. Clarke," said Tess, very softly.

"Oh?"

"Yes. You know what the key opens," said Tess. "It opens that triptych."

There was silence, after which she went on with breathless violence, appealing to Dr. Fell:

"It's a big flat wooden thing, hanging up on the wall in the study, covered with gold and enamel work. It's got two leaves that fold together; and there's a concealed keyhole so that you can lock it up. I've seen triptychs with keyholes in Italian churches: you'd never find the keyhole unless you looked closely. That's what the key was for, and Mr. Clarke can't deny it."

Andy Hunter snapped his fingers. His startled look had become one of certainty.

"If that thing fell on the floor," he declared, "it would make a noise exactly like the noise I heard last night. By Jove, Tess, you've got it! And once before Mrs. Logan wanted to look inside the triptych. And—"

He broke off, for Clarke was chuckling. Swishing the light cane against one leg, he turned round to Dr. Fell.

"The triptych," said Clarke, "has no keyhole, concealed or otherwise. It contains a religious painting, the Adoration of the Magi. Do you think Mrs. Logan would get up and go downstairs in the middle of the night to look at a religious picture?"

"How do you know she got up and went downstairs?" I inquired. "Nobody here has said anything about it."

Again we saw Clarke's teeth. It was a sight which was beginning to affect me with an uneasiness like nausea.

But he said nothing in reply. Politely, he got to his feet. Politely, he stepped down off the porch.

"Will you follow me, please?" he requested. "All of you."

We followed him, even Dr. Fell. He walked along the smooth grass beside the porch, past the end of the porch, and up to the great north window which gave into the study. This window, composed of six mullions, was set up some eight feet from the ground; you could see into it only by standing on a chair, or using some other form of support.

And Clarke stopped short with a whistle of what sounded like genuine surprise. Underneath the window was an unplanted flower bed. In the flower bed, set close against the wall, was an upended wooden box.

"Somebody," he observed, "has already been using this vantage point to look inside. Never mind." He whirled round to me. "Mr. Morrison. Will you be good enough to stand on that box, speak to whatever policemen are in there, and ask them to open the triptych?"

I climbed up. It brought my head well above the sill of the window, so that I was looking straight across the study toward the fireplace and the two windows in the other wall.

A man with a black satchel, presumably the police surgeon, was bending over Logan's body: which had now been carried more toward the center of the room. A constable was packing away camera and insufflator. Two other men—Elliot, and a uniformed inspector of police—were engaged in a task whose grisly logic became clear.

They were unwinding a steel tape measure. While Elliot held one end of the tape measure against the hole in the wall where the bullet had lodged, the uniformed inspector was playing out the other end of the tape until it touched the muzzle of the .45 revolver hanging above the fireplace. It formed a straight line. At a word from the inspector, the constable came and stood behind the typewriter in Logan's former position. He was about Logan's size, too. And the tape measure would have passed dead through the center of his forehead.

"No doubt about that," growled Elliot.

I rapped on the window, one of whose panes was partly open, and Elliot came over. Raw-boned and sandy-haired, he looked more worried than I had ever seen him.

"Well?"

"That triptych. Over there. See if you can open it."

"What about it?"

"See if it's got a keyhole. If it has, that may be the explanation of the key."

Elliot stared back for a second. Then he strode across to the triptych, dulled now in shadows: for the day was darkening, and a damp wind blew against our backs.

The triptych hung in the middle of the west wall just over the line of low bookshelves. Elliot pulled open its leaves. Even from where I stood, it became clear that Clarke had told no more or less than the truth. It contained a conventional treatment, of somewhat crude line but fine color, of the Adoration of the Magi in the manger of Bethlehem.

Elliot looked at it, and then turned his head round to look with exasperation at me on my perch. The gilded wood winked; the robes of the Magi burnt with somber hues under the glow of the child's halo.

"Yes?" said Elliot. "What about it?"

"Has it got a keyhole?"

"Yes, it has," said Elliot thoughtfully; and I could have yelled aloud with exasperation. Why should Mrs. Logan, flustered and disheveled, have made a great secret out of this? Riddle piled upon senseless riddle.

"Will the inspector," came Clarke's voice with great urbanity from below, "assure himself that there is no deception? That, for instance, the paint is several hundred years old?"

"Yes, it's old enough," agreed Elliot. He shut up the triptych. He opened and closed his hands. "Will you ask Dr. Fell to come in here?" he added. "This thing looks worse and worse."

A drop of two of rain stung the back of my neck. Clarke was laughing.

X

It began to rain in earnest just after lunch, a lunch which nobody ate.

They removed Logan's body. Gwyneth Logan suddenly collapsed in tears and hysterics, after throwing a glass at a completely inoffensive Andy Hunter just because he had asked her whether she would like some coffee. Julian Enderby tried to sneak back to London, but was intercepted leaving the house and told to stay.

Nobody except Dr. Fell had been allowed into the study, and the police had remained closeted there from the beginning. But at three o'clock they sent for me.

The study looked evil and gloomy; the floor a pale lake; and rain pattered against the windows. Dr. Fell's bulk gravely endangered one of the chairs. Elliot introduced me to the Inspector from Prittleton, a long-faced intelligent-looking officer with thick eyebrows and a powerful hand shake.

"It seems," Elliot said grimly, "that I am going to get the case after all."

Inspector Grimes made his position clear. "I tell

you straight," he returned, "that I want nothing to do with this business if I can help it. Neither does the Super, and neither does the Chief Constable." He hesitated. He glanced at the place where Logan's body had lain. No trace now remained of Logan except some bloodstains on the floor, and a few more blood spots low down against the plaster wall in the corner.

"I'd just joined the force, seventeen years ago," Inspector Grimes went on abruptly, "when that other thing happened. You know—the chandelier falling on the butler. I was here."

He jerked his head in the direction of the dining-room.

"Polson, his name was. William Polson. Old man: eighty-two if he was a day, and served the Longwood family all his life. It nearly killed Mr. Longwood (that was the last of the old Longwoods) to have Polson die on him.

"Well, the Superintendent . . . not the one we have now, but a good man . . . the Superintendent, he tried to solve it himself. And a fine gum tree he got up. We didn't find any explanation because there wasn't any explanation. Murder, they said. Murder! Who'd murder old Polson? And how? I'm telling you, that old gent of his own free will jumped up and grabbed the chandelier and started to swing on it." Inspector Grimes was growing excited. "So it wasn't accident either. But what in blazes was it?"

Elliot eyed him curiously.

"Yes. We want to hear all about the last of the Longwoods—"

"We do," rumbled Dr. Fell.

119

"—but in the meantime," pursued Elliot, "we want some more facts." He turned to me. "Look here, I'll put the cards on the table.

"Logan was shot by a bullet from that revolver hanging on the wall." His face darkened angrily. "Your friend Miss Fraser made one fine mess of things by handling the gun afterwards. Her finger-prints are on it, and so are Logan's own. What other prints are on it we don't know; but we think no others.

"Now at some time, either late last night or early this morning, somebody came in here; hid the old cavalry pistol that was on those three pegs—we found it behind some books over there—and put the .45 in its place. You've told us that this .45 belongs to Logan himself. Are you sure of that? Do you know it to be a fact?"

It was my own turn to hesitate.

"Well, it looks like the gun he had down here last night."

"Never mind that. Are you *sure* of it?"

"No, I can't swear to it. But his wife seems to think it's the same one, and she ought to be able to identify it."

"Yes," said Elliot slowly, "she ought to be able to identify it." He went to the table, sat down in a cane chair, produced his notebook, and rapped a tattoo on it with a pencil. "Now, when did you last see that gun—assuming it's the same one—before you saw it in here to-day?"

"Last night, about one-thirty. I mean this morning; but it'll be less confusing if we call it last night."

"Where was the gun then?"

"In the pocket of Logan's dressing gown."

"You've said that you and Mr. and Mrs. Logan were in this room, while Logan hunted round for somebody he thought might be hiding here?"

"Yes."

"And what did you do after that?"

"Went upstairs to bed. The Logans went to their room, and I went to mine."

"Was the revolver still in Mr. Logan's pocket? That is, might he have taken it out and left it down here?"

"No, I don't think so. It was still in his pocket, so far as I can remember."

Elliot made another note. Then he looked up. "Who, besides you and Mrs. Logan, knew that he had a gun here?"

"I can't tell you. Nobody, so far as I know."

"You didn't meet anybody else — in the halls, or prowling about?"

"No."

The rain pattered steadily, drearily, bringing out an odor of old wood and old stone.

"Now," continued Elliot in a quiet, insistent voice, "I want you to look at something, and think hard if you ever thought in your life. Walk over to the fireplace and look at that row of pistols. Study it. Then tell us whether you see anything different, anything at all different from the arrangement of the pistols last night. I don't mean the substitution of the .45 for the cavalry pistol; but is anything else different?"

He spoke with such urgency that I grew uneasy. Even Dr. Fell's wheezing breaths seemed to come faster; the doctor struck a match for his dead cigar, with a sharp plop and a core of light like a start, which was reflected back from his eyeglasses.

I went to the mantelpiece. There was a dead silence except for the dreary monotone of the rain. At first nothing emerged. The rain went on. Then a half-memory grew in my mind, and twisted, and took shape . . .

"Yes, by the Lord Harry there is!"

"Well? What is it?"

"Somebody has been monkeying with more of the guns."

"So? How?"

Memory returned as flat and clear as a picture postcard.

"Somebody," I said, "has taken down three or four of the pistols off the wall, and hung them back up again in a hurry."

Inspector Grimes whistled. Elliot's eyes did not waver; his hard, probing voice went on insistently. "You're sure of that, now?"

"Dead sure. The murderer was trying to find the right height for his gun trap, and set the .45 in several other places first. And he did it clumsily. Last night the muzzles of those pistols were in practically a straight line. Now somebody's been messing them about, and they're uneven."

"As a matter of fact," Elliot admitted, "that's what Mrs. Winch and the maid Sonia tell us. Sonia swears that two of them have changed places: that the Bow-Street-runner gun is now where a dueling pistol used to hang—"

"And she's right!"

"Is she?" asked Elliot. He put down his pencil.

"There's a film of bright polish on all of them," he added. "Would it interest you to know that there isn't a fingerprint on any of 'em: not even a smudge where they might have been handled with gloves? *Nobody* has touched those guns."

"But, hang it, that's not true! Ask anybody. They've been changed about all over the place!"

"Nobody," said Elliot tonelessly, "has touched any of those guns."

"But if there's a secret passage—"

Elliot suddenly grew human. He picked up his notebook and slapped it down on the table. "For the love of Mike," he said, "stop babbling about secret passages. Will you, once and for all, get that obsession about secret passages out of your head? That mantelpiece is just what it pretends to be: a solid brick mantelpiece. There's no secret passage, or trick door or whatnot, anywhere in this room."

He turned to Dr. Fell.

"Well, sir, have you any ideas? What do you say?"

Dr. Fell stirred. He scowled at the lighted end of his cigar, drawing in several chins for weighty speech, and replying in a voice of such concentration that it seemed to come from deep down in the earth like the first rumble of an earthquake.

"I do not deny," he replied, "that I have an idea. A faint o'erglimmering of an idea, which"—he gestured vaguely with the cigar, scattering ash—"flickereth and goeth out. There is one very strong objection to it. Before committing myself, I should like to hear what Mr. Enderby has to say."

Elliot got up, went to the door, and spoke to the constable in the drawing-room.

"Ask Mr. Enderby," he said, "if he can come here at once."

What Julian had to do with this was a mystery to me, but Elliot made no comment. However, when I started to go, he motioned me to remain where I was.

He went to the typewriter table, where he picked up six opened envelopes: presumably the envelopes of the letters Logan had received that morning, and which he had been sitting down to answer when he was shot. These Elliot put in a neat pile on the center table. With them he placed a collection of articles which were probably the contents of the dead man's pockets. They included nothing which appeared very significant: a notecase, a key ring, a fountain pen, two pencils, a small address book, some loose change, and a bent cigar in a crumpled cellophane wrapper.

Elliot was arranging these things in a line when Julian entered. In that dim light, with eternal rain smearing the windows, his tubby figure was reminiscent of someone else. But, when he opened his mouth, he could be nobody but Julian. Elliot motioned him to a chair, and he sat at attention.

"Now, sir, as a formality . . ."

"I don't suppose, Inspector," said Julian, "that any attention would be paid to me if for the dozenth time I asked to get away from here? Good Lord, I know nothing of the case. Nothing! If I did, I should be only too pleased to help you."

Elliot had an admirable way with witnesses: brisk, and yet deferential; pleasant, but implying that nonsense was nonsense in anybody's phraseology.

"In that case, sir, the sooner we get the routine

inquiries over with, the soon you'll be able to get away. Would you mind giving me your full name, with both your business and home addresses?"

Julian took out a super-neat cardcase, extracted a card from it, disengaged it gingerly from the intervening tissue paper, and laid it on the table.

"Just so, sir. And the home address?"

"Twenty-four, Malplaquet Chambers, Finchley Road, N.W. 6."

Elliot wrote it down.

"How long have you known Mr. Logan, sir?"

A shadow of exasperation crossed Julian's face. "But that's just the point. I didn't know him. I never saw the man until after he was dead. Consequently—"

"Have you ever met Mrs. Logan?"

Julian reflected.

"I'll tell you what, Inspector," he confided. "That's something I've been trying to remember ever since I saw her. I think I've met her somewhere before, or seen her; but for the life of me I can't remember where. Anyway, for all practical purposes you can say that I didn't know her."

"Yes. I see. Now, at what time did you arrive at the house this morning?"

"At just before ten o'clock. I'm afraid I cannot be precise as to the minute."

"You went straight into the house?"

"Of course. I wished to pay my respects to our host. I—er—was not acquainted with him either."

"But you didn't find Mr. Clarke?" .

"No," returned Julian, fiddling with his already perfect tie, and then leaving off to brush at the lapels of his coat. "The housekeeper (I think it was the housekeeper?) told me he was 'out back.' I went out into the garden, as I have already told Bob Morrison." He flashed a side glance. "I was in the garden when I heard the shot which presumably killed Mr. Logan."

"You heard the shot?"

"Of course."

"Whereabouts in the garden were you then, sir?"

It sounded like routine questioning. But I, who knew Elliot, could hear a faint undertone, a faint suave lift which suggested traps amid courtesy.

Julian considered the question. His voice was persuasive.

"I'm not quite sure about that, Inspector. It's a big garden: you may have seen it. There is a lot of grass, with a crazy-paved path, and then a sunken garden beyond. I was startled when I heard the shot (naturally); and I can't be positive."

"Just try to tell me your approximate whereabouts, sir. Were you near the house?"

"No, not very near."

Elliot turned round and inclined his pencil toward the great window facing north, toward the gardens. It was blurred and darkened by skeins of rain, which tapped back at him. One of the tall panes still stood partly open, so that rain sluiced down almost on the top of the radio-gramophone under it.

"You weren't near that window, for instance?"

"No. Not very near it, that I remember."

Elliot put down the pencil and folded his hands.

"Mr. Enderby," he said, like a schoolmaster across a desk, "I'd be very grateful if we could cut out all this and come down to business. What did you see when you climbed up on that up-ended wooden box outside, and looked in through the window just as the shot was fired?"

"Looked in . . ." began Julian; the rain was like a roar in all our ears.

Elliot made a restraining gesture. His tone was patient.

"Just a minute, sir. I'm not bluffing, and I'm not third-degreeing. As you know, you're not compelled to answer my questions. If you refuse to answer, that's your own affair. But I'd like to point out the trouble it will save you at the inquest if you help me now by telling the truth. It will certainly save your face," here he looked hard at Julian, "and it may save you other unpleasant consequences as well. When you drove up to the house this morning, did you notice a gardener working beside the front drive-way—in a flower bed just outside the two front windows? There?"

He pointed.

"I noticed somebody. Perhaps," said Julian, "a gardener."

"Yes. This gardener, Mr. MacCarey, was standing not six feet from the front windows when the shot was fired. He dropped his hose, and ran to see what had happened. The front windows (you notice?) are built much nearer the ground than the back one. It was easy to look in."

"Well?" said Julian. He began to twirl the end of his watch chain; and twirl it faster.

"Mr. McCarey," continued Elliot, "is prepared to swear that he saw you standing outside that big back window, on the box, looking in. He couldn't see the box; but he distinctly saw you. He also says that your hand was inside the window, through that partly opened pane. And this was only two seconds . . . two *seconds*, sir . . . after the firing of the shot."

Again, this time with a sharper movement of his hand, Elliot forestalled the other.

"Just a minute, sir. I'm not suggesting that you had anything to do with this crime. You're all right: you were clear outside the window at the time. But what we do want, and want very badly, is a witness. You are that witness. You must be. If you were on that box, and with your hand partly through the window, only two seconds after the shot . . . well, it's twenty to one you saw what happened when the gun went off. Mrs. Logan tells what seems to be an impossible story. You're in a position to confirm that story, or demolish it. Considering that, and considering what your plain duty is, are you ready to change your mind and tell me what happened? What do you say?"

XI

Julian's response to this was interesting, to those of us who know our Julians. He turned round on me.

"*You* got me me into this," he said accusingly.

Which was confounded cheek, to say the least of it. When you considered Julian puttering up and down, saying in an agony of logic, "Let us consider the factors involved," and, "I have no concern with this!" it became too greased and slippery for anybody's liking. But Julian pulled himself together in a second. He did not bat a round eyelid as he returned Elliot's gaze.

"Inspector," he said, "can the person who is being questioned get in a word edgeways?"

"I'm waiting, sir."

"So am I," retorted Julian. "You see, your proposition does not follow. Even if it were true—"

"Is it true? Were you outside that window?"

"Not so fast, not so fast!" Fussed and fussy, but always alert, Julian hit back. "Suppose what you say is true. I say: suppose it, that's all. Why am I, *per se*, your chief witness? What about the gardener? Why can't he substantiate, or deny, Mrs. Logan's testi-

129

mony?"

"Because, sir, he wasn't at the window when the shot was fired."

"Then," said Julian, "have you any reason for supposing that *I* was?"

"Look here—"

"No, no! It's a fair question, Inspector. The gardener arrives at the window a few seconds after the shot. Very well. Why shouldn't the same apply to me? Why shouldn't I hear the shot too, and look through my window on the other side? Have you one scrap or shred of evidence to show that I looked through my window before he looked through his? You haven't; and you know it. Then why should I be expected to know so much more than he?"

Elliot's patience was wearing thin.

"Because, Mr. Enderby, the gardener looked through the wrong window."

"The wrong window?"

"I mean," continued Elliot, putting the palms of his hands flat on the table, "that even if MacCarey had been at the window when the shot was fired, he still couldn't have seen anything. Do you follow that? He looked through the window that had the typewriter table against it. That one there. So he couldn't see Mrs. Logan, because she was over at the other side of the fireplace; and the projection of the mantelpiece cut off the view."

Julian turned to look.

"That," he conceded, "would appear to be true."

"Whereas you had a grandstand seat from the opposite side. Now that's all I've got to say to you, sir. I've practically gone down on my knees to you. If you don't tell the truth now, it'll be at your own risk. Were you looking through that north window when the shot was fired?"

"No, I was not."

"Did you look through the window at any time?"

"No, I did not."

And that, for the moment, appeared to be that. For the life of me, I couldn't decide whether or not Julian was lying. He has one of those rubber faces which can be as noncommittal as a sponge.

What attitude Elliot might have taken was not apparent, for Elliot never got a chance to speak. There was an interruption. Dr. Fell, clearing his throat with a noise which could have been heard upstairs, rolled forward in his chair. His cigar had gone out again. He blinked at it vaguely, and compromised by dropping it into his pocket. He leaned forward with his hands over his crutch-headed stick, and an expression of Gargantuan distress on his face.

"Mr. Enderby," he said, "where is your chivalry?"

"Chivalry?"

"Chivalry," repeated Dr. Fell firmly. "Here is a lady in distress. Mrs. Logan tells an incredible story. Archons of Athens! Unless you back her up, don't you see that she will probably be arrested for murder?"

Julian's voice had a note of heavy skepticism.

"That won't do, Doctor."

"No? Why not?"

"To begin with, why should I be interested in backing her up?" inquired Julian, lifting his shoulders. "*I* don't know the lady. It's no concern of mine."

"Chivalry, sir. Chivalry."

Julian seemed genuinely amused. "Besides, Mrs. Logan is in no danger of being arrested. Ask Bob Morrison. There is the reason (a) that the revolver was hanging against the wall when it was fired. See powder marks. There's the reason (b) that there were no fingerprints of hers on the revolver. Oh, yes, I know that!" He grinned round at us. "As a matter of fact, I happened to overhear Inspector Elliot and Inspector Grimes in consultation."

Dr. Fell blinked at him.

"And is that," he inquired in a hollow voice, "all the reason you have for thinking she wouldn't be arrested?"

"It's a good enough reason."

"Oh, tut, tut!" said Dr. Fell. "Tut, tut, tut, tut!"

"I don't understand you."

"Listen to me," urged the doctor in a confiding tone. He edged forward. "I will make you a fair offer. *I will undertake to fire that revolver, while it is hanging on the wall, without touching it — without coming within six feet of it — and without using strings, mechanical devices, or flummery of any kind.*"

There was a silence.

"Five bob you can't," growled Inspector Grimes under his breath; but nobody was listening.

"In other words, you can explain the miracle?" asked Julian.

Dr. Fell nodded, and nodded again.

"I rather think so, my lad. Harrumph — Elliot. Where's the revolver? Give me the revolver."

The revolver had been laid down on top of a bookcase. Elliot, after staring at the doctor with hard suspicious eyes, yielded and went to get it. We have since learned that to trust Gideon Fell with a loaded revolver is about as safe as entrusting him with a packet of nitroglycerin. But at the moment we were all too absorbed to consider the little possibility of getting our ears blown off.

"Ahem. Now watch me closely, gentlemen," he invited.

He lumbered over to the fireplace, with the gun in his hand, and turned his back to us. It was impossible to watch him closely, since his back blotted out the whole center of the mantelpiece. But we heard a sharp click.

"I do not," he continued, "I do not anticipate results of an—um—dangerous nature. But at the same time, Inspector Grimes, you had better stand to one side. Just a little to one side."

"Look here," protested Elliot, "you're not going to fire the thing?"

"If possible, yes."

"But can't you show us? Why disturb the whole house again?"

"Ready," said Dr. Fell.

He was not listening to Elliot. He was utterly absorbed. Moving well to the right of the fireplace, he took up a position as though he were standing by a blackboard with his cane for a pointer.

Even in that dim light you could see the .45 hung on its three pegs, below the glistening tier of pistols. Nobody moved or spoke. The windows were a crawling mass of rain; a faint gurgle came from the chimney, and chilly air crept along the floor from under the door.

JOHN DICKSON CARR

"You observe," Dr. Fell went on, "that not even any magic words need be spoken or any cabalistic designs drawn. I merely—"

"*God!*" said Inspector Elliot.

To my bedazed eyes, it seemed that Dr. Fell merely made a mesmeric pass like a conjurer. The explosion of the shot blasted in that confined space. A streak of fire opened and closed across the dark bricks as the revolver, as though twitched by a diabolical life of its own, flung itself upward and backward into Dr. Fell's face. It struck his upthrown arm, and fell with a ringing clatter on the hearthstone. When the noise had quivered and died away, I glanced toward the left. There was now a second bullet hole in the white wall, almost overlapping the first.

Dr. Fell wore a guilty expression.

"I must apologize," he said, "for causing such a row." He nodded toward the door. "But, do you know, I already hear sounds of response from the house. It should be very interesting to see who is the first person to come in here."

"But what did you do?" demanded Julian.

"It's quite simple," the doctor assured him, scowling hideously and rubbing a bruised arm. "Er . . . will you pick up the revolver, Mr. Morrison?"

I did so.

"Thanke'e. First of all, you see, I cocked the gun by drawing back the hammer. Thus. Then . . ."

Julian interposed. He had got a bad shock. "But do you need to cock a modern revolver before you can fire it?"

"No, sir, you do not. The point is that a .45 has a hard trigger pull, and requires considerable pressure.

134

By cocking it, you make the gun a hair-trigger which can be fired by the lightest touch. Now observe the three pegs which held the pistol to the wall.

"The center peg, obviously, is used to support the revolver under and inside the trigger guard. I place the weapon back in a certain way. It points toward the left. I make sure that the center peg is placed against – and in front of – the trigger. I stand to the right, well to the right. The slightest touch against the butt of the gun will push the trigger against that wooden peg. So I reach out with the end of my cane, and . . ."

"Don't fire it again!" snapped Elliot. "Let it alone! Come away from there!"

"H'mf. Well. If you insist."

"So all that's necessary," muttered Elliot, "is to make the gun jump: so that the peg touches the trigger."

Dr. Fell spoke in a curious tone.

"Yes," he agreed. "By thunder, but there never was a happier choice of phrase. All that's necessary is to make the gun jump."

After a pause, which we were to remember afterwards, he turned to Julian.

"You follow the demonstration, Mr. Enderby?"

"Yes, I follow it all right," Julian said with peevish violence. "But, frankly, I'm disappointed. I don't see that that's so very clever. It looked like magic, just because we didn't see you touch the butt of the gun with your stick . . ."

"Aha!"

"What do you mean, 'aha'?"

"Then you still don't see the real point?"

Julian hesitated. "Technically, I admit, it disposes of the two objections. It shows how Mrs. Logan could have fired the shot without leaving fingerprints or taking the gun off the wall. That is, if she were foolish enough to try a trick like that."

"H'mf, yes," said Dr. Fell. "But it also shows (d'ye see?) how the shot could have been fired by somebody who wasn't in the room at all."

That latest experiment had roused the house. Faintly, you could hear running footsteps and a confused noise of calling. Dr. Fell paid no attention to it.

"As I understand it," he went on argumentatively, "the morning was dark and overcast. Everybody talks about the sun 'trying to struggle out.' So it didn't come out, except for a gleam or two, until after the murder. I say, Elliot. Did you get a statement from Mrs. Logan?"

"I did, sir."

"And what does she say? Does she say it was dark in this room when Logan was killed?"

"Yes, she does," returned Elliot calmly.

"Now suppose," said Dr. Fell, lifting one finger with fiery emphasis. "Suppose I were standing outside that big north window." He pointed. "Suppose I were standing on a box, with one pane open and my hand inside the window.

"Suppose (hey?) I had in my hand a long, thin, fine rod, like an elongated fishing rod. Suppose in the gloom of the room that rod went unnoticed by an overimaginative and not-too-observant woman. Suppose, after touching a hair-trigger pistol, I let the end of it fall to the floor; and drew it back unobserved by a gardener at the other window. Suppose — "

He paused.

With a leisurely motion, as though pondering this, he took a large red bandana handkerchief out of his hip pocket, and proceeded to mop his forehead. He replaced the handkerchief, shook his shoulders, and spoke in a pleading tone.

"Be chivalrous, Mr. Enderby. You've got nothing to fear. You're all right, as Elliot has told you. The police haven't suspected you so far. Why not be chivalrous and support the lady?"

"The suggestion is nonsense," yelped Julian. "What you say is p-p-preposterous."

Dr. Fell grunted.

"To be quite frank," he admitted, "it is. I can think of nothing more unlikely than that you were hanging about with a damned great rod fifteen feet long, and fished for a revolver without being seen. But, do you understand, it is one way of explaining a miracle? Perhaps the only way. That method, if suggested at the inquest, would at least cause you more embarrassment, publicity, and lurking suspicion than any simple process of telling the truth. Can I persuade you, Mr. Enderby?"

Julian contemplated his neat brown shoes. He looked very tired. He was in a corner, and he seemed to know it. When he raised his head, his eyes were squeezed up so that the fine wrinkles round them showed in pin-point detail.

"Very well," he said, exhaling his breath. "If you must know, you must. Rather than be pestered like this, and be threatened with blackmail (which is what it is, as you very well know), I'll tell you. Yes. I was

137

looking in through that window."

"When the shot was fired?"

"Yes."

At this point Inspector Grimes created a diversion by falling over the coal scuttle. But it was Elliot who picked up the questioning, without inflection.

"You couldn't have told us that before?"

"I didn't choose to tell you before."

"You climbed up on that box?"

"Yes; about half a minute before the shot. I didn't put the box there. It was already there. I saw it, so I just climbed up."

"Why? What made you climb up?"

Julian's eyebrows drew together. "Because I heard voices in here. Because of something I heard."

"Oh? And what did you hear?"

"I heard—"

He got no opportunity to finish the sentence. The view-hallo noise of searchers, which had been going from room to room but nervously avoiding this one, at last plucked up courage and rushed at the door. The first person into the room was Gwyneth Logan, with the marks of tears still on her face. Just behind her, his hand on her shoulder, was Clarke.

XII

I have always been attracted but puzzled by those detective stories in which the narrator is in on everything. He tags about everywhere without any real excuse, and yet the police never seem to notice him. At least, they never object to his presence. They never say, "Oi! What are you doing here, my lad? Get along home."

This grouse is inspired by the fact that, just as Julian Enderby was going to give some really important evidence, they tossed me out of the room.

I regret to say that once the closing door had shut me out into the drawing-room, I dropped a sofa cushion on the floor and gave it a swift kick. This was witnessed by Tess and Andy, who directed withering glances, but were as seething with curiosity as I was. Our state of mind remained no better because Gwyneth Logan and Clarke had been allowed to stay in the study.

"Well?" prompted Tess. "What happened? Is somebody else killed?"

"No. They were only experimenting with the gun. But they've got a witness who saw the murder too:

Julian himself."

"Julian . . ."

"Yes. In the flesh."

"But what does he say?"

"I don't know. That was where they slung me out. If he backs up the Logan woman, the crime is more impossible than ever."

Keeping my voice down, straining without success to catch the muffled mutter of voices from behind the study door, I told Tess and Andy what had happened. It was too dark in the drawing-room to see their expressions. You could hear the noise of Andy rubbing at his already bristly jaw.

"Swine!" commented Andy. He meant Julian. "Told you what he'd be like, didn't I? Ass! Why? Why deny it? Being at that window, I mean."

Tess spoke thoughtfully. "I can understand that. Julian's awfully dignified. He heard something interesting, and eavesdropped on it; but he'd rather die than have to admit it in a witness box. So it had to be dragged out of him with pincers. They must have given him a bad time, Bob. Poor Julian."

"Poor Julian my eye."

"Anyway," said Andy, "it'll clear Mrs. Logan."

You could feel the breath of relief which he exhaled, the loosening of taut muscles, and the fall of sinewy hands to his sides. This was new and disturbing. Tess felt it too.

"And poor Andy," she laughed.

"What do you mean, poor Andy?" demanded that harassed man.

"The lady-in-distress would appeal to you," said Tess, linking her arm through his. "Don't fall, Andy.

For heaven's sake don't *you* fall."

"That," I said, "was what I advised him this morning."

"I don't know what this is all about," said Andy, disengaging his arm. "I said she was a dashed fine-looking woman. So she is. Why not? And I'll swear she's telling the truth."

Tess regarded him curiously. "What if Julian says she isn't telling the truth? What if he upsets her whole story?"

"He can't. Damn little bounder!"

"Steady, Andy."

He drew a shuddering breath, and became himself again. Sitting down on one arm of the sofa, he took out his pipe, turned it over in long fingers; and seemed to be listening, with his head on one side, to the fall of the rain.

"See here, Bob. What did you mean when you said that if this Julian Whatshisname backs up Mrs. Logan, the crime will be more impossible than before?"

"Just that. It will be another hermetically sealed room."

"Eh?"

"Look at it. We now know there was a witness guarding every entrance or exit to the room. MacCarey, the gardener, covered the two south windows. Sonia, the maid, was in this room and covered the only door to the study. Julian covered the north window. All can testify that nobody left the study after the shooting. So no outsider—say—could have shot Logan and nipped out of the room without being seen."

JOHN DICKSON CARR

"Well?"

"Gwyneth Logan was alone with her husband. If she told the truth, and didn't shoot him . . . there you are. It's a hair-raiser of an impossibility. Something or somebody moved the revolver; but what?"

It was ten minutes past four. The shadows were closing in, both literally and figuratively. In a short time it would be just twenty-four hours since we had first crossed the threshold of Longwood House, and something with fingers plucked at Tess's ankle from the floor.

Night came on again. From behind the closed door to the study, I heard Martin Clarke's high, hearty laugh. There seemed to be an exchange of courtesies. Then the door opened, and Gwyneth Logan came out.

Gwyneth was transfigured. Considering the temperamental atmosphere she carried with her, you could tell that even in the dim light. Her blue eyes, wide open, shone with relief or gratitude near tears; her lower lip, moist and with the color now of a sepia painting, quivered before she set her teeth in it. She had both hands pressed against her breast, and ran toward us as though for sanctuary.

"My dear friends," she said; "my dear, *dear* friends!"

The reason for this emotional outburst was not clear. It left us uncomfortably wondering what we had done to deserve it. But Tess, easily touched, sat her down on the couch and put her arm round Gwyneth's shoulder.

Tess's voice was strained.

"They—they didn't keep you long."

142

"No," said Gwyneth, with blurred eagerness. "I'd seen them before. They wanted to ask me about Bentley's revolver. And where he kept it. And whether he locked our bedroom door at night. Bentley always kept it locked; which I've told him is *vulgar*, when you're in the country." She brushed this aside. "But that isn't it. That isn't what I wanted to tell you. They *believe* me now."

"Ah!" growled Andy.

"Don't you understand? They know I'm telling the truth. That nice Mr. Something, the one with the fair hair, the one who only got here this morning, you see: he saw it all. And he told them."

"Julian Enderby?" murmured Tess.

"Is that the name? Yes, I believe it is."

Tess bent closer. "But tell us. What was Julian doing, standing on a box outside the window?"

Gwyneth stopped in mid-flight. Her tone changed. "I—I can't tell you. It's nothing, really. Just something I said to poor Bentley, and he said to me. I didn't tell the police before, because why should I?"

"But, my dear," said Tess, "you'll probably have to tell it at the inquest."

"At the inquest?" screamed Gwyneth. "In public?"

"Unless it's adjourned, of course."

"I'd die before I'd told it, even in front of you," declared Gwyneth; and then, evidently at her wits' end, proceeded to tell it. "It was the reason why I went in to see poor Bentley this morning, when he sat down to his typing. I—I was frightened," she went on breathlessly. "You see, I'd been wondering. I—you know—I slept with Bentley last night, without—you know—using precautions."

Even in that gloom, her face was pink. She gulped out the words.

"So that," grated Andy, "that was why he was so full of beans this morning."

"Andy!" said Tess, shocked.

"And I didn't want to think I might be going to — you know — have a baby," explained Gwyneth, making a flapping gesture. "I wanted to tell him so. So I waited for him in the study this morning. He came in, and saw me, and said, 'Hullo: what are you doing here?' So I told him, I said: 'I didn't use any precautions, any at all, and you don't think I might have a baby, do you?' " Gwyneth paused. She added simply: "And just as he laughed, the revolver came off the wall and shot him."

Then she began to cry.

Perhaps because of the eternal rain, the drawing-room felt even more chilly. Through the open door to the hall, and from across the hall in the dining-room, a rattle of plates and saucers indicated that the table was being set for tea.

"*Explicit* the situation," murmured Tess.

"*Explicit* Julian," said I.

"Now, now!" said Andy gruffly.

Gwyneth gulped. "Yes; I'm being silly, aren't I?" she decided, and sat up and passed the back of her hand across her eyes. "I expect I haven't got anything to be afraid of, really. But I'm always worried whenever that happens."

"Of course," said Tess.

"And the main thing is," insisted Gwyneth, "the m-main thing is that they believe me now. When I said the revolver just got up off the wall and killed poor

144

Bentley, they know it was the truth. I feel awful. I
expect I look awful too. I know! Come with me, Tess,
while I powder my nose; and then let's all go and have
some tea. What do you say?"

Andy and I walked across the hall to the dining-
room, while the other two, with that unmistakable air
of women who intend to communicate secrets to each
other, disappeared upstairs.

Two wall lamps were on in the dining-room, barely
glowing through the twilight but striking hard against
our eyes. The cheerful Mrs. Winch — completely un-
moved by anything that had happened — flew about
and cackled at us, pointing out in succession the
nutritive value of everything on the table. She
smacked Sonia for some serving enormity which I
forget, and swished her out into the kitchen.

It was the first time we had been given tea in that
house, and I could do with it. But Andy eyed the
table with disfavor. Wrestling with himself, he
flopped down into a chair and stretched out his long
legs.

"Poor girl!" he said moodily.

"Who? Sonia?"

"Sonia! — Mrs. Logan."

"H'm. Maybe. But if she got worried every time
THAT happened, her married life must have been
one long terror."

This stung Andy on the raw. He opened his eyes
with an incredulousness which gradually changed to
dogged and baffled exasperation.

"Bob," he said in all seriousness, "what's the matter
with you? Haven't you any sense of the—" he gestured hard, groping for words—"of the fineness of

145

life? Of the—of the fine things—of the spiritual things, what I mean; and all that? You know what I mean."

"Yes, I know what you mean."

Andy brooded.

"He was thirty years older than she is. He must have led her a devil of a life. All I wonder is, who . . . ?" This seemed to be the torturing problem, the recurrent problem never absent from the back of Andy's brain.

"You wonder who Gwyneth's boy friend is?"

"We oughtn't to be talking about it," Andy said stiffly. "Rotten business, talking like this. All the same." He looked round to make sure we were not overheard. "All the same, who the hell is it? That's what I'd like to know."

"What about Clarke?"

Andy sat upright. "Clarke?" he repeated, with a hollow incredulity which must have carried as far as the hall. "Nonsense! *Nonsense!*"

"Why?"

"Clarke? Why, man, Clarke's as old as Logan! Older, if anything. Clarke!"

"All the same, he doesn't strike me as being any Trappist monk. Also, Clarke is the museum expert. Also, Clarke himself admits that he and Logan began by hating each other's guts; and I would lay a tanner that their relations haven't improved much, in spite of surface appearances. Also, it would be more comfortable to know why he's got a thousand gallons of petrol stored in the cellar."

"A thousand gallons of what?"

"Petrol. The stuff that burns."

"Bob," said Andy, "you must be dotty. There's no petrol in this house. I ought to know, oughtn't I?" He whacked the table with his fist. "I've been over every inch of those cellars. And I've been visiting this place for weeks, nearly every day except last Wednesday and Thursday. I tell you, there's not —"

This was a point on which I had conferred long with Tess at lunch. And she had given me the facts.

"Ask Mrs. Winch," I suggested.

"What's Mrs. Winch got to do with it?"

"As a matter of fact, Clarke had the stuff brought here and stored on Thursday. Even the Winch, who wouldn't bat an eye if she found a skeleton sitting on her dressing table, has got the wind up about that. She told Tess. Tess told me."

Andy's face had darkened.

"Look here, Clarke can't do that!"

"Is it against the law?"

"Well, no. Not unless he's tried some funny business with the insurance company. What I mean: the stuff's dangerous. Suppose — ?"

"Exactly."

Andy spoke after long consideration. He had pushed his chair back, jarring it on the hardwood floor and seeming to draw an answering ring from the great chandelier. He sat in the same chair he had occupied at breakfast; and again the chandelier, its triple crown of white candles massive under a weight of shadow, hung almost above his head.

He blurted: "We'll get out of here. To-day. Not that I don't trust Mr. Clarke, mind! But there was something I was going to tell you, this morning, when we were interrupted."

147

"Yes?"

A massive tread, clacking first on the tiles of the hall and then down the two creaky steps into the dining-room, drew a definite vibration from the chandelier.

It was Dr. Fell, followed by Inspector Grimes. Dr. Fell's eyes were fixed on that same chandelier, with such concentration that he almost lost his balance. His crutch-headed stick poked ahead of him, feeling like a blind man's. He was (in fact) staring so hard at the chandelier that he did not see us until he had come well into the room.

"Eh?" said the doctor, pulling up with a grunt. "Oh, ah!" He blinked at the tea table. "I beg your pardon, gentlemen. I had forgotten that this is tea hour in any civilized country. Inspector Grimes was going to—"

I offered bitter courtesy for the interruption.

"Will you join us?"

"Thanke'e, my boy," said the doctor vaguely, still staring at the chandelier. Then he woke up. "I beg your pardon. What did you say?"

"I asked whether you'd join us."

"In what?"

"Tea."

"Oh, ah! Tea!" cried Dr. Fell, suddenly enlightened at last. "With pleasure, with pleasure! I was—er—muzzily concerned with other matters." He turned to Inspector Grimes. "Then this is the room where the chandelier fell and crushed the butler's skull?"

"This is it, sir."

"You were here at the time?"

"I was that."

"H'm, yes. Now tell me: is it the same chandelier, or a different one?"

Inspector Grimes hesitated. He frowned at it. "Well, sir, that's a bit hard to say. It looks like the same one, right enough; but I don't see how it could be. You'd best ask Mr. Clarke."

"It's the same one," interposed Andy. "Mr. Clarke dug it out of the cellar and had it refurbished. There's a spike on the under side of the thing, if you look closely enough." Andy looked as though he were cold. "Rotten way to die. I know *I'd* hate to peg out like that."

Dr. Fell nodded.

Since the window curtains had been drawn, we heard the noise of the rain only as a murmur. The well lamps, behind yellow shades, turned the twilight to a kind of luminous mist in which woodwork, china, silver, and even faces assumed a golden patina as though painted with a Dutch brush. The tea urn steamed, as yet untouched. The sandwiches were high-piled.

Though the table was in the way, Dr. Fell reached up with his stick and just managed to touch the lower part of the chandelier. It swung; and a sharp *crack* issued from the beam.

"I'd be careful with that thing, if I were you, sir," said Inspector Grimes, in rather too loud a voice. The crack had made him jump. "You never know, do you?"

"Rot. It's all right," declared Andy. "Or at least, it was all right."

"What about the dining table?" asked Dr. Fell, paying no attention to either. "When the last of the

Longwoods lived here, did the table stand where it does now? Almost under the chandelier? What do you say, Inspector?"

"That's right, sir."

"But I presume the butler didn't get up on the table as well as a chair? That is to say, he didn't whang up a chair on top of the table, and then climb up on top of both?"

Grimes shook his head.

"No, sir. When we got here and found him in the mess, the table was pushed away to one side. Done it himself, evidently. Then he'd put a chair like these ones here" — Grimes pointed — "tallish old chairs. He put one of them just under the chandelier, and stood up on it."

"So. How tall a man was the butler? As tall as you?"

"Taller than me, sir." Again Grimes pointed. "About as tall as that gentleman there."

"About as tall as Mr. Hunter?"

"That's right."

With an absent-minded word of apology, Dr. Fell lost no further time: he laid hold of the table and gave it a Gargantuan shove. There was a clatter of crockery which brought Mrs. Winch flying from the kitchen; pink-and-white cakes whirled; the tea urn toppled, and was righted by Andy only at the expense of a burned hand that made him swear.

Dr. Fell next picked up a chair. It was a high-backed, high-seated Jacobean chair in a carved oak. I remembered that story, told at the Congo Club, of a chair endowed with life: particularly since Dr. Fell regarded this chair with as much malevolence as though it had done him a personal affront.

From the corner of my eye I could see Tess and Gwyneth Logan come in from the hall; and stop short.

"I am not," wheezed the doctor, "I am not, unfortunately, spry enough for the next maneuver. You, Mr. Hunter, appear to be the same height as the late William Polson. Would you mind climbing up on that chair?"

"Right. Anything else?"

The yellow-shaded lamps were against the north wall of the dining-room. Across the south wall, across dark-red window draperies and the china plates on the panel rail, they threw a tall shadow of Andy: elongating like a pair of scissors when he set his feet apart to balance himself.

"Good!" Again Dr. Fell nodded. "Now stretch your hands up above your head."

"Clear up?"

"Yes. How far are your hands below the chandelier?"

"About six inches. If—"

"For God's sake, look out! It moved!"

You should not have thought the soft-voiced Gwyneth Logan had so much strength in her lungs. Her cry, beginning as a sob and ending as a screech, brought out the sweat on my body in one convulsive start. It made Andy stumble; it made him jump down from the chair, and back away with a white face. It brought running others who must have been in the hall then: Martin Clarke, Inspector Elliot, and Julian Enderby.

Clarke's voice, firm and authoritative, spoke from

behind Gwyneth.

"What's going on there? What moved?"

"The chandelier moved," screamed Gwyneth at the top of her lungs. "Just as if a hand had p-pushed it. Like that!" She illustrated with a frenzied gesture.

"My dear Gwyneth! There's no hand there. See for yourself."

"Why not?" asked Tess quietly. "Why not the same hand that caught my ankle in the entry last night?"

The idea that we were dealing with a hand, only a hand, a little shriveled, ever-watchful hand which twitched when you least expected it, was a far from soothing one. But it was an idea which evidently did not appeal to Inspector Elliot. Pushing through the group at the door, Elliot came down into the dining-room and strode up to Dr. Fell.

"What happened, sir?" he asked harshly. "You were watching the chandelier. Did it move?"

The doctor nodded his massive head.

"Oh, yes," he said. "Like the revolver. Like the chair. Like the fingers in the entry. It moved."

XIII

"And now, Doctor, suppose you give us your real opinion of this case," suggested Clarke.

You might not have thought that we would sit quietly down to have tea. But why not? Eight of us were ranged round the big table, with Gwyneth Logan presiding at the urn and pouring. Julian Enderby alone refused to join us: he was sulking, he eyed us with defiance, and he marched out of the room. Both Elliot and Inspector Grimes were at the table, though the latter under protest and with throat-clearing reluctance.

Elliot's air indicated firmly that the subject, for the moment, was shelved. But no sooner had we drawn up our chairs than Clarke fired off the question.

Dr. Fell chuckled, a homely and heartening sound. His constraint had gone. He was one vast substantial beam, towering above the table like the Ghost of the Christmas Present, with a napkin stuck into his waistcoat.

"My real opinion," he mused. "Why, sir, I don't mind if I do. It may perhaps clear the air if I am permitted to talk a little. That is a privilege of which I seldom fail to avail myself."

"You mean you know what did it?" demanded Gwyneth.

From where I sat, beside Tess, I could see only one side of Gwyneth's face behind the tea urn. Her hands were remarkably steady for those of a woman who has been given another bad fright.

"I thought we agreed," smiled Clarke, "that it was done by Eric the Hand. If only for the sake of convenience, he ought to have a name. Shall we call him Eric?"

"Don't be horrible," said Gwyneth, jerking her head. "How many lumps, Dr. Fell?"

"Hey? Oh. Just one. Now, what would you say was the chief riddle, the most puzzling trail of all, the problem to which we have been given no clue? I'll tell you. It is the problem of the Longwoods. I cannot fathom the Longwoods."

"The Longwoods?"

"Look round you." He moved his head. "For more than three hundred mortal years, up to the year 1920, this house was occupied by the descendants of one family. It is crusted thick with the air of living. Births, deaths, marriages, family rows, all should have given this house character for more than ten generations. Yet who were these Longwoods? What were they like? What do we know about them?"

Clarke was watching him keenly. Clarke signified two lumps, and accepted a cup from Gwyneth, still without taking his eyes from Dr. Fell.

"Isn't that point rather—esoteric?"

"No, by thunder, it isn't!" said Dr. Fell, smiting the table so that crockery rang. "It's the key to this whole affair, if we can grasp it. But so far we have nothing to grasp. Where is Uncle Mortimer's hobby? Where is Aunt Susanna's needlework? What is the reason for these hauntings? The Longwoods seem to have been an extraordinarily colorless crowd."

Clarke grinned.

"Be careful that Eric the Hand doesn't hear you say that," Clarke warned. "He might throw something off the sideboard, just by way of protest."

Tess involuntarily turned round and glanced at the sideboard.

"It's true," pursued Dr. Fell, "that a hundred years ago we have a Longwood — Norbert — who met a violent death somehow. But what do we know about him, even? Except that he tampered with devils, drugs, and doctors, nothing. No picture emerges except a pair of D'Orsay side whiskers and a cloudy medical or scientific interest. How did he live? And die? He has not even left a legend."

More undercurrents! I could have sworn that there were deeper waters here than you could find in a teacup. For at this point Tess darted a swift glance at Dr. Fell, colored slightly, and spoke.

"I don't know about that," she said. "Wasn't it Norbert's death which started the story of the thing that catches at your ankles?"

"It was," affirmed Clarke.

"And of the corpse with the scratched face?" asked Dr. Fell.

"It was."

For a moment Dr. Fell stirred his tea. A silence fell at the table. Tess, Elliot, and Grimes, signifying their needs in the way of sugar, had been supplied with cups. You might have said that this conversation about legends was mere byplay, an exuberance of the doctor's; yet I noticed that Inspector Elliot's shoulders had grown tense, and his eyes regained their hard watchfulness.

"Finally," said Dr. Fell after a long pause, "there is the death of the butler seventeen years ago."

His voice grew big and emphatic.

"Mind you, that was only seventeen years ago! A bagatelle in time, against the history of this house. A Longwood, the last of them, was master here then. But what do we know about HIM? Again, absolutely nothing."

Inspector Grimes coughed.

"*I* can tell you about that, sir," he volunteered.

"Eh? Did you know him?"

"I knew him well. And a nicer gentleman you wouldn't want to meet. That's why we were all sorry when it happened."

"At last," grunted Dr. Fell, "we appear to be learning something! Well? What sort of person was he? A terror in the countryside? Addicted to sinister studies, like Norbert?"

Inspector Grimes, unexpectedly, gave a loud laugh which was not without its effect on Gwyneth Logan. The cup skittered in her hand; she dropped in three lumps, pushed it across to Andy, and hurriedly turned off the tap of the urn as it ran over. Inspector Grimes checked himself with equal hurriedness, and apologized. But his sincerity did not lessen.

"Him, sir? Not likely! It's just as I say: a pleasanter gentleman you wouldn't want to meet, and with a good word for everybody."

"He didn't encourage ghosts, then?"

Grimes reflected.

"Well, sir, I shouldn't go so far as to say that. There never was a man so fond of his little joke. If he could have you over a trick matchbox, or anything like that, it made him happy all day. So he liked to joke·people about the old Longwoods getting up out of their graves and walking.

"You see, he came from a distant branch of the family. Oxfordshire, I think it was. He never expected to come into the money or the estate, and was pleased as Punch when he did. Little, brisk-walking man like a professor, with a bald head and a high collar. He came here just about the time the war was over: the end of '18 or the beginning of '19, I forget which. And said he was going to remodel the house, and have a Longwood living in it again."

Inspector Grimes paused.

He had lost his air of sitting gingerly on the edge of the chair, and stirring tea like a chemist with a mortar and pestle. He was remembering old days.

"Married? Any children?" asked Dr. Fell.

Clarke intervened, with startling asperity. "My dear doctor, can you tell me what the devil difference it makes whether he was married or had any children?"

The violence of the outburst drew everybody's eyes.

"In good time, sir, I can," Dr. Fell thundered in reply. "Go on, Inspector."

Grime hesitated. "He was married — and a very nice lady, too — but he hadn't any children. I don't rightly know what else you want me to tell you. He was proper gentry, but he liked working with his hands. Do a proper job of work, too; and draw you a little

157

plan of it as slick as Joe Partridge down at the water board. He had to work—wanting to get the house rebuilt, that is." The inspector's tone grew grim. "In '18, and for a part of '19, there wasn't an able-bodied man to be got for love or money. Mr. Longwood had to get laboring-men from Guernsey to finish the house. I hope that doesn't happen again, soon."

"It will happen again," said Clarke softly.

"What will?"

"War," said Clarke.

Though his voice still was not loud, the word had a rounded and ominous distinctness.

You might have thought that he was only trying to change the subject, for he spoke in his usual smiling and quizzical way. He even emphasized this by picking up a small sandwich, and taking a very large bite out of it.

"We were not," I protested, "discussing the international situation—"

"Discuss it or not," said Clarke. "This year, next year, the year after: war. You mark my words. That's partly why I decided to pull up my roots and leave Italy." He finished the sandwich. "However, I only make the remark in passing. As you say, we were not discussing the international situation. Let's return to the matter of murder on a smaller scale. What does the ghost party expect for tonight?"

This was the time to run up the colors.

"There will be no more ghost party for Tess and me," I said, and put my hand over hers. "I'm taking her back to town to-night."

A stir ran round the table. Clarke picked up another sandwich before replying. His eyebrows showed that his hospitality had been affronted.

"I'm sorry to hear that. Sorry, and disappointed. I hardly thought you would be the first to run. The question is, my dear fellow, will the police let you go?"

Elliot also hesitated before answering.

"I'd rather you didn't any of you," he told me curtly.

"That's not the point. Have you any authority to keep us here?"

"Inspector Grimes has the authority here, as yet. He can't compel you to stay in the house, of course. You're at liberty, any of you, to stay at the village or close at hand. But we can't allow you to get off to London just yet. I'm sorry, but there it is."

Clarke chortled.

"In the village!" he repeated, munching the sandwich. "Come, come, will you and Miss Fraser put up at the *Startled Stag*? That's a clear admission of defeat. What is it? Are you afraid of Eric the Hand?"

(*"Bob, don't let him get your goat!"* whispered Tess. She did not hiss this, there being no aspirate in it, but the general effect was much the same.)

"Not of Eric, surely?" prompted Clarke.

"Not of Eric's ordinary pranks, no."

"Well, then?"

"But if Eric should take it into his head to toss a lighted match into a thousand gallons of petrol in this cellar . . ."

"Right!" said Andy.

There was general uproar, so much that you could see Clarke laughing: you could see the strong sharp teeth and the unhealthy red gums exposed: without hearing any sound. He lifted his hand to quiet the noise.

"I was wondering," he declared, "how soon some-one would mention that. I assure you, it's quite all right. I have explained the matter to Inspector Elliot, and he has the only key to a locked cellar. I further assure you that I am no pyromaniac. The presence of the petrol is merely an instance of my acumen and foresight. The late Bentley Logan always testified to my acumen and foresight."

"Meaning what?" demanded Andy.

"There is going to be a war." Clarke spoke simply. "Need I say more?"

"Yes."

"I expect it next year. The one article nobody will be able to get is petrol. But if I lay in my supply so far ahead, if I make a plain business gamble of it before there is any noise of danger, I shall be allowed to keep it. That's all."

Clarke finished the sandwich, licked his fingers, and wiped them on a handkerchief. He seemed to be calculating something.

"I estimate that such a supply will keep my modest car running for over two years," he went on.

"You don't take many chances, do you?" asked Andy.

"My boy, I never take *any* chances," said Clarke.

After surveying Andy with an unruffled and know-ing eye, he turned back.

"That, my friends, is my sinister secret. You can't in honesty say that you're afraid of a petrol-hoarder. Why, even Mr. Enderby, who is not (I should say) remarkable for courage, has consented to remain. So it must be something else. If our good friend Morrison is afraid of Eric — "

"That's a lie, and you know it."

"Is it? My dear fellow, I'd like to bet you five pounds you won't stay the night here."

"Done. And I'll offer a further five pounds that you're scared out of this place before I am."

"Done," agreed Clarke.

"Oh, men!" said Tess despairingly. "Men!" She got up and did a kind of dance beside the table.

Andy spoke through stiff jaws. "I say. Not to interrupt. No. But isn't anybody going to ask Mrs. Logan how *she* feels about staying?"

This pulled us up short, a good deal ashamed. Andy's face was fanatical. Tess drew a despairing breath and sat down. Gwyneth, mechanically receiving cups and filling them again, set down the latest cup.

"I don't know," she answered mechanically. "I'll have to ask . . ." Her voice trailed away. Her eyes acquired a fixed look. Wonder grew in them, and then a wandering edge of terror. "I was going to say, I'll have to ask Bentley," she breathed. "But he's dead. I depended on him for everything; and now he's dead. My God, what am I going to do? There's nobody to take me home, even. What am I going to do?"

"We're your friends, Gwyneth," Clarke told her. He took her hand.

"Yes, I know, Martin. I know. You're probably the realest friend I've got." Her voice was hasty and caressing. She returned the pressure of his hand. "But you don't understand. I'm on my own. I haven't been on my own since I left the convent. I can't stay here. I

161

can't. Alone, in that room—"

"You could share Miss Fraser's room."

"Could I? Could I, Tess?"

"Of course."

Inspector Elliot got to his feet, brushing away crumbs. His whole manner had changed. It seemed to announced that the interlude was over, and that we could now return to business.

"Then that's settled," Elliot said briskly. "I'm bound to say I think you've chosen the wisest course, all of you. As soon as we get the statements we want, you can get back to town just as soon as you like. In the meantime, Dr. Fell and I must be getting back to town ourselves; and there are one or two points to clear up first."

His tone became very dry, though he did not smile.

"For instance, there's been a good deal of talk about this 'hand.' Miss Fraser: would you like to come out in the hall and show us exactly where you were standing when it caught your ankle?"

"But . . . I . . ."

"You don't mind?"

The single unshaded electric bulb was burning in the hall. It looked more bleak than last night, since the noise of the rain beat thickly now. Our footsteps rapped on the red tiles. Dr. Fell, Elliot, and Inspector Grimes took up a position at the rear, looking toward the front.

"Just show us what happened, please," requested Elliot.

Tess was indecisive. She stood under the light, which kindled her hair to black silkiness, and threw shadows of her eyelashes down across her cheeks.

Her arms were straight down at her sides. She was like a nervous actress at a rehearsal, stiff and unnatural. Behind her was the big nail-studded front door, with a window on either side of it, and the tall grandfather clock in the corner.

"I — I — " she began; but Clarke helped her out.

"This door was open then," he explained. He bustled across, drew the big wooden bar, and opened the door. A gust of cold air whisked in, stung with raindrops blown through the peaked hood of the entry. Tess shivered, and her skirt was blown wide. I went over to Clarke, yanked the door out of his hands, closed it, and shot the bar again.

"Steady. Is this necessary? Clarke, Andy Hunter, and I were all standing outside. You don't want us to go out in the rain now, do you? You've seen the place where it happened: that wooden-walled entry, with the door mat. Does she have to reconstruct it for you?"

Clarke frowned.

"My dear Morrison, I was only trying to be of assistance. What's wrong? Do you think the hand is out there now?"

"One moment!" interrupted Dr. Fell.

For some moments he had been sunk in a brooding meditation which did not seem to please him. Waving us to one side, he lumbered forward. But he did not go near the door. Instead he stopped in front of the grandfather clock, which he scrutinized up and down.

"Am I correct in assuming," he continued, tapping the case, "that this is the clock which is supposed to have stopped on the night Norbert Longwood died over a hundred years ago?"

"That is the clock."

Dr. Fell pulled open the long door in the case of the clock, and peered inside. He fished a box of matches out of one capacious pocket, struck a match, and peered closer. There was nothing inside, as I could see for myself, except the pendulum, the chains, and the weights. Though crusted dark with age, they had been given a dusting and the weights were wound up. Dr. Fell closed the door.

"Archons of Athens!" he muttered, puffing out his cheeks. "The original clock. The original chandelier. The original . . . h'mf. And the clock, presumably, was stopped by our ever-present 'hand'?"

"No," returned Clarke firmly.

"No?"

Clarke looked earnest and excited. "Don't believe any such rubbish," he advised. "I was telling these people last night, it's the one part of the story which is obviously pure foolishness. Why? Because it's such an old, dreary, hackneyed legend. You meet it over and over again."

Slowly and massively, Dr. Fell turned round. He took several steps forward.

"Admitted," he said. "But then the story of the corpse with the scratched face isn't very new — is it?"

Though it may have been an effect of the electric light, Clarke's features seemed to blur as though they had grown muddled. He had retreated until he was standing almost against the door to the drawing-room. His heels and toes were springy, like a boxer's. But he kept his smile.

"I don't understand you, Doctor."

"Why, sir, if this incident occurred in 1821 (as I think it did?), the legend is surely of rich and ripe vintage? The ghost with the scratched face is of at least tolerable antiquity?"

"Oh. Yes. Of course. I thought—"

"What did you think I meant?"

"Nothing at all," affirmed Clarke, regaining his good humor. "Your thunders are apt to be a bit confusing, Doctor. Not, mind you, that I lose any faith in the hand just because it didn't stop the clock. I daresay Eric could *start* the clock again, if it wanted to." He looked round the hall, grinning, and whistled as though for a dog. "Where are you, Eric? Can you hear us?"

"Don't!" cried Tess.

"I beg your pardon," said Clarke abruptly. "I am not fond of bad taste myself."

Inspector Elliot was patient but weary.

"I shouldn't be alarmed about that, if I were you," he told Tess, with a shade of a smile. "The lights are full on, and it isn't likely that your 'hand' could try any games with all of us looking on." He considered. "We needn't rehearse what happened last night, but I'd like to see this entry. Open that door again, will you?"

While Tess stood back, I drew the bar and let gusty rain blow the door open. Yellow light streamed out through the hutch, illuminating bare tiles, a crumpled and muddy door mat, the wooden sides and roof: nothing more. Elliot studied it. The blood of exasperation came up under his eyes. He strode into the entry, felt the walls, and knocked his knuckles against them.

"How far were you inside here, Miss Fraser? How far from the entrance, I mean?"

"Nearly touching the front door."

"And facing this way, of course?"

"Yes."

"But the light wasn't on in the hall?"

"No. It . . . *listen!*" said Tess.

Tess, like Gwyneth Logan once before that day, turned round a face of pure superstitious terror. The violence of her gesture struck us all motionless. She turned on a scraping heel, and the gold clasp of her blouse glittered against her breast. Outside, the rustle of the rain deepened to a roar; but this was sharply disassociated from the faint, rustling noise which crept into our heads and knocked there with as measured a beat as it knocked in the brightly lighted hall. We all turned to look in the same direction.

Elliot had his answer.

The clock was ticking.

XIV

The second tragedy occurred at three minutes past two in the morning.

I was awake, and so was Tess, for she was sitting by the fire in my bedroom with a quilt round her shoulders. Mrs. Winch, that thoughtful woman, had lighted a fire in all the bedrooms against the damp which had begun to seep and soak through the bones of Longwood House. With that fire, we were almost comfortable.

But only physically. It had been early dinnertime before Elliot and Dr. Fell left, after taking from each of us a separate statement whose exhaustiveness left its mark. What the others said I don't know. Tess left the inquisition room flushed but defiant. The longest interview was with Clarke, and seemed to be of a somewhat rowdy nature. But (to be quite frank about this) it was impossible to overhear much through those thick doors: Sonia told Mrs. Winch, and Mrs. Winch told Tess, and Tess told me, that the conversation had been something about a letter.

The puzzling thing was that Julian Enderby elected to remain in the house rather than finish his Whitsun holiday at the *Startled Stag*, or whatever the name of the pub was. Julian's whole attitude had become one of concentrated wariness. He had a long talk with Clarke in the library after dinner, at which Clarke was affable and Julian so wary that he could not sit still.

I knew at least that he was worried, for they had given him the bedroom next to mine; and after we retired I could hear him pacing up and down, up and down, in a pair of slippers that creaked.

The rain had stopped. You could feel the whole house creaking and contracting after it. I put on pyjamas and dressing gown, and sat down in an easy chair by the fire to smoke a cigarette. Julian's slippers were squeaking intermittently, like mice, beyond the plaster wall. I considered the idea of going in and talking to him, though it did not appear likely that he would prove rousing, rollicking company. The person I badly wanted to go and see was Tess; but Gwyneth Logan was sharing her room, and Tess would probably have her hands full quieting that imaginative lady's nerves in the dark hours.

I had just come to this decision, when there was a light knock at the door. It opened, and Tess slipped in.

"Sh-h!" she whispered, putting one finger on her lip, and pointing to the adjoining room.

The pacing of the slippers stopped, hesitated, and resumed as Tess noiselessly shut the door. She was wearing a peach-colored negligee of heavy lace and silk, about which she seemed to be a little nervous and self-conscious.

"But what about—" I began in a normal voice.

"Sh-h!"

"It's all right. He can't hear what we're saying, even if he can hear voices."

"But I don't want him to think . . . You know what Julian's like."

"Frankly, I don't. I wish I did. Every time something important happens, like a grandfather clock set going under our eyes without a soul coming within ten feet of it" — the image of that placid clock, jarring and beginning to tick, returned with infuriating vividness — "every time something like that happens, Julian carefully isn't on the spot."

"Bob, it must have been strings or wires!"

"It wasn't string or wires. You know that. Hold on: I was going to say, what about Gwyneth?"

Tess drew a sharp breath. "Asleep, thank God. You know her husband took sleeping stuff? I gave her a double dose of it, disguised in barley water, and tucked her up within fifteen minutes."

She came across to the fire, swishing; she spread out her hands to the blaze, looking up at me questioningly. I put my arms round her and kissed her hard. For a few seconds she returned the pressure, turning round fully; but, as Julian resumed his pacing in the next room, she jerked her head and broke loose.

"No!" she said. "Not to-night. Not here."

"Maybe you're right. But — "

"Sh-h!"

I sat her down in the easy chair, gave her a cigarette, and lighted it. The bedroom was chilly despite the fire, so I got a quilt from the bed and draped it round her shoulders. She began to speak rapidly, through puffs of smoke.

"Besides," she went on, "you weren't here at all when I came in last night. That's why I followed you downstairs. You saw me?"

"I saw your hand."

"Don't say 'hand'!" She shuddered. "Bob, I've got to talk this out or go mad. I know everything now."

"You know—"

Well, nearly everything. Everything except what killed Mr. Logan. Gwyneth and I got confidential, embarrassingly confidential, before she turned in. I know what the key was for, and all about that. You may say the explanation isn't important, and won't help us. But *I'm* jolly sure it will."

Tess's elbow was on her knee; the arm upraised through a draping of the blue quilt, fingers turning the cigarette round and round as she stared at it. Its fire burned pale against the flame in the grate. She shook her head fiercely.

"I like Gwyneth, Bob. She's a dreadful little liar, of course. Not that *I* should ob—" Tess stopped, and bit her lip. "Not that that matters, I mean. But I'm sure she was telling me the truth about the key."

"What about the key?"

Tess stirred.

"It's perfectly simple. You've noticed how matey Clarke is with Gwyneth. Last night, after dinner, he got even more matey. She's heard (haven't you?) about the museum at Naples where they have all the lurid exhibits from Herculaneum and Pompeii. Clarke thought it was an excellent joke to tell her that the triptych . . . which is a perfectly harmless Florentine altarpiece . . . was actually one of the lurider exhibits from Naples. He gave her the key to it. And her curiosity was strong enough to make her go downstairs in the middle of the night for a private view. Naturally, she wasn't anxious to explain afterwards. That's all."

"Hell!"

"Sh-h!"

"Yes, but —"

"Gwyneth was so startled at finding only an ordinary painting that she let the thing drop off the wall. Hence that bump in the middle of the night." Again Tess drew a deep breath. "Then, this morning, Clarke denied he had given her any key. That was bogus chivalry, of course: pretending to be protecting her. You remember how he laughed? He even made it more difficult (as he loves to do!) by solemnly saying there was no keyhole in the triptych. And laughed again, because it was nothing to do with him. But he carefully told Inspector Elliot and Dr. Fell all about it this afternoon." She paused. "Gwyneth didn't tell me that. I heard it from listening outside the window."

We stared at the fire.

"Tess, I'm beginning to think this fellow Clarke is a first-rate, hundred-carat swine if one ever lived."

She opened her eyes. "You're 'beginning' to think so? Bob Morrison, when on earth can I drive it through your thick head that he *is*?"

"All right. But at least, if this is true, we've cleared the air a bit. This incident can't have anything to do with the murder of Logan."

"Can't it?"

"I don't see how. If it was just Clarke's idea of humor . . ."

"Me, I think it was more than that. Listen, Bob."

171

She threw her cigarette into the fire, snuggled closer into the quilt, and shivered. "Please don't underestimate Clarke. That's what you're doing. He's sly; and he's horribly, horribly clever. I doubt if there's anybody who's a match for him, except Dr. Fell, and even then I shouldn't like to bet on it."

"Very well: we won't underestimate him. What about it?"

"He persuaded Gwyneth into going down to look at the triptych, *so that* Mr. Logan would follow her. So that her husband would think she was going to meet a man. So that he wouldn't believe her if she tried to explain. So that it would cause trouble, trouble, trouble, trouble. Don't you see?"

"It's quite possible."

The pacing of the slippers in Julian's room had stopped. We were automatically speaking in low tones, and there was no other sound but the rattle and pop of the fire.

Tess shrugged her shoulders under the quilt.

"He's stage-managed the whole thing, if you just look back over it," she said.

This was undeniably true.

"And you think he killed Logan?"

"Bob, I'd swear to it! But I can't think how or why. It's no good asking Gwyneth about things like that. So far as she knows, Clarke and Mr. Logan were the best of friends. All the same, I'd bet you anything he hated Mr. Logan like poison: whenever he forgets himself for a second, you can practically hear it in his voice."

True again.

"H'm. Yes. You didn't manage to ask Gwyneth

anything about her boy friend?"

A wry expression went over Tess's face. Her eyes were bright and mocking, her mouth pursed up.

"That," she pointed out, "was a bit more difficult to approach. Even when I intimated that I'd over-heard her husband's accusations last night. I had to finesse that bit most tactfully, or she'd have flown out at me; and serve me right." Tess's eyes, the whites very luminous round the hazel, grew demure. "I did it by pretending I'd thought you were the mysterious lover; and telling her I'd been horribly jealous; and then admitting, almost in tears, that I'd misjudged her."

"Yow!"

"Sh-h!"

"All right. Go on."

Tess spoke swiftly. "Of course, darling, naturally I never really thought any such thing."

"Of course not. Er—what did she tell you?"

"Not much. First she said she'd never been unfaith-ful to her husband in word, thought, or deed. It's her choice of phrase: 'word, thought, or deed.' Then she confessed she might have had a little affair meeting the man in the Dante Gabriel Rossetti Restaurant at the Victoria and Albert Museum—"

"In the what?"

Tess frowned.

"There's a restaurant in the museum that was designed by either Dante Gabriel Rossetti or William Morris. I forget which; and I never could keep them straight anyway. That's where Gwyneth met the man. But she says it wasn't serious; that she's never been his mistress; and, finally, that wild horses wouldn't make her tell who he is."

"Clarke?"

"I don't know."

"Clarke!" I said bitterly. "Clarke, Clarke, Clarke!" The man's image moved behind every screen and stuck its head out of every cupboard. It was omnipresent. "We'd at least have something to work on if we knew what Clarke was doing, and where he was, at the time Logan was shot. But the police aren't inclined to be communicative."

Tess looked surprised.

"I can tell you that," she informed me. "At least, he's been volunteering the information to everybody. He *says* he was out for his morning walk, down on the dunes by the coast a mile or so from here. He says he's very sorry poor Mr. Logan was shot in his absence."

"Has he got any witnesses?"

"Not that I've heard of."

This was the point at which someone knocked heavily on the communicating wall. Any such noise at Longwood House was apt to give you a start, and Tess shot up out of her chair with the quilt flying. Next I thought it was only Julian asking us to pipe down, stop talking, and let him go to sleep. But instead he must have meant it as a kind of delicate warning.

He came out of his room coughing loudly. He tapped at the door, waiting for my reply, and then put his head in.

"I can't sleep," he said miserably. "I—do you mind if I come in?"

This was a new Julian, one I at least had never seen before. One or two strands of his pale hair, unfas-

tened from their adhesiveness, stood up straight at
the back of his head. He had pulled round him a
black wool dressing gown, with white edging, and the
monogram JGE. Out of his handsome face, thinly
lined across the forehead, the light eyes looked out
with the hesitancy of a dog that wants to make
friends. Again, as once before that day, I was haunted
by a vague impression of his similarity in face or
build to someone else.

"Hello, Julian," smiled Tess, drawing the quilt
round her. "Please do come in. We were only talking."

"I can't sleep," he complained again. "You're sure
I'm not intruding, Bob?"

"Not at all. Have a cigarette?"

"Thanks."

He had already taken a cigarette case out of the
pocket of his dressing gown and extracted a cigarette;
but he put it back again and took one of mine, mildly
thankful for the saving.

"Nothing wrong, is there?"

"No, no!" Julian accepted a light, his head on one
side. He inhaled deeply, walked to the window, drew
back the curtain, peered out, and dropped it again.
He fidgeted. Finally he sat down on the edge of the
bed, and faced us. "Yes, there is," he added flatly.
"There is something wrong. And I can't help it. I've
come to you for advice."

"*You* have come to *us* for advice?"

"No joking, Bob. This is serious. Very serious."

His tone sounded desperate. It was still more
effective in the thin middle of the night, when each
syllable was weighted with significance to tired
nerves, and you could hear Julian's watch ticking

loudly from the pocket of his dressing gown.

"Anything I can do, old son. What's on your mind?"

Julian took another clumsy draw at the cigarette, his fingers so far out on it that the fire must have scorched them. He then, out of earnestness or night-nerves, made what must have been one of the few melodramatic speeches of his life.

"First of all," he said, "I want you both to swear by Almighty God that you will never repeat a word of what I'm going to tell you to anybody, unless I give you leave. Will you swear?"

"Yes, if you insist."

"What about you, Tess?"

"Yes. All right." Tess was impressed. Then her quick intuition flew, and she half got up. "Julian, for heaven's sake, wait! Stop a bit! You're not going to tell us you committed the murder, or anything like that?"

"No, no, no." His forehead wrinkled. "Though — since after all, you know, I am a respected and respectable professional man; and not a word's ever been said against me — I'm not sure it's not almost as bad. I can't make up my mind what to do. I've got to find out how it sounds to disinterested persons. Do you swear?"

We raised our hands.

"Yes. Now go on: speak up. What is this enormity you've committed?"

Again Julian drew deeply at the cigarette before answering.

"You remember," he said, "the testimony I gave the police this morning? I first of all said that, though I

176

was in the garden and heard the shot fired, I did not go near the back window and didn't look into the study at any time."

"Yes."

"Then, under their infernal blackmailing tactics"—his forehead wrinkled up—"I changed that. I said that I *had* looked in at the window, and confirmed Mrs. Logan's story. I said I'd climbed up on the box just before the shot was fired. You remember?"

"Definitely. What about it?"

Julian sat up.

"Well," he said simply, "every word of my original statement was gospel truth. I was never within twenty feet of that window. I never climbed up on their blasted box. I never looked in through the window at all, either before or after the shot. Now you know."

XV

"That's torn it," breathed Tess.

Otherwise nobody spoke for some seconds. To see this complete upheaval of the evidence, to realize what it might mean in the long run, was not easy for weary wits at a quarter to one in the morning. My first question, with a hit-between-the-eyes feeling, was not very sensible.

"Man, are you off your chump?"

"I hope not," replied Julian, continuing to puff at the cigarette pretty steadily, and looking straight ahead of him.

"Then what in blazes did you have to go and tell them that for? If it's not true?"

"Because I was — ah — not very frank at the beginning. So they got me cornered. And it seemed to me that I adopted the best way out."

"But if you weren't the man at the window," asked Tess, "who on earth was it?"

Julian huffily called for silence.

"Perhaps I had better tell you what happened. Then you'll understand. I want advice; not recriminations.

"I arrived here, as you know, just before ten o'clock this morning. As you also know, I went out into the garden to find our host. While there, I heard the shot. At this time I was standing on the grass, about thirty feet from the window, and just at the edge of the sunken garden."

He paused, and swallowed.

"Something, however, had attracted my attention just before the shot. I heard a woman's voice speaking in that room. It was not only speaking, it was shouting: just as you have heard Mrs. Logan shout at other times today. Since one of the lights of the window stood open, I heard it distinctly. She was saying she thought she might be going to have a child, and pouring recriminations on someone. I looked toward the window. And I saw a man standing on that wooden box, with his back to me, looking into the window."

"You saw WHAT?"

Julian snapped at us.

"I saw a man standing on the box," he repeated querulously, "in just the position that was later ascribed to *me*."

"Who was it?'

"How can I tell you that? It was a dull day, with shadow along the back of the house; he had his back to me; and he was thirty feet away from me.

"Immediately afterwards I heard the shot. The man, still without turning round, jumped down from the box and ran like the devil round the west side of the house. All I can tell you is that he was wearing a brown suit and a brown hat. You remember I also wore a brown suit and hat?"

"Yes."

"Well, what did I naturally think?" demanded Julian. He could hardly hold his cigarette in his hand. "I thought that man was the murderer. I thought that probably the woman was addressing him. I thought that certainly he had fired a pistol through the window, since his hand was inside. And so I resolved to have absolutely nothing to do with it."

"But why?"

"Bob, you don't understand these things. You're one of these"—his hands expressed anguish—"one of these happy-go-lucky people. I'm not. I tell you, Caesar's wife isn't in it with the reputation a professional man has got to keep. It isn't merely that you mustn't become involved, however innocently, in a shady business. You mustn't come within a mile of any shady business.

"And that's not all. Did you know I'm going to be married? Well, I am. Probably this autumn. To one of the . . ." He mentioned a family so illustrious that I didn't believe him, though I have since had reason to know he was telling the truth. "Consequently, this morning I thought to myself, 'What will they think?' That is, if I figured not as an ordinary witness, but as The Man Who Saw the Murderer? The man who would have to fight it out in court. The man—"

He stopped.

"I decided to forget him," Julian concluded. "It wasn't as though I were telling a lie, you see. It was only a slight *suppressio veri*."

We all exchanged glances.

"A mere bagatelle," moaned Tess. "An amiable indisposition. And then?"

Julian's face grew red. "Then, as you know, those swine got me into a corner. I mean Inspector Elliot and Dr. Fell. When I told my original story, I didn't know there was another witness. I didn't know this accursed gardener MacCarey had seen the man in the brown suit; and, by one of the worst bits of ill-luck in the world, had identified him as me."

Julian got up. Holding his dressing gown round him as though he had got stomach-ache, he waddled over to the fire and flung the cigarette into it. Gulping smoke, he returned and sat down again on the edge of the bed.

"I was already in it too deeply," he pointed out. "If I now told the story about the man in the brown suit, they wouldn't believe me. And I should be landed back with the trouble I wanted to avoid. They were actually going to blackmail me by as good as saying *I* committed the murder. My God, do you call that fair? Do you call that justice?"

"What they obviously wanted me to say was that I had been looking in at the window. If I said that, they as good as promised I shouldn't be involved in any notoriety. So I took the line of least resistance; and admitted it. That's the whole story."

There was another long silence.

Tess, reaching a slippered foot out from under the quilt, kicked at a clinker that had fallen into the grate. The fire was sinking to ash-crusted red. A faint wind had begun to blow round the house at the turn of the night, getting up from the beech trees beside the garden.

"Julian, my lad," I said, "you've done it now."

"Why so? Just tell me that! Why so?"

"Because now — isn't this true? — you can't really confirm Mrs. Logan's story after all? You don't know what did happen in that study?"

"No, I don't."

"But who," persisted Tess, "who was the man in the brown suit, if it wasn't Julian?"

I could tell her that.

It wasn't inspiration. It didn't even feel like inspiration, at that drugged hour of the morning. But that last movement of Julian's across the room, when he went to throw his cigarette into the fire, had unlocked the door and let the blinds fly up. I knew now why there was something tormentingly familiar about him. I yelled at him to stand up, and he bounced off the bed as though he had been stung.

"Sh-h!" hissed Tess.

"Tess, who does he remind you of? Look at him! Not in his actual features. But in his build, every pound of it; in his height; in his way of moving; and, above everything, in the shape of his head and face? Who else is it who nearly always wears a brown suit and hat?"

After a long stare, Tess nodded.

"Clarke," she said.

"Clarke. Right."

"But Clarke," she protested, willing to believe but squirming under it, "wasn't wearing a brown suit this morning . . ."

"He wasn't, at least, when you and I saw him first. He was wearing a white linen suit and Panama hat. And that's why we were all thrown off. If we had seen those two together, side by side in brown suits, we couldn't have missed the similarity between them.

That's what misled the gardener, in a bad light and through a window. Would you like to make a bet that the man who was standing outside that window was really our host?"

Julian, having so nearly lost his dignity, was now struggling to regain it. There was a curious air about him, which I did not like at all. A keen, wary air, reddish of eye and heavy of breathing.

"As a matter of fact," he conceded, "I had — er — already thought of that."

Immediately afterwards, as though regretting that he had said so much, he took a handkerchief out of the pocket of his dressing gown, and wiped his mouth. The watch in the dressing-gown pocket ticked loudly.

"Then the man was Clarke?"

"I've told you, I don't know it was. I could not swear to anything."

"But you think it was Clarke?"

"I don't want questions," said Julian. "I want advice. Through no fault of my own, absolutely none, I've been maneuvered into this position. Believe it or not, I don't like telling lies. It upsets me. And my digestion too. I've got a conscience. Just tell me: what would you do if you were in my place?"

"That's very obvious. Go straight to Elliot and tell him the truth."

"Why is that so obvious?"

"Get him to arrange an identification parade. Have the gardener look through the front window again. If the gardener picks Clarke as the man, or even if he admits it might have been Clarke, the police will believe you."

Julian hesitated, evidently distraught with perplexity. He contemplated the bedpost, and drummed his fingers on it. You felt that once more hesitant nets were being lowered into his conscience, sweeping after very elusive fish.

"That's very easy to say, Bob. But it isn't quite as simple as all that."

"Why not?"

"This Mr. Clarke," said Julian, staring at the bedpost, "is a man of considerable property."

"Well?"

"Very considerable property," continued Julian, getting into his stride again with the old fluent smoothness. "I ascertained that before I accepted this invitation for the weekend."

"Yes; well?"

"A friend of mine in the city tells me that he's worth, at a conservative estimate, over a quarter of a million. My friend says Mr. Clarke is a very keen man. He says Clarke has only once been done down in a business deal; and that by someone in the grocery trade, who nicked him for ten thousand and made him look like a thundering fool into the bargain. But that's by the way. What I mean is that Clarke is a man who knows how to get on in the world."

Julian hesitated.

"The fact is," he went on, plucking at the bedpost, "he seems to have taken quite a fancy to me. We've had several chats to-day. I hope I'm not conceited; but I'm a sensible man and I'm fully conscious of my own capabilities. Now that Clarke is more or less retiring as a country gentleman, it appears he wants someone to — er — manage his affairs for him. You see that? He as good as told me the job was mine for the asking."

Here Julian struck the bedpost with the flat of his open hand, and whirled round on us.

"Do you know," murmured Tess, "I believe we're getting to the root of this. Julian, darling, has Clarke bribed you to say you didn't see him at the window?"

"No, certainly not! I'm astonished at the suggestion. Astonished; yes, and hurt too! You know me better than that, Tess. The subject was never discussed between us."

"All the same, this proposed job would go whingo"—Tess raised her hands, palms upwards—"if you said you saw him at the window?"

"Probably. Yes."

"Julian, my dearest fathead, *will* you listen to a bit of advice from me?"

"I don't like your tone, Tess. But go on."

"Don't touch it," said Tess, with extraordinary intensity. "Don't touch it with a barge-pole! Whatever Clarke wants you to do, you just take my advice and shut your ears and run. And I'm not just preaching, either. I don't mind its being crooked. If I could push Bob here into a job where he'd make two or three thousand a year—my dear, I wouldn't care if it was so crooked you couldn't see it for the whirls."

"Here! Hoy!"

"Be quiet, Bob. I'm sorry; but it's true. You're such an honest lummox that you'd never get on otherwise."

"Are you advising Julian or me?"

Tess, who had got to her feet, sat down again. She spoke in a low voice, but with no less earnestness.

"I'm advising everybody: have nothing to do with

Clarke. Don't you see he's at it again? Julian: please, please do what I ask you. Go to Inspector Elliot and tell him what you've just told us. That man in the brown suit (otherwise Clarke) must have been the murderer."

"I think not," retorted Julian coolly. "Aren't you forgetting something? If it was Clarke at the window, how did he fire the revolver?"

And once more the old puzzle appeared and leered at us, in itself like a face through the window.

Julian was now enjoying himself.

"Let me make the position clearer," he suggested in his most persuasive way. "It is absolutely certain that the revolver was hanging up on the pegs against the wall when fired. You two helped to prove that. The police accept it. They admit that their fishing-rod idea is rubbish which would not stand a minute's real scrutiny. Nobody standing outside the window could have managed to reach across fifteen feet of space: definitely not without being seen by either Mrs. Logan or the gardener. Whoever was at the window, it wasn't the murderer. If Clarke was at the window, the murderer can't possibly be Clarke. Q.E.D."

"You are giving me," said Tess, "the most amazing and painful headache I have ever had in my life."

"Isn't it true?"

"No, it isn't," returned Tess crossly.

"But, my dear girl—"

"I'm not your dear girl," said Tess. "I'm not anybody's dear girl; not even Bob's, just now. I'm horribly tired and yet I can't sleep. I know Clarke did it and yet I can't think how. Ugh! Julian, you beast. Why don't you be a dear and go and tell Mr. Elliot about this? I've a good mind to do it myself."

"You swore an oath—"

"Pfaa!" said Tess.

"Are you going to hold by that solemn oath, or aren't you?"

"Oh, all right. I don't promise anything, though."

Julian hesitated. "Think it over until morning," he urged, pressing his fingers over red-rimmed eyes, and taking them away with a bleary look. "I want sleep. Maybe I can sleep now. Thanks for—er—promising, anyhow. Good night."

His creaking slippers crossed the room. The door opened and closed.

Now here I must confess, in attempting to reconstruct it afterwards, to something like a hiatus in time. I was not conscious of it as a hiatus then. I remember being extremely drowsy, in one of those feather-witted states of drowsiness when the head jerks, and the furniture seems to spill together under a blur of lights; yet all the while you are conscious of pygmy voices talking, with pygmy movement, so that you could swear you never lost consciousness at all.

Thus I can remember Tess saying, "There's something awfully fishy about that." To which I said, "About what?" and she replied, "About Julian telling us—" At which the whole conversation was blurred as though in the roar of a plane's motor, and senses dipped like the wing of a plane.

In the following moment someone was whispering "Bob!" and shaking my arm, while a fierce crick in the back helped to shock dulled senses alert.

Tess's face as close to mine, and it was white.

The fire was nearly out and the room deathly cold,

though the light still burned thinly. As Huckleberry Finn once put it, it even *smelt* late. I stirred in the hard chair; it gave a creak of inordinate loudness, a creak that seemed to echo back from the white walls. It warned me to whisper when I spoke to Tess.

"What is it?"

"You've been asleep. Sitting bolt upright."

"Nonsense."

"Well, I've been asleep in my chair." It was barely possible to hear her, the ghost of a whisper. She had discarded the eiderdown, and was kneeling on the edge of my chair, staring at the door. "Bob. I think there's something downstairs."

"Something downstairs?"

"A—a noise," said Tess. "It sounded like somebody moving the table in the dining-room."

I got up, cramped, and she followed. Both of us took care that the slightest jar of woodwork should not betray any sound. I put her back in the easy chair, draped the quilt round her shoulders, and crossed the room on felt-soled slippers. My wrist watch was in the drawer of the bedside table, which rasped like the noise of a bad wireless when I pulled it open. The time was one minute past two o'clock.

"Listen! There it is again."

I went to the door, turned the knob clear round, and, holding it there, eased the door open noiselessly. My room, at the back of the house and about the middle in a transverse corridor, was not far from the head of the stairs.

By craning my neck, I could see down the stairs past the door of the dining-room. Though the door was closed, there was a very dim thread of light under

188

the sill.

Tess had run out, and was frantically dragging at my arm to pull me back into the room; but there is such a thing as being baffled to the point of mania. You could distinguish noises from the dining-room too. First a faint shuffling, as though very light wood were being moved. Then a creak or two. Then a ringing or jingling, growing a little louder with an indescribable rhythmic swing which created images out of the past . . .

The yell of terror that woke Longwood House then, at exactly three minutes past two in the morning, would have jabbed the nerves even of a person under drugs. It was a man's voice.

You heard it piercing even through other things. It was exactly as though the whole floor up here had snapped and twanged like a gigantic bowstring; intensified by the long, ripping noise of iron tearing loose from wood; and swallowed up in the vastness of the crash when two hundredweight of spiked iron struck a hardwood floor.

But there had been a more muffled, more sodden quality about it too. When the chandelier fell in the dining-room, it fell on something besides the floor.

About twenty seconds after the crash, Martin Clarke came out of his bedroom, tying on a dressing gown, and began quietly switching on the lights in the upstairs hall. He stopped short when he saw me, but he made no comment. We stared at each other for a moment, and then we went downstairs together.

The dining-room door was closed, but not locked.

JOHN DICKSON CARR

The wall lamps were burning.

We hauled Andy Hunter out from under the wreckage of the chandelier, and from the wreckage of a step-ladder. It was not a very bad sight to look at, since the weight had caught his head only glancingly, and missed his body altogether except for the left shoulder. But there could be little doubt as to the result. His eyes were closed, and there was a little sluggish blood trickling from one nostril. He moaned once, twitched his right hand, and then lay still.

Whitsunday, May 16th, came on the following day.

The tide was out at Southend-on-Sea. A vast expanse of gray pitted mud, looking rather like the end of the world as imagined by Mr. H. G. Wells, took up the beach and apparently a good deal of the ocean as well. Even the Pier, a white centipede with black legs, hardly reached to the end of it.

It was too early for the full surge of Sunday holidaymakers. The sun was strengthening and brilliant like the air. In one of the steep, pleasant, shady streets leading down to the front, I was waiting in the antiseptic front parlor of Dr. Harold Middlesworth's nursing home when Inspector Elliot arrived. Elliot took the front steps two at a time, brushed past an angry nurse, and confronted me.

"Well? Is he — ?"

"No. He's not dead. Yet. But he's got a fractured skull, with other minor injuries. It's remotely possible, even, that he may recover. The question is whether his mind will ever be the same again."

This pulled Elliot up short. For the first time he showed concern. "How do they know that?"

"X-ray photographs. Bone pressing on the brain or something. I don't know. Ask the doctor."

"Look here . . . You feel pretty badly about this, don't you?"

Just how badly I felt I was not going to let anybody see.

"Andy's one of the best blokes alive. That's always the kind who seem to get it in the neck. Why the ruddy chandelier couldn't have fallen on"—I was going to say Clarke, or Julian Enderby, but I substituted "somebody else" instead, "is one of the major mysteries in the cussedness of all human affairs. Incidentally, if you hadn't insisted on keeping everybody at the house last night, this wouldn't have happened."

Elliot turned over the pages of a magazine on the waiting-room table. He turned them back again before he replied.

"Sorry," he said quietly. "But I doubt that."

"What does that mean?"

"Hunter knew too much. If you want to claim a bull's-eye, claim one for saying that yesterday. He had discovered something about that house which the murderer was afraid he might tell. So the murderer had to get rid of him, one way or the other."

The blood came up under Elliot's eyes. He raised a bony, freckled hand.

"Wait! Don't say I should have foreseen that, and prevented it. Yell at me all you like; but don't expect miracles. I had no idea what line Dr. Fell was working on, and he didn't tell me until last night. He wasn't positive, because there was no objection to it; but I'm dead certain he's right and it's a point we can settle to-day."

I stared at him.

"You mean you've got the solution?"

"Yes," said Elliot briefly. "I think so," he added with innate caution. "That's for your consolation."

With a significant wag of his head, he perched himself gingerly on the edge of the table.

"Dr. Fell," he went on, "spent last evening at the Congo Club, buying pink gins for one of your writing friends. It concluded with a long and expensive telephone call to this fellow's father at Manchester. Satisfactorily, I'm glad to say." He paused. "As for me, I spent the evening collecting — information received. All very satisfactory too." He looked hard at me. "I admit it was a hell of a shock to go down to Longwood this morning, and find out what happened. But I got some of the facts from Mr. Clarke. I also had a very interesting interview with Miss Fraser."

Tess had spilled the beans.

Meeting Elliot's eye, I had no doubt whatever about that. She had undoubtedly repeated to him Julian's story and everything else; and it was difficult to blame her. Elliot had the air of a man who intends to put up with no nonsense.

"Stop a bit," I said. "I can guess what you want to talk about. But before you do . . ."

"Well?"

"There hasn't been any time to think about this: Andy's accident, I mean. It's been all crash-bang-and-run-for-the-doctor. But, if this was a deliberate attempt on Andy's life, how was it done? If the murderer deliberately made the chandelier fall, how in blazes did he manage it?"

Elliot considered.

"I didn't say it was a deliberate attempt on Mr. Hunter's life."

"The devil you didn't! You said—"

He stopped me. "No. I said that if this stroke of the chandelier falling hadn't been managed either by luck or accident, sooner or later the murderer *would have* tried to kill him: whether you people were at Longwood House or not. Haven't you still got any idea of what happened?"

"No."

"You probably will have," Elliot said grimly, "when you know why I'm here. Do you think there would be any objection on the part of the doctor if I took Mr. Hunter's fingerprints? It will only take a minute; and, even if he's unconscious, it won't disturb him." He paused. "You see, I've had a good look at that fallen chandelier, and at the oak beam in the ceiling. The beam was wrenched back and forth again. There are two distinct sets of fingerprints, left and right hand, on the lower rim of the chandelier. The prints match others that are all over a dozen articles in Hunter's bedroom, and it's almost certain they're his. But if I could get his fingerprints here, we could be absolutely sure."

Insane puzzles were gathering round again.

"Do you mean," I yelled at Elliot, "that this is the Case of the Agile Butler all over again? Did Andy jump up and start to swing himself back and forth on the chandelier too?"

"That's what the facts indicate."

"But why?"

"Why did the butler do it? That is, why did the butler apparently do it?" asked Elliot, choosing his words with care. He struggled between his inclinations to give a hint, and his caution in keeping a professional lip buttoned. "If you'll only concentrate for a second, you can't miss it."

"That's what *you* think."

Elliot consulted his watch. He spoke in a colorless tone.

"It's a quarter to one, and we can't stand here arguing. Dr. Fell is down on the front, sampling the local beer. I've got to meet him in fifteen minutes. Where's this Dr. Middlesworth? Oh, and by the way." His look became sharp. "I understand Mrs. Logan came in to Southend with you. Where is she now?"

His question was answered by both Dr. Middlesworth and Gwyneth Logan, who came downstairs then.

And I had to admit that Gwyneth, under the stress of trouble that was not her own trouble, had acted with a firmness and a practicality you would not have expected. Tess (who can blame her?) had completely cracked under the strain. But Gwyneth's character seemed to have changed, like an actress's, into that of a nurse.

Her step was firm, her hands cool, her blue eyes anxious but determined. You might almost have had an unpleasant suspicion that she was enjoying the excitement of all this, if her shock and horror had not been so manifest when she first learned of Andy's accident. She was wearing the same dark green frock she had worn on Friday afternoon. And I cannot help it if the simile sounds trite or even grotesque, against that white antiseptic parlor, but it is what I thought of: she looked like a taller wood nymph.

"I'll only be a few minutes," Elliot told us, before he went into conference with Dr. Middlesworth. "Then, if you don't mind, I want you both to come along with me."

"Of course," Gwyneth smiled; but no sooner had the door closed behind Elliot and the doctor, than her attitude changed in a flash.

"What on earth do you suppose they want now?"

"More questions, probably."

"But I've already answered their questions. Three times yesterday! Over and over." She made a gesture as though she were about to stamp her foot on the floor. "Oh, it's all so beastly!" She studied me. "Have they found out anything? You're a friend of Mr. Elliot's: won't you tell me whether they've found out anything? Please?"

Here was an opportunity.

"They know why you went downstairs with that little key on Friday night."

She had taken a step toward me, but she stopped. Her hand went up under her heart as though she had received a shock, and her eyes widened.

"Tess Fraser told them!" she said quickly.

"No. Tess hasn't said a word. It was your friend Clarke who told them."

"Who?"

"Your—friend—Clarke."

Now you might have thought that this would have had some effect on her. You might have thought it would have struck her to anger, or at least some show of displeasure with Clarke. But, so far as appearances

196

went, she never gave it a second's consideration. Instead she was covered with confusion, which she veiled with modestly lowered eyelids and a fine appearance of not being there at all, while her mind stuck insistently to another point.

"Tess told you too, though," she said, with soft accusation.

I lied, and swore Tess hadn't.

"Yes, she did. I know she did. What else did she tell you?"

"Nothing!"

"Please?"

"Not a word."

This appeared to satisfy Gwyneth. She wandered away from me, scuffing the soles of her shoes on the carpet, and paused by a window. The window was open to the green avenue. Sunshine poured in, kindling the little room which had a hard white glaze like the polish on a tombstone. Distantly, a band was marching and playing, "I Do Like to Sit beside the Seaside"; behind it, through all the town, was that tremble of hurrying feet which marks a holiday. Gwyneth breathed deeply the warm, somnolent air.

"Oh, dear," she complained. "To-morrow I've got to face life again. There will be lawyers and chief clerks and all sorts of dreadful people crowding round, with 'Sign this,' and 'Do that.' I don't mind the reporters so much . . . one of them took a photograph of me this morning . . . but I do so hate the others, because I never did know anything about poor Bentley's business and I don't want to know anything about it. He took care of all that."

Again she breathed deeply. And she spoke with

197

sudden violence.

"He would have *loved* being alive this morning," she said.

The band went on playing in the distance.

Gwyneth dabbed a small handkerchief at one corner of her eye. This was genuine, I think. It was as much grief as she was capable of feeling.

"Anyway," she went on, "I've got to go up to town, if only to get some decent mourning. And I mustn't think of myself alone, either." She reflected. "He's an awfully nice boy, isn't he?"

"Who?"

"Mr. Hunter." She spoke with the greatest formality. "Not that I would—good heavens!—not that I would—you know—think about anything like that, with poor Bentley not even buried. But it's odd. Do you know, I never used to think I liked men of Mr. Hunter's type at all. I always thought I liked someone more—more—"

"Mature?"

She turned round. "Why do you say that?"

"It's the obvious idea. You mean someone more like Clarke, for instance."

"Well, yes." She considered this, and nodded solemnly. Then doubt flashed into her eyes; she took hold of the lace curtain, pinching it between thumb and forefinger. But, instead of challenging the subject, she slid off at a tangent and calmly approached another.

"I do hope, anyway, that Inspector Elliot can tell us what's been happening at that house. And whether it was an accident, and all. I should dearly love to know what poor Mr. Hunter was up to last night. He was up to something, right enough. I could have told you that last evening, though I didn't say anything about it at the time. I knew it when he stole something out of my room."

"Andy stole something out of your room?"

"Yes, when he thought I didn't see him," answered Gwyneth. "He stole a paper of pins."

There was a silence.

She made this astonishing statement with the simple candor of a child. But there was nothing at all childlike about her face or her manner.

"Did you say a paper of pins?"

"Yes. You think I'm lying." She pounced on this. "It's easy enough to prove, though. He wanted them for something last night. The paper of pins was in his left-hand jacket pocket when he — when that dreadful thing happened. If you don't believe that, just ask the nurse here who undressed him."

"But what in the name of sanity did he want with a paper of pins?"

"I can't think. You people are clever; and I'm not at all clever; so I thought you might be able to tell me." Then she stiffened. Her soft voice grew sharp. "Do be careful what you say! There's somebody coming."

It was only Elliot, striding down on us with a grimly sardonic but grimly satisfied air. He wiped his fingers on a soiled handkerchief, which he stowed away and buttoned up in the brief case he was carrying. Then he turned to Gwyneth.

"And now, Mrs. Logan, I've finished here. There's nothing more that you can do either, I'm afraid. I wonder if you'd mind coming along down with me to the Priory Hotel?"

"What for?"

Elliot smiled. "Well, I'd like to offer you a sherry or a lemonade before lunch, for one thing. For another, I'd like you to talk to Dr. Fell. He rebelled at climbing up this street, so I had to leave him there."

"You only want to ask me more questions!"

"Frankly, Mrs. Logan, we do. And if you're straight with us this time, as I'm sure you will be, we may be able to nail your husband's murderer before the end of the day."

Gwyneth did not move, nor did her color change. But the atmosphere of fear was strong about that lady who conveyed most things by atmospheres.

"I have been — s-straight with you!"

"No, Mrs. Logan, I'm afraid you haven't. Don't let it worry you, because I think we can convince you that you're protecting a fool and a semi-maniac who would cut your throat as soon as look at you." (Here Gwyneth opened her mouth as though to protest, but thought better of it.) "What's more, one of the things we want you to tell us probably isn't a lie on your part at all: it's just a mistake. This isn't a trap. I can assure you of that."

Gwyneth regarded him curiously. She seemed to be speculating.

"Oh? What if I won't go?"

"Then it will just take a little longer, that's all. And cause more worry for you." He turned to me. "We shall want you too, my lad. Very much so."

"Why me?"

"In the absence of Mr. Enderby — "

"Enderby!" cried Gwyneth, with sudden shrillness.

"—in the absence of Mr. Enderby," Elliot pursued blandly, "and also Miss Fraser, you'll do very well to confirm some things that were told you last night."

"So Tess Fraser did tell you," whispered Gwyneth. Her whole aspect changed again; she lifted her dreamy eyes and mouth. "Very well. I'll go with you. I'll answer your questions. And, as I hope to go to heaven, I'll tell you the truth."

"Ah!" said Elliot.

Groping, but now apparently on the right path, we were approaching the end. In a few minutes more, I knew, we should hear at least a good part of the answer: which may be already apparent to the reader of this narrative, but which still remained a blur to me. The riddle of Andy Hunter's "accident" merely completed that blur. As we went out into the sunlight, with the bands on the hill beating hymns into our ears, I could think of nothing but four words as meaningless as the accident or the murder.

A paper of pins. A paper of pins. A paper of pins.

XVII

"Sit down here, Mrs. Logan," invited Dr. Fell.

Though the Front was crowded and strident, swept with good sea-air, Dr. Fell had managed to choose the gloomiest and most deserted corner of an oak-paneled smoking-room at the hotel.

But perhaps the doctor needed shade and quiet. For he was in a warm condition. Let loose from under Elliot's watchful eye, he had made off instantly for the amusement fair: where he had spent an absorbed hour at noble games of skill involving pitching pennies, throwing wooden balls, firing rifles, and hammering nails into boards.

As a result of this, he had accumulated a large golden-haired doll, which he gravely presented to Gwyneth; a vile cigar, which he smoked; five small boxes of assorted toffees, which he distributed among us; and a large brass stickpin, value one farthing, which he wore in his tie as proof of victory over a sporting gentleman who gamely but rashly offered to guess his weight. He had also got his fortune told twice, and taken a ride in the Dodgem.

Since I did not know him well at this time, I would not have guessed that he was worried. But just how badly worried he was under those snorts and chuckles, even upset, even Elliot never heard.

"The proprietor of the Ghost Train," he said, "I consider a dog and a varlet, probably destined for irremediable spiritual ruin. The same, with knobs on, applies to the proprietor of the Witching Water Mill. Neither would let me in. The proprietor of the Royal Alpine Slide, on the other hand—"

"All right, all right," interposed Elliot. "Though what you find to amuse you in that stuff, sir, for the life of me I can't—"

" 'Ark at 'im," scoffed Dr. Fell. He adjusted his eyeglasses. "You think that my morning was wasted?"

"Wasn't it?"

"No. Hear my tale. While engaged in tucking in an ambrosial delicacy vulgarly known as a hot dog, I met a clergyman shepherding a troop of Boy Scouts. The parson turned out to be a very good fellow. He also turned out to be the vicar of Prittleton. Waiter!"

Gwyneth Logan put down the doll beside her chair, and said nothing.

It was so dim in our corner that they had turned on a light in the wall over the table, economically leaving dark the rest of the big smoke-room before the pre-lunch rush. Gwyneth had not spoken since our entrance: she had that eternal quality of patience we had noticed before: but she seemed a trifle nervous of Dr. Fell. And this was the curious thing. For you could have sworn that Dr. Fell was equally nervous of Gwyneth.

Except to give her the doll, he had not looked directly at her; now, as he put down his cigar and rapped on the table to summon the waiter, he turned a fiery and embarrassed face.

"But that, ma'am," he said apologetically, "is another matter altogether. The vicar can wait. Yours is a sherry and bitters, isn't it?" He cleared his throat. "The maid, Sonia, says you always take sherry and bitters."

"Yes. Please."

It was not until we had received our drinks, and the waiter had gone, that Dr. Fell exploded.

"Elliot, I don't like it," he roared. "By thunder and Long John Silver, I don't like it!"

"Steady, sir."

"Do you mean you don't like to question me?" asked Gwyneth quietly. She seemed to know how to deal with men like this. Her expression was grave, sweet, and anxious: the same expression she had worn on Friday night, when Bentley Logan caught her with the key to the triptych. As she had addressed him, so she addressed Dr. Fell. "Please do question me. I don't mind, really. In fact, I'd rather you did."

"Then, damme, madam," said Dr. Fell, "how long has this affair between you and Clarke been going on?"

He flung the words at her. She replied without either hesitation or excitement.

"There never has been anything between Martin and me. Never in the world. I don't see how you could think that."

Dr. Fell and Elliot exchanged glances.

"In that case, Mrs. Logan," Elliot took up the

query, "who was the man you've been meeting at the Victoria and Albert Museum?"

"Tess Fraser told you that."

"Information received, Mrs. Logan. Like to tell us who the man was?"

Gwyneth looked bewildered. "But I don't s-see what that has to do with it. You're not interested in my morals, are you? Not that it was ever anything but a harmless flirtation! It has nothing to do with Bentley's death. If you must know, the man was nobody you've ever even heard of."

Dr. Fell shook his head.

"No, ma'am. D'ye see, the conclusion is almost inescapable that your squire of the Victoria and Albert Museum was at Longwood House yesterday, and that he was the person who shot your husband."

"Oh!" said Gwyneth.

"Yes, ma'am. Exactly."

"But that's im—what makes you think so?"

Inspector Elliot intervened.

"Mrs. Logan," he said, "the first job we had was to identify the revolver. Yes, I know both you and Bob Morrison thought it was your husband's. But that wasn't good enough: we had to have positive identification before we could get anywhere. Last night we checked up. The revolver belonged to Mr. Logan, right enough. And that gave us a straight lead."

Elliot paused, moving his pewter tankard round on the table. He peered up.

"The next question was: Who knew Mr. Logan had taken a gun to Longwood House? It seemed to be generally agreed that he hadn't mentioned it to anyone. The only persons who came to know about it, from that little scene late Friday night, were yourself, Bob Morrison, and Miss Fraser.

"Of course, Mr. Logan *might* have dropped a sly side hint to someone else. Or someone *may* have seen him carrying the gun on Friday night: though we know that the house was dark when he went downstairs, and he had the gun in his pocket when he went upstairs again. Take any of those possibilities you like.

"But look at what comes after that! At one-thirty in the morning, you and Mr. Logan went back up to your bedroom. He put away his revolver in a Gladstone bag, in a cupboard of the bedroom; and you turned in. Correct?"

"I've told you all that," moaned Gwyneth wearily.

"Mr. Logan always kept the bedroom door locked at night? He locked it that night?"

"Yes. I've told you that too!"

"Good! Now, at just before half past eight the next morning, Mr. Logan got up; dressed; went downstairs; had his breakfast, and was out for his walk by nine. He left you asleep, since you didn't get up until nearly ten?"

Gwyneth shrugged her shoulders.

"I was dozing," she answered. "He woke me when he got up, and then I drifted off to sleep again. I'm a very light sleeper."

Elliot pushed the pewter tankard to one side. He nodded as though well satisfied.

"So you see, Mrs. Logan, the revolver must have been taken out of that bedroom between half past eight and ten o'clock in the morning." He paused. "I just want you to think for a second what that means.

The murderer had to get this revolver, and hang it on the wall for his death trap. So the murderer had to walk openly into your bedroom — where you were, as you say, 'dozing,' at a time in the morning when it's easy to awaken anybody — he had to rummage all over the place after the revolver, and get out again without being seen or heard by you. Mrs. Logan, he ran an awful risk. He ran a senseless risk. He ran an almost incredible risk. Unless . . ."

"Unless what?" cried Gwyneth.

Elliot smiled without any amusement at all.

"You see how it is. I'm forced to the conclusion either that you were an accomplice — " Gwyneth cried out at this, getting to her feet and jarring the table so that the small glass spilled; but Elliot made her sit down again.

"Or," he said, "that the murderer was desperate and didn't much care whether he woke you or not. In other words, the murderer was your lover, who meant to kill Mr. Logan, and thought you would protect him if you did happen to wake up.

"The likeliest person to have known about the revolver was your lover. Why? Because you'd have told him, of course! You'd have warned him. Hang it, Mrs. Logan, people don't take .45 army revolvers to the country for a week end as a general thing. If your husband carried a gun, you knew why he carried it; and it couldn't have made you feel very easy. So you tipped off your lover. He probably even knew where to find the revolver. You must have known all about it when you unpacked the bags on Friday afternoon. And so, next morning, he took a chance and nipped in to get it."

Gwyneth clenched her fists.

"I was asleep," she said piteously. Her face was full of a tragic earnestness which shone like that of a saint on canvas. "I tell you I was asleep. I *didn't* wake up. I didn't see anybody come in. I didn't even know the revolver was gone."

"Agreed. We believe you."

"You – ?"

Elliot grinned in a twisted but more human way. His tone was dry.

"That's right, Mrs. Logan. It's not very likely (is it?) that, if you'd known what was going to happen, you would have gone and planted yourself smack in the room where it did happen?"

"No. No, of course not."

"So, if you could make up your mind to tell us who the man is, you'd be helping us a lot."

"What else do you want to know?" asked Gwyneth quietly.

Dr. Fell, either from worry or perplexity or some other cause, now wore an expression which would have been considered hideous even by Mr. Harpo Marx. He puffed out his bandit's mustache; he shook his head, so that the big mop of gray-streaked hair tumbled over one ear. Once, by internal evidence, he seemed about to protest. But he did not speak.

For my own part, though I meant to remain neutral in this, it struck me that Elliot had better stick closely to her if he wanted any reply. Otherwise she would ease her slippery body away, as the nymph escapes in the story. And again, if several contradictory similes seem to have been used in describing Gwyneth, that is only natural. She was not a woman, but a dozen women; and at least ten of them desirable.

"What else do you want to know?" she repeated.

"I'm sorry you don't choose to answer, Mrs. Logan."

"It isn't that." She shook her head firmly. "You may think I'm evading, but I'm not. Are you telling me there aren't any—any ghosts?"

"Oh, Lord," groaned Elliot.

"Don't laugh. I believe in ghosts. Still, if I say that you'll think I'm evading you again. Just tell me if there's anything more you want to ask me, and we can clear it all up at once."

Again Elliot exchanged a glance with Dr. Fell. Some indecipherable signal passed between them.

"Very well," agreed Elliot. His tone was so casual that I had all my ears alert. "Just for the sake of clearing things up, I want you to think back to the exact moment your husband was shot."

Gwyneth shivered.

"Got that? Good! You saw the man in the brown suit, of course?"

"The man . . . ?"

"The man who was standing outside the north window. The one who gave you an alibi."

"You mean Mr. . . . oh, dear, I never can think of his name! The one with the fair hair. Wait! Mr. Enderby. That's it." Having evidently got this established, Gwyneth frowned and ruminated. "I sort of saw him vaguely," she admitted, "after poor Bentley was hit. That is, I'd got an idea someone had looked in to see what had happened after the shot. I hadn't known he was there beforehand, naturally. I hadn't known there was anybody there. Otherwise I shouldn't have spoken out so frankly about — you know — what Bentley did to me the night before."

"You recognized Mr. Enderby, did you?"

"Yes, I — No, I didn't *recognize* him in the way you mean," Gwyneth corrected herself, with another pretty frown followed by a smile. "I'd never met him before. I knew him afterwards."

Elliot nodded thoughtfully.

"You're quite sure it was Mr. Enderby, Mrs. Logan?"

"Pardon?"

"I said: you're quite sure it was Mr. Enderby?"

It was already warm in that corner of the dim smoking room, with the one light beating down on our faces from a glass shade; but now the temperature seemed to go up several degrees. Elliot waited. Dr. Fell waited. I waited, staring at a garish sign extolling the merits of Bass. Even my neckband felt warm.

"Oh!" murmured Gwyneth, with a soft start. "But it must have been Mr. Enderby," she protested, after more reflection. "He said he was, didn't he? You said he was? Why should he say he was, if he wasn't? This is becoming terribly mixed up, but you know what I mean. And, anyway, how could he have known what I said and what happened in there, unless he was?"

"At any rate, you've got no doubts?"

Gwyneth hesitated.

"It's a peculiar thing. I only got a tiny look at him, because he jumped down afterwards and anyway I never saw him properly. But I had a sort of ghosty idea — at the time, this was, before I knew — that it might have been someone else."

"Someone else? Who?"

"Martin," said Gwyneth. "Martin Clarke."

Not a muscle moved in Elliot's face. Picking up the tankard, he took a deep pull at it, set it down, and folded his arms on the table.

"Mrs. Logan," he said, "Sometime in the future, maybe, somebody's going to suggest to you that *I* put that idea into your head. Can you say here and now, before witnesses, that I didn't?"

"No, no, it was my own idea," Gwyneth declared. She looked frightened. "Why? Have I said something I shouldn't? In any case, if the man was Mr. Enderby he couldn't have been Martin."

"But at the time you thought it was Mr. Clarke?"

"Yes, I did."

Once more Elliot and Dr. Fell exchanged glances.

"He had his hand inside the window, I think?"

Gwyneth seemed dubious. "I can't say about that. As I keep telling you, I never got a proper look. It was like this." She moistened her lips. "Did you ever, when you were a child, play that game where you whirl yourself round and round and round, deliberately getting dizzy, and seeing how long you can keep it up without falling. Everything I saw seemed to be like that. Just a—z-z-z!

"He had a brown suit and hat, I think. His face wasn't very clear behind the glass, and in a darkish room, though I could almost swear to the outline. And I didn't pay any attention even to the little I saw, because I thought he'd only jumped up there after the shot. So I truly can't tell you whether his hand was inside the window or not. I'm sorry."

"That's all right, Mrs. Logan. You've said

enough."

"Madam," observed Dr. Fell heartily, "you have. And, oh, Bacchus, but you speak in parables!"

"It isn't a parable! It's the truth."

Dr. Fell made an apologetic gesture. He picked up his own tankard and polished off the whole pint before setting it down. It kindled his color to a marked degree, but seemed to do little toward curing his mental or physical indigestion.

"I referred," he said, "to something else. I referred to the game of spinning one's self round and round, deliberately inducing dizziness, yet trying to remain upright. THAT's a parable, if you like."

Here he looked very hard at me.

"What do you say, friend Morrison?"

"Only that I'd like to know what it means."

"The parable?"

"No; hang the parable! This. This mess. I want to know what makes a revolver come off the wall and fire itself. I want to know how an invisible hand can first grab Tess's ankle, and then start a clock in full sight of all of us. I want to know what makes Andy Hunter—a quite sane man, or at least as sane as old Polson the butler was—jump up and swing on the chandelier with a paper of pins in his pocket. Among other things."

Nobody commented on my mention of the pins, though you could tell from Elliot's expression that it was no news to him. Dr. Fell pointed a large finger.

"A perfect example," he said.

"Of what?"

"Of the parable," insisted the doctor. Then his mood changed. He sat back mildly deprecating, with a troubled brow. "See here. I don't wish to make mysteries. But then I am not making the mysteries. You are."

"As how?"

"By words. By the wrong implications. By your manner of stating the facts, or what you believe to be the facts."

He ruffled his hands through his hair.

"It was the same thing, d'ye see," he went on, "with your young friend at the Congo Club, who in a sense started all the trouble. I am a member of that club, though I don't often drop in. Last night I tracked him down there. Eventually it required a phone call to this chap's father, who had been a guest at Longwood House in nineteen-twenty, to clarify a slight misunderstanding."

"What misunderstanding?"

"About a chair," more or less explained Dr. Fell. "The chair had me completely puzzled. But, as it turned out, it wasn't a dining-room chair. It was a porch chair. And that makes all the difference in the world."

I didn't say anything.

It would have been a breach of manners, for instance, to have got up and emptied the remnants of my beer over his head. It would have been a breach of manners to say, in front of Gwyneth, what I thought of this kind of talk. But if I had then known the reason for what sounded like mere hocus-pocus, if I had known why he was so worried, I should have begged his pardon instead.

Elliot intervened.

"It may sound a bit cloudy," he conceded. "You'll

see how simple it is, though. If you should happen to be at Longwood House at about teatime . . ."

"Elliot, I wouldn't do it," snapped the doctor. "I swear I wouldn't do it!"

"But, sir, what else can we do? It'll nail things dead to rights, won't it?"

"H'mf. Hah. Perhaps. But it will cause trouble, my lad. You are heading for a bigger row than you have ever dreamed of in all your natural life."

"Since when, sir, have *you* been afraid of trouble?"

They were not going to get away with this. I was still smarting with the effect of double-dealing mysticism, which can be the sorest salve on earth. Police or no police, I tried a challenge.

"Doctor, you've evidently got this thing taped. You've discovered the murderer . . ."

"Or think we have," muttered Dr. Fell, with a curious grimace at me. It was as though I had mysteriously got entangled in the middle of the business without knowing how or why.

"Or think you have. All right. At the same time, you claim that the facts have been misstated. I quote a list of things that happened. You then say I'm making mysteries by my manner of stating facts, or what 'I believe' to be the facts. Is there anything in that whole list of occurrences which isn't a fact?"

Dr. Fell hesitated.

His cigar had gone out unheeded in the ash tray. He picked it up, and turned it over in his fingers.

"Only one," he growled.

"Only one thing which isn't a fact?"

"Only one thing," said Dr. Fell, "which is a deliberate, flat, spanking lie."

"But, look here, sir! It's all in the record. I haven't told any lies."

Dr. Fell inclined his head. He did not seem either angry, or accusing, or heavily reticent. His expression was made more difficult to read by the light shining straight down on his eyeglasses, and by the upthrust of the pendulous, grim underlip into the mustache. He grunted once. His fingers, toying with the amusement-park cigar, broke it in two pieces.

"No," he said. "But your *fiancée* Miss Fraser has."

XVIII

Once again a warm, pinkish-tinted twilight had gathered to the west of Longwood House. We were approaching a little episode that few of us had expected, and that none of us ever wants to go through again.

I got down from the bus at the stop some thirty yards from the gate. There had been Andy's car to use up to the middle of the afternoon, but Gwyneth had pinched it and disappeared. I walked along the road, passing nobody but a boy on a bicycle, and went up the gravel driveway. The somber beauty of the house flamed with windows against black-and-white *fleur-de-lis*. In the hood of the doorway, scanning road and drive, stood Tess. She ran down to meet me, lithe and light-footed over the rolling green.

"Bob, I'm glad you're back. Where on earth have you been?"

"Southend."

"Yes, darling. I knew that. But what have you been doing?"

"Various things."

Tess glanced back over her shoulder. "Clarke and I are alone in the house. Ugh! He's given the servants the day off until late to-night. Gwyneth hasn't come back. And Julian — Julian's done a bunk for London. I don't know what the police will say. How's Andy?"

"Bad."

"Clarke's talking war again. He says there's certain to be a war. He's sitting out in the sunken garden, with a bottle of cheap grocery champagne; and he frightens me worse than ever."

"Does he?"

The grass was velvety and still fragrant after last night's rain. Two yards of it separated us; we were alone on the lawn, very much alone. Tess was all in gray, gray skirt and jumper with a bow-and-arrow design in red across the left breast. Her mouth opened as she stared back at me: it was as though you saw the flesh tighten across the cheekbones.

"Bob," she said, "what is it you know that I don't know?"

"Is my dial as easy to read as all that?"

"Yes." She struck her hands together.

"You've been standing in that entry again. Aren't you afraid the hand will catch your ankle again? Tess, that story of the 'hand catching your ankle' was all a damned lie; and you know it."

The colors of twilight changed and shifted across the windows of Longwood House. It wasn't easy to hate Tess, and I didn't hate her. I only felt dull-witted and hot with resentment. I wanted to find and

criticize every flaw in her: every flaw of face or figure
or innermost mind. She pressed her hands together,
making no comment.

"I ought to have guessed it, of course. From the
way Dr. Fell looked at you when you first told that
story. From the way you looked at him, and colored
up and got uneasy, every time *he* mentioned it. From
the way you acted when Elliot asked you to show him
how it happened. From last night, when you practically admitted to me that you weren't to be trusted;
but then I never thought of that."

She broke her silence.

"Bob, for God's sake—"

"There never was any hand. There never was anything in the entry. It doesn't matter about your
starting everybody on this crazy wild-goose chase.
But why did you do it? In the name of sanity, why?"

"You've been talking to Elliot."

"Sure I've been talking to Elliot. Where else could I
have learned about it? You wouldn't tell me."

She was still clasping her hands together, her head
a little on one side.

"Bob, I tried to tell you! And I couldn't."

"But you could tell Elliot and Dr. Fell. You told
them last night, Tess. Last night, after that 'recon-
struction' scene. That's why you came out of the
inquisition room in such a grand defiant state. Last
night. All right! And yet you couldn't tell me. You
kept on acting . . ."

She flashed out at me:

"You're talking like a child."

"It was a child's hand in the entry, wasn't it? The
same one?"

This was the first time we had ever had a real row, and yet it couldn't be called a row at all. There was no flare-up about it. It was too bitter to the taste, like dry medicine, and you felt it all the way down. But before we began saying foolish things I was pulled up with a start by the realization that at least she was not acting now: she was desperately sincere.

"Did Elliot tell you why I made up that story?"

"No."

"Can't you guess?"

"No."

"You will guess," said Tess, "when they come up here to have a talk with Clarke. That is, if they ever do."

"They're coming up here this evening. In fact, they're due here now."

Tess nodded blankly. "Yes; and there comes the car. Oh, Bob!" One moment we were standing there like marionettes, in stiff and unnatural poses; then Tess ran to me, and I put my arms round her. For these states of mind, thank Longwood House. Thank the influence which had been only too successful. Thank the murderer.

The engine of a police car throbbed loudly against that early evening hush; you seemed to hear each individual gravelstone crunch as it drew up before the front door. It contained Elliot, Dr. Fell, and Gwyneth Logan. They climbed out. Elliot, evidently not too well pleased, strode across the grass toward us, slapping his brief case against his leg.

"Inspector," said Tess in a high, clear voice, "will you please tell Bob that —"

"Yes, miss. All in good time." Elliot was polite but

curt. "Can you tell me where Mr. Clarke is?"

(So they were gathering for the kill.)

"He's in the sunken garden out at the back. Drinking champagne."

Elliot's sandy eyebrows went up. "Drinking champagne?"

"It's that cheap Italian stuff Mr. Logan used to stock for the World-Wide Stores," explained Tess.

"Oh. And where's Mr. Enderby?"

"Cleared out. Gone back to London."

"So I heard." Again Elliot slapped the brief case against his leg, savagely. "We must see about that. In the meantime, I'd appreciate it if both of you would go out and stay with Mr. Clarke. Dr. Fell and I will join you as soon as we've had a look in the house." He turned away, and then swung back again. "And by the way. There will be a couple of workmen, with tool kits, here looking for me in a few minutes. Don't send them away."

He nodded curtly, strode back to Dr. Fell and Gwyneth; and all three of them entered the house.

That something was going to happen grew more apparent with every breath we drew. I started to speak, but Tess stopped me. We circled the house, crossed that long and beautiful plain of grass behind it, and went down into the sunken garden. There we found Clarke at his ease.

The garden was circular in shape, some twenty feet across, and almost as deep as the height of a man's head. Shallow crazy-paved steps led down into it. The inside of the bowl was ringed with hollyhocks, not yet in bloom; with delphiniums, hardly a blue blaze, but full of a richness of bursting buds; with the rock plants, the lemon of primroses threaded by orange-red polyanthus. In the middle was a big open space, circular, having circular concrete benches built round it, and a sundial in the center.

Clarke sat back with lounging ease on one of these benches. A bright-painted garden table had been drawn up to the bench. There was a wine bucket on the table, with the gilt-foil neck of a bottle leaning over its edge. Clarke was hatless, and wore his white linen suit. A Panama hat, a book, and a pair of spectacles lay on the bench beside him. As we came down the steps, he was just holding an empty wine-glass up to the light, with every appearance of having drunk appreciatively.

"Hell-o!" he said with warmth. He set down the glass. He uncrossed his knees, but did not get up.

"Excuse my apparent discourtesy. I do not offer you any of this stuff"—he gestured toward the wine cooler—"because it is bad as champagne can possibly be. But please sit down. How is the rash invalid?"

It suddenly struck me that the man was looking ten years older, and wicked as a joke that is scurrilous without being funny.

"You mean Andy?"

"Yes, of course."

"He is dying," I said.

The word fell with thick weight into that colored garden. Clarke looked startled, and sat up. Tess let out an involuntary cry.

"Bob! It's not true!"

"It's true, right enough. That's why I've been so long in town."

"Indeed. I am sorry," murmured Clarke. He

221

sounded genuinely sorry. "He is in most respects an admirable young man. And a proficient architect. I had not thought his injury was so serious."

"They didn't think so either. He took a turn for the worse this afternoon. I'm going back there as soon — "

"As soon as?" Clarke prompted.

"As soon as the police finish here. They're in the house now. They know the murderer, the motive, and the method. They may be able to make an arrest to-night."

Clarke passed no comment. Reaching out for the neck of the bottle, he splashed and paddled it in ice-lumped water before drawing it out, streaming, and filling his glass. The bottle was three parts empty.

"I have just been sitting here musing," he had begun, when Elliot and Gwyneth Logan came down the steps into the garden. There was no sign of Dr. Fell, though Clarke appeared to be looking out for him. Clarke, with great smoothness, merely nodded to the newcomers and included them in his remark. "I have just been sitting here musing (sit down, my friends) on life and death, and the sources of both. And particularly on our ghost party."

While Gwyneth shrank back to a bench at the opposite side of the circle, and Tess and I stood like dummies, Elliot put down his brief case on the sundial.

"Yes, sir," Elliot said briskly. "I want to talk to you about that ghost party."

"With pleasure, Inspector! But in what way?"

"The fact is, sir, that all your ghosts are fakes."

Clarke laughed, and settled himself back more comfortably against the bench.

"Consequently," pursued Elliot, "there's something we ought to have out here and now. Were you ever acquainted with the late Herbert Harrison Longwood?"

"Herbert — Harrison — Longwood," repeated Clarke, as though ruminating.

"Let me help your memory. Herbert Harrison Longwood, of the Oxfordshire branch of the family, was the distant relative who inherited the estate in 1919. When an old servant was killed here, by the chandelier falling, Mr. Longwood was so cut up that he went abroad with his wife and never came back to England. Dr. Fell met the local vicar at Southend today. The vicar tells me that Mr. Longwood went to live at Naples, and died there four or five years ago. Did you ever know him?"

Clarke glanced up blandly.

"Yes. I knew him."

"You admit that, sir?"

"Readily."

"Then you also knew that he owned a trick house?"

"A trick house?"

Without moving his eyes from Clarke, Elliot jerked a thumb toward the windows at the other end of the garden behind us.

"A house," he said, "where ghosts can be produced, by natural means, as easy as snapping your fingers. I'm going to suggest that that's why you bought the place; that that's why you assembled your ghost party; and that that's how you murdered Mr. Bentley Logan."

The sun was setting.

Here in the garden, the smell of earth seemed

stronger than the smell of flowers. Clarke was absolutely at his ease. He picked up his glass of champagne, tasted it, and set it down. He regarded Elliot with what appeared to be real curiosity.

"See here, Inspector. Am I by any chance under arrest?"

"No, sir. If you were under arrest I couldn't question you like this."

"Ah, that's a relief. So I murdered poor old inoffensive Logan. How do you suggest I went about it?"

Elliot unfastened the catch of his brief case.

"First of all, you had to direct people's attention away from the real history of the house. You didn't want anybody to learn the actual facts, either about 1820 or 1920. You got very annoyed when Bob Morrison looked up the house in the *Reports of the Historical Monuments Commission*. In fact, you get annoyed every time someone steers the conversation toward the history of the place, as we saw yesterday. But — since this was supposed to be a haunted house — you had to provide them with SOME kind of legend. So you had to invent a ghost.

"But you weren't even clever enough to invent a ghost, Mr. Clarke. You cribbed one. That whole story of the 'corpse with the scratched face,' which you attributed to Norbert Longwood, was cribbed straight out of a collection of real-life stories by Andrew Lang.* Because the book was published forty years ago, you thought nobody would spot it. Here's the book."

The Book of Dreams and Ghosts, by Andrew Lang (Longmans, Green & Co., 1897).

Diving into his brief case, Elliot drew out a gray-bound volume and put it on the sundial.

He added:

"Don't ever try games like that on Dr. Fell, sir. It won't work."

It was as though he had struck Clarke across the face. Clarke's stocky body tightened up. His eyes remained, fixed and unwinking, on Elliot's face.

"But you tried a much cruder trick than that one," Elliot went on easily. "Much cruder. You tried to make the story a little *too* good. Now, I'll be frank with you. Miss Fraser here" — he nodded toward Tess — "has always thought you were a wrong 'un. She thought so when she first met you months ago. She believed you were going to try some kind of jiggery-pokery when you got the ghost party down here. So she decided to test you out."

Clarke's eyes swiveled round toward Tess. He smiled at her and raised his hand as though in greeting.

Elliot continued:

"The minute she stepped into the house, she said something had caught her ankle. To test you. To see what use you'd make of it, if any. You were all a bit nervous that night, and she didn't have to put up much of a show of acting. And you used it, Mr. Clarke. It was a boon to you. You thought in her nervousness she believed something had caught her. So, just like that" — Elliot snapped his fingers — "you instantly tacked it on to the story of the corpse with the scratched face. You claimed that a clutching hand

225

was an old legend at Longwood. You said that
Norbert's ghost was in the habit of catching at
people's ankles. Whereas the whole thing had been
invented on the spur of the moment by Miss Fraser
not fifteen minutes before."

Elliot paused.

He shook his head, with abrupt Scots dourness
which made him look older than his thirty years. He
added:

"That wasn't very intelligent of you, either, Mr.
Clarke."

"No, Inspector?"

"No, sir. It showed us that as a matter of fact you
were a wrong 'un without any doubt."

"And, of course, it proves that I killed Bentley
Logan?"

"If you don't mind," said Elliot, with the same
stolid and patient plodding, "we'll go on and talk
about that."

A large black shape darkened the garden from
above. It was only Dr. Fell, his box-pleated cape
billowing out behind him and his shovel hat pushed
down firmly on his eyes; but he seemed to tower over
us and to take away light. His face was puffed with
uneasiness, polished and shining, when he lumbered
down the steps among the flowers. Also, he wheezed
hard.

Tess, I knew, was about to scream, "Get on with
it!" It would have made anybody's scalp crawl to see
the leisurely and smiling way in which Clarke drained
his glass, shook out the nearly empty bottle, and
poured more sweet champagne.

Whatever else Martin Clarke was, he was a vain

man. And his vanity must have been scraped raw. Yet he gave no sign of it.

"Ah, Doctor," he said. "I was wondering whether you would honor us. The inspector was just about to tell us how Logan was murdered. Weren't you, Inspector?"

"Yes."

"Then do it!" cried Gwyneth Logan, coming to life. It was the first time she had spoken. She sat bolt upright, in a green Robin Hood hat, her fingers twisting a handbag until it was almost doubled in two. "I was there. They thought I was a (what do you call it?) an accomplice, until I told them different. What did happen?"

Dr. Fell bowed gravely to her, swept off his shovel hat, and indicated by pantomime that he wanted to sit down beside her.

"By the way, ma'am," said Dr. Fell. "We may as well clear up rather an important point here." He extended his crutch-headed stick and pointed it at Clarke. "That is the man, isn't it, whom you've been in the habit of meeting at the Victoria and Albert Museum?"

"Yes. That's the man," answered Gwyneth. "Oh, Martin, why deny it?"

"I knew it!" whispered Tess, and pinched at my arm.

Clarke's suavity had begun to turn.

"You were saying, Inspector?"

"About the secret of this house," continued Elliot; and a dead silence fell in the gaudy garden.

"The question was this. What did we know about the real history of the Longwoods, either in 1820 or

227

1920? About Norbert in 1820, only that he was a scientist writing pamphlets in that year with three others whose names were Arago, Boisgiraud, and Sir Humphrey Davy; and that he died mysteriously in that year. That's all.

"But about Herbert Harrington Longwood in 1920 — well, that's different. We've got a good deal of information about him. He thoroughly rebuilt this house." Elliot paused. "He installed electric light and modern plumbing. He built the billiard-room annex of the east wing. He raised the ceiling of the dining-room, making the room more spacious but destroying the usefulness of the bedrooms just above it. He tore the paneling out of the downstairs hall. Finally, he built a new fireplace, a brick fireplace, in the study. And he did all this using a gang of workmen imported from Guernsey, who would not be likely to talk much hereabouts afterwards.

"An interesting character, that fellow. Everybody hereabouts testifies to his character — "

Tess interrupted him. She had put her fingers to her temples, with a wild air of concentration. She peered through them at Elliot, and spoke with difficulty.

"Wait! Please wait! Is that the same man who was mad about his family history and records? And loved the idea of having a haunted house? And was mad about practical jokes? And so, since there weren't any children to frighten, he *made* it into a haunted house? Is that what you mean?"

"Bull's-eye," observed the heavy and grimly affable voice of Dr. Fell. "Whang in the gold."

"But how?"

"Yes. Let the doctor tell it," requested Clarke, with

unshaken urbanity. "After all, what the inspector said was only His Master's Voice. He was only repeating a parrot lesson. Not very intelligent of you, Inspector. And rather dangerous. Can't Dr. Fell speak for himself?"

Dr. Fell, at the moment, looked rather dangerous himself.

"Why, sir, it will hardly be necessary for me to speak. You can see for yourself. In a very few minutes we shall have a couple of workmen here. With your permission (and even, I fear, without it) we are going to begin some alterations of our own. Frankly, sir, we are going to tear your blasted house to pieces, in the firm expectation of revealing as cruel and ingenious a murder trick as comes within my experience." His face became fiery. He struck the ferrule of his stick sharply on the stones. "And we shall begin by opening up that brick fireplace in the study."

Clarke's voice grew shrill.

"Opening it up? God help us, are you back on Morrison's old obsession of a secret passage? That is a solid mantelpiece. You proved as much yourself."

"Granted," agreed Dr. Fell.

"Well?"

"It is a solid mantelpiece. No crack or crevice exists in it. Every brick is safe and smooth-joined with mortar. But there is something buried in it. A small thing, d'ye see: not half as big as my hand." Dr. Fell held up his hand. "A dead thing, too. Yet something which can become, on occasion, horribly and viperishly alive."

Nobody spoke, though I thought Gwyneth Logan was going to scream. The sky had darkened so that the beech trees above and beyond stood out against clear silver; and the garden was being drained of its color.

"You will easily spot the truth," continued Dr. Fell, "if you clear your minds of atmosphere, and forget the spell which our friend Mr. Clarke has tried to throw over your wits. Just ask the simple question: What happened here? And get a reply in plain words.

"Here is the reply, in plain words. A number of articles have been made to move. That's all. Kindly note that not one of those articles is at all difficult to move, nor did any of them move very far. A revolver was made to 'jump.' A chandelier, already so delicately balanced that the lightest draught will make it move, was set swinging. The pendulum of a clock, a very delicate balance, was also set swinging. Finally, we were first told that a wooden chair — perplexity of perplexities! — was made to 'jump.' But, by thunder, it wasn't a wooden chair! It was a flimsy iron chair on greased wheels, such as you see on the back porch. And now the sun breaks out. Now the darkness divides and the birds sing again. For we see at last the connecting link: that each one of these objects was made of *metal*."

Dr. Fell leaned forward, making a face like a Dame in a pantomime.

"Do I need to tell you now what is buried in that mantelpiece? Buried just below the surface, under the thickness of half a brick? Buried cunningly an inch to the left of a revolver muzzle? Buried in such fashion that, when the current was switched on, the revolver would respond by jumping forward a fraction of an inch?"

He paused.

With infinite labor he propelled himself to his feet, grunted, growled, and swung round on Martin Clarke. His big voice sounded clearly in the darkening garden.

He said:

"I mean, of course, an electromagnet."

XIX

Dr. Fell resumed, as though speaking confidentially to the sundial:

"Any schoolboy knows about electromagnets, and could construct you one in a few minutes. Take a small piece of soft iron; wind it round with as many coils of insulated copper wire as you need; and send an electric current through it. You then have a powerful magnet which can be turned on or off at will.

"The strength of the magnet depends on the number of ampere turns, the strength of the current employed, multiplied by the number of turns in the coils. In plainer words: the more wire you wind round her, the stronger she is. You could construct a magnet big enough and strong enough to lift a ton of scrap iron—in fact, they're used commercially for just that purpose. But all we need here is a miniature, matchbox affair.

"To set a chandelier swinging! Embed your magnet under a plaster ceiling just beside the beam. Give her 'bursts': That is, keep turning the current on and off until the iron chandelier gets up momentum and begins to swing wildly. The same neat effect can be managed with the metal pendulum of a clock, by burying the magnet just under a plaster wall in the angle where the clock stands cater-cornered. I need hardly add that the power of an electromagnet is not materially affected by intervening surfaces, such as wood or plaster or brick, provided the surface is not *too* devilish thick. The late Harry Houdini (upon whom be peace!) used to stand in front of a bolted door, and draw the inside bolt by using on ordinary magnet from outside.

"I myself, as a boy, once constructed an electro-magnet for the purpose of . . ."

"When you were a boy?" cried Tess. "Were they invented then?"

Dr. Fell blinked at her.

"My dear," he said mildly, "you overwhelm me. Do you know when the principle of the electromagnet was first discovered?"

"No."

"In the year 1820," replied Dr. Fell. "It was discovered almost simultaneously by three eminent scientists whose names, curiously enough, were Arago, Boisgiraud, and Davy. They were not doctors, as Mr. Clarke misled you to believe: or at least they are not remembered as doctors. They were men of science. But then Mr. Clarke had not mentioned them, you know. It was young Morrison who brought them up, so a bit of misdirection had to be used. Norbert Longwood appears to have made a fourth to this trio of scientists who even then were experimenting with electricity, in the form of the galvanic battery, and 'bombarding each other with pamphlets.' "

Clarke had not moved.

You could see his white hair against the gathering dusk, and his white teeth as he smiled. He was as quiet as a tarantula. Dr. Fell never once glanced in that direction.

"Go to hell," Clarke said softly and pleasantly.

Still the doctor did not look round.

"That," he explained to Tess, "is the sort of obscure and good-for-nothing information I enjoy collecting. It—harrumph—made me look out for electromagnets before I had been hearing about the case for ten minutes.

"We don't know how Norbert Longwood really died. Since he was experimenting with electricity, it must have seemed to the whole countryside so weird and devilish that foul play would have been suspected if he had died of green-apple colic. He passes, leaving only a smell of smoke and burning.

"But, by thunder, we do know how the butler Polson died in 1920!

"Reflect. The late Herbert Harrington Longwood, in all probability, had no criminal intentions at all. He thought he was only playing a harmless joke. We learn that he was a great one for studying family records: it seems likely that he heard of old Norbert's interest in crude and primitive electromagnets; and suddenly realized how, with a modern application of the method, he could create a 'haunted house' as a rich, ripe joke with which to bedevil his friends.

"Herbert Harrington Longwood had the house wired for at least three—very probably more—electromagnets. They would work off the ordinary house current. The wires would be hidden in the walls, and would lead to concealed switches . . . where? That, d'ye see, is the point. For the ingenuity of the scheme is that the man who works the magnet need not be in the same room or anywhere near at the time.

"Poor old Polson's death was the result of a tragic accident; yet an accident which should have been foreseen.

"The butler goes downstairs late at night to lock up. His employer, chuckling at the joke which is to be played, tries out the mechanism. Well, what would be the effect of that? What would be the effect on an old family retainer who — contrary to all laws of sense or reason — sees a chandelier begin to swing, with more angling and wilder momentum each second? I think he would lose his head. His first impulse would be to stop it: stop it any cost. He drags a tall chair under the chandelier. He stretches up his fingers to arrest that unholy movement. But he cannot quite reach it. He stands on tiptoe, groping. He loses his head completely. He makes a final, desperate little jump; his fingers close on the iron; he loses his balance . . .

"And his employer, white and horrified, hears the weight fall. This employer's only intention was to frighten a servant with the spectacle of a swinging chandelier. Instead his joke has killed an old friend."

Dr. Fell hunched his shoulders under the box-pleated cape, and looked at me.

"You see, my lad. Polson never swung himself back and forth on the chandelier. Like everybody else, you put the cart before the horse. The chandelier was already swinging; and it swung him."

After this, two voices spoke almost together.

"Andy—" cried Tess.

"Pins—" I said.

Dr. Fell scowled. His voice was angry.

"Yes. You perceived the masked truth. Young Hunter, during the repairs to this house, must have uncovered certain wires for whose purpose he could not account. The death trap was still here, hidden and unimpaired by time. Hunter did not know what the jiggery-pokery was, except that it somehow concerned electricity. Let us say that he tumbled to the trick just before tea on Saturday, when I asked him to climb up on the chair under the chandelier; and the chandelier very slightly moved. (You noticed his expression then?) He said nothing. But he got some pins—"

"Why pins?" I demanded. "Why pins?"

"Because iron, when once acted on by an electro-magnet, becomes in its own turn magnetic. Is that clear? If such a force had been used, the chandelier would be magnetic in its top parts. Get some pins. Climb on a stepladder. If the pins adhere to the iron, your theory is proved with a resounding Q.E.D. Unfortunately, something happened to the too-curious Mr. Hunter."

The doctor's voice was heavy and grim. He hesitated, puffing out his cheeks.

"That is all I have to say," he growled. "Elliot, this is your affair."

Clarke laughed.

Those constant chuckles, that tireless amusement, rasped against the nerves each time it occurred. And you gradually realized, not without uneasiness, that it was not bravado. Clarke was not alarmed in the least. I felt in my bones that some new twist was coming—

some new devilry would spring out of ambush — some further upheaval would strike us between the eyes again.

This case was not finished.

"You've been sunk in a long, long silence, Inspector," Clarke remarked. "Have you no observations of your own? No accusations? I deplore your lack of originality."

Elliot's jaws shut up hard.

"Plenty of accusations," he said. "You deny you're responsible for all this?"

"Oh, *God*," breathed Gwyneth Logan, from her quiet corner at the other side. The words came as though with realization or inspiration. She put her hands to her forehead as once before we had seen her do, when recalling the details of her husband's murder. Clarke paid no attention.

"I deny it absolutely."

"Do you deny that an electromagnet was used to fire the gun that killed Mr. Logan?"

"I neither affirm it nor deny it. I leave you to prove it, if you can."

Elliot nodded. Reaching into his brief case, he took out a .45 revolver, dark and wicked glinting in dusk. From his lapel he detached an object too small to be seen in that light; but you could guess what it was. He held it near the barrel of the revolver. There was a short, slight click. He held out the weapon barrel foremost, so that we could all see the pin adhering to its polished curve.

"Proof, Inspector?" inquired Clarke.

Elliot ignored this. "Do you deny, sir, that you took this gun out of Mrs. Logan's room on Saturday morning?"

"I do."

"Do you deny that you were standing on a box outside the north window of the study, when Mr. Logan was shot?"

"I do."

"And with your hand inside the open window?"

There was a silence.

It crept up and closed. If Clarke could get away from the python of accumulated facts which was gradually tightening round him, tightening and crushing against arms, legs, and even neck, he must be a miracle-worker. We waited. It was so quiet that we could hear the deep hum of evening traffic along the Southend road.

"I said, sir: with your hand inside the window?"

"It would be very interesting, Inspector, if you could prove that. How do you propose to prove it?"

"By two witnesses." Elliot swung round. "Mrs. Logan. Is that the man?"

"Yes," said Gwyneth. "Yes, yes, yes!"

"Well, well, well!" beamed Clarke, mimicking her tone, though not unkindly. "And your other witness?"

"Mr. Enderby."

Clarke laughed outright. "But where is Enderby? Can you confront me with him? Did he tell you he saw me outside that window?"

"No. He told—"

"Ah, hearsay evidence! But surely even a policeman knows enough law to be aware that that won't do."

"We'll have Mr. Enderby presently."

THE MAN WHO COULD NOT SHUDDER

"I doubt it."

Tess and I exchanged glances. It was growing intolerably hot down in our bowl, with a baking heat which despite the dampness seemed to breathe out of the ground itself. And doubtless it was only caused by excitement.

"Do you further deny, sir, that you did all the decorations for that house? Arranged the furniture, and so on?"

"Of that dread crime, Inspector, I admit I am guilty."

"Yes. Good. Then," said Elliot, "why did you put the typewriter table by the south window?" As Clarke started to speak, Elliot made a sharp gesture and continued. "A south window, I don't have to tell you, is the worst of all places for anyone who wants to use a typewriter. You get the sun in your eyes all day. You also get the traffic from the main road — "

(There must have been a lot of traffic going to Southend that night.)

" — whereas you had a big north window, giving the ideal light and facing a quiet garden. Why didn't you put the typewriter table by the north window?"

"Inspector, you should have been an interior decorator."

"Isn't it a fact," said Elliot, within an ace of losing his temper, "that you put the typewriter table there so anybody sitting at it would face a gun hung above the fireplace? Isn't that why you got Herbert Longwood's old collection of guns out of the attic and hung them up? Isn't it a fact that there's a concealed electric switch under the window sill of the north window; so that all you needed to do was glance through the window, see Mr. Logan's position, and press the switch when he picked up a typewriter carefully planted in the right place?"

"Is it a fact?" inquired Clarke, with interest. "But what about the others?"

"The others?"

"The other two (or three, or four, or perhaps five, six, seven) switches? I was in your company, remember, when the grandfather clock was started. Was I near any possible switch? Weren't my hands free and unoccupied?"

Elliot smiled grimly.

"Maybe they were. But your feet weren't. I just happened to remember that swaying movement you kept making, back and forth from your toes to your heels, when you stood over against the wall in the hall." His eyes narrowed. "Not a bad idea, sir! The switch for the magnet under a loose tile in the floor. Set your weight on the tile; take it off; set it on again. Nobody suspects you, because you're in plain sight. And yet . . .

"The only trouble with your scheme, Mr. Clarke, is that you're now caught flat-heeled. It's a fine trick so long as nobody tumbles to the magnet. But, once we dig the magnet out of the mantelpiece in the study, and the switch out of the sill under north window, you're for it. We can prove you were at the window. And, the second we find that switch—"

Tess held up her hand to implore silence.

"That noise isn't traffic," she said.

Looking back on the events now, it is difficult to describe what happened: or, rather, to remember which of many pictures comes first in a nightmare.

I think our first full intimation that Longwood House was afire was not the dull and growing roar, with a crackling that spread and ran beneath it like fat in a skillet. It was not the explosion which followed. It was, instead, the blue-yellow curl of flame which curved up gracefully, with the lightness of a dancer, as melting glass splintered in one pane of the study window. Then the whole place seemed to light up inside like a gas range.

It was the stolid Elliot whose voice rose to a snarl of defeat and despair. We heard it clearly above the gathering roar; but so confused were movements, voices, faces, in that overset garden that it was impossible to tell who spoke.

"God damn us for slow-poke fools!" the voice said, as the back kitchen gushed flame. "There goes the evidence. That's what he wanted the petrol for."

"Down!" said somebody else. "Down! Get down! Some of that stuff is in airtight tins—"

There were only two explosions, neither of them very heavy. But it was as well that we were in a garden nearly as deep as the height of a man's head, bulwarked against attack. Broken glass sang in the wind of the first blast; you saw it glitter before you ducked. A fire-arrow of burning shingle, thrown high, sailed into the hollyhocks behind, and another, which Elliot stamped out, fell at the foot of the sundial.

It was holding Tess's head down as though I were trying to drown her. I remember Gwyneth crying, "All our clothes," or, "My fur coat," or something of the sort. Sound had become a blur under the one overwhelming noise of the fire, and the air turned greasy with smoke as an intolerable yellow brightness

241

glimmered through.

Elliot ran up to the top of the garden steps, but turned back at the second explosion. In pantomime he asked Dr. Fell whether anybody had been left inside; and the doctor returned a, "No, thank God," with his face much less ruddy in the growing glare of light.

That was when we all thought to look at Clarke.

You might have thought he would show triumph. But he didn't. His white suit was smudged. He leaned back against the bench as though exhausted: half sick, and wholly venomous. His light eyes showed up clear against the tanned face. The last glass of bad, sweet champagne stood untasted on the table.

"My house," he said. "My beautiful house."

"You didn't want this to happen, of course?" Elliot shouted at him.

"You parcel of thick-witted fools," said Clarke, with a kind of sick suavity. "Of course . . . I didn't. I didn't kill Logan."

Someone coughed. Heat was descending scorchingly: prickling the eyelids, fanning the ears, feeling over the whole face, while the tang of smoke crept into the nostrils and stifled them. A burning ember flew high, and drifted down softly by Clarke's knee. He paid no attention.

"I didn't kill Logan," he said again. "If you said I wanted him dead for making a fool of me, that would be true. But I didn't kill him. I never take *any* chances."

And then:

"Do you think I'd set fire to my own house? You can't prove I did kill Logan—now. But I can't prove who did."

"We'd better get out of here," shouted Elliot. "There won't be any more explosions. Up the stairs and run for it. Come *on*."

"Fire engines," said Clarke, suddenly getting up off the bench. "What good are you? Why are you standing there? Can't you get the fire engines?"

"It's too late for that," said Elliot. "She'll have to burn now."

At the top of the steps we faced a solid glare which turned us blind. I threw my coat over Tess's face, and ran her round the side of the garden to a point far back from the burning house which was now hardly to be recognized as a house. Elliot took care of Gwyneth Logan, Dr. Fell followed, and Clarke trotted at the rear.

The next person we saw was Inspector Grimes. He came pelting across a field to the west, his face turned sideways to the blaze. In the distance we could hear a yowling of motorcar horns being punched in the main road. Inspector Grimes vaulted over a rail fence. By the light of a pillar of fire which sketched out shakily every detail in the landscape, down to the pattern of a leaf and the fine hairs on the backs of Grimes's hands, the inspector's face seemed to jump about in front of us.

"Oo-er!" was all he said, from deep in his throat. "Ooer!"

"Alarm —" began Elliot.

"Turned in alarm," gasped the other, making a telegraphic gesture. "A. A. Box. Down there, though. All safe?"

"Yes."

"See you later. Important evidence."

"What evidence?"

"Murder," said Inspector Grimes, gulping back his breath. "Never mind now. See you later."

"Man," said Elliot, "what do you think you can do? Niagara Falls wouldn't put that one out. She's gone to glory and our proof with her."

"Mr. Clarke," Grimes confided. "Where is he?"

"He's here. Just over there. What about him?"

"He didn't do it," said Grimes simply. "Didn't do the murder, I mean."

Everywhere we were being invaded by alien shapes and presences. A cow, fire-stung, galloped past from somewhere. A motorist, having left his car in the main road, ran round charitably to shout and ask whether we knew there was a fire. But every other interest or feeling had been blotted out.

"Why couldn't you have told us, sir?" demanded Inspector Grimes. "He wasn't down on the beach, like he said." Grimes turned to Elliot. "He was in the village street at Prittleton, or inside the pub. From a quarter to ten on Saturday morning, to ten minutes past eleven anyway, he was either sitting on a bench outside the *Startled Stag* or inside in the bar. He deliberately made us think he hadn't got an alibi, and set us looking all over the seaside in the wrong direction, when he's got the best alibi there ever was in the world."

"Is this true?"

Grimes shouted back at him.

"There's half the village to prove it. Two or three people with him all the time. Including the bank manager, who stopped to speak to him outside the pub at just ten o'clock. What do you think of that?"

"Ah!" said Clarke, softly and richly.

He was attempting, with a handkerchief, to clear the smudges from his coat and face. Also, he was himself again.

"But it can't be," snapped Elliot, staring alternately from Clarke to Grimes. "Two witnesses say they saw him look through the north window here at just ten o'clock . . . "

"Can't help that." Grimes's tone was flat. "Four witnesses (double on you, my lad) four witnesses including Mr. Perkins the bank manager, say he was sitting outside the *Startled Stag* at ten. They don't open till half-past."

Elliot swung round.

"It's quite true, Inspector," Clarke forestalled him.

"Then why didn't you tell me? Why give me that lie about being down on the beach?"

"To be quite candid, Inspector, because I hoped you and the good Dr. Fell would make fools of yourselves," replied Clarke.

He bent down a moment, hiding his face from the brilliant glare of the fire so that it should not again show itself convulsed with inner amusement.

"The fact is," he resumed, after coolly dusting his trousers with the handkerchief, and trying not to let a broad smile show, "the fact is, it is now time for me to say checkmate.

"Your case (you realize?) is up the spout. An alibi for me means that I am unquestionably cleared. Whatever I might have done with an electromagnet, and however I might have used it, I assuredly didn't operate it by remote control. If you admit — as, ultimately, you must — my presence among witnesses in Prittleton when Logan was shot, you can't possibly connect me with the murder. Your clever demonstration about the magnet makes that certain. You've overshot yourself, my friend. Who, may I ask, is unintelligent now?"

The brassy clanging of a bell, careening along the main road and beating up above the roar and crackle of flames, brought Clarke alert with a jerk. He finished wiping his face and neck with the handkerchief, and stowed it away. He brushed back his whitish hair with both hands.

"That will be the fire engines," he said. "You must excuse me."

Elliot, himself now looking a trifle ill, tried to restrain him.

"Then who was the man in the brown suit?" he demanded. "Who did look through that window at ten o'clock?"

"I am sorry," apologized Clarke. "Someone burned my house for me, and so I cannot tell you. Now you must excuse me, I repeat. I am going to a fire."

He pulled his arm loose, arranged the sleeve of the coat, and took several steps more. But he stopped once more, for he met Dr. Fell.

None of us is ever likely to forget the two of them standing there, silhouetted against the fire. Fine ashes were sifting down, some fiery and some a soft gray. There was Clarke, shortish and dapper in a white suit. There was Dr. Fell, a bulky weight with a red face and eyeglasses. Their brief exchange of words had a curious eighteenth-century flavor, with the fire bell clanging in the background. But Clarke so far forgot his famous good manners as to the laugh in the doctor's face.

"Sir," he said, "acknowledge yourself beaten."

"Sir," replied Dr. Fell, "apparently I must."

"Badly beaten, I think."

"So it seems."

"In fact, made a fool of."

"So it would seem. But I think, Mr. Clarke, that sometime in the future you and I will speak about this matter again."

"I think not," said Clarke, not without smugness. "As I am never tired of pointing out, I never take *any* chances."

XX

"Of course," said Dr. Fell thoughtfully, "you realize who was really at the bottom of it all, don't you?"

Both Tess and I can easily remember the precise day on which we heard the truth.

It was in the first week of September, 1939. Tess and I had been married for over two years. I had long ago finished the preceding narrative, and put it away in a drawer as eternally unfinished.

The Gargantuan doctor had dropped in (as he often does, living so close by) for tea. We were sitting in the garden of our place at Hampstead, which is small but very much loved by both of us. Clear and bright, the evening was drawing in. From that garden you could just manage to see in the sky the silver shape of a barrage balloon; but there was nothing else to remind you that, elsewhere, the great earth stirred.

The doctor, spread out in a wicker chair, smoked his black pipe and had an evening paper in his pocket. He made this remark out of as clear a sky as the one above us.

"Believe me," he went on, with a long rumbling sniff in his nose, "I have had a good reason for not being communicative about this. And, in any case, the question was rhetorical. You *don't* know who set the death trap. You don't know who stole the revolver out of Gwyneth Logan's room, and hung it up on the wall over the fireplace. You don't realize who wanted to kill Bentley Logan more than anything else in the world."

"Who?" asked Tess.

"As a matter of fact," said Dr. Fell, "it was your friend Andy Hunter."

This was the point at which Tess dropped the crossword puzzle she was doing, pencil and all. I dropped the match with which I was lighting a cigarette. But neither of us spoke, and presently the doctor went on.

He said:

"You see, my young 'uns, I never for two seconds believed that the button which controlled the electro-magnet was *in* the study itself—either under the window sill, or anywhere else. That would have been too easy for Herbert Harrison Longwood.

"What Elliot seemed to forget (and what I allowed him to forget) was that the last of the Longwoods had not confined his building operations to the study, the hall, and the dining-room. Not at all! He had carefully built on an extra wing: an excrescence: a destroyer of line: by adding that billiard-room on the east side. It is a curious fact that from the windows of the billiard room you got an excellent view into the nearer window of the study across the way."

He looked at me.

"It is still more curious that you and Andy Hunter were standing in the billiard-room, looking out, when Logan was shot. It is most interesting of all that you could both distinctly see Logan when he picked up the typewriter and brought the muzzle of the pistol in line with his forehead.

"Obviously, the person who shot Logan had to be somebody who could *see* Logan. Furthermore, the likeliest person to be the murderer was an impassioned and idealistic young man who for four months had been desperately in love with Gwyneth Logan—"

I stopped him.

"Hold on, Doctor! Wait! Are you telling us that Gwyneth and Andy had known each other before that week end?"

"Of course. You make that plain enough in your manuscript, even if you do not appear to realize what you are writing. Perhaps you've forgotten that within five minutes of their having apparently met for the first time, Andy Hunter gravely handed Mrs. Logan a sherry and bitters without even inquiring what she wanted to drink?"

Tess and I looked at each other.

"You carefully record how he asked each other person what that person wanted to drink. It was just after your arrival at Longwood House in a body. But he handed out the sherry and bitters automatically, without a word. Both of them were a bit rattled, as we can understand.

"Curiously enough, precisely the same thing happened the other way round. It was at tea on Saturday. I saw it happen. After asking each other person how many lumps of sugar we required, *she* put three lumps (three, observe) into *his* cup and passed it over without a query. She knew how many lumps he took. After all, they had met often enough in the restaurant at the Victoria and Albert Museum."

"But Clarke—" began Tess. She hesitated, shook her head as though to clear it, and was silent.

"The first of these instances," pursued Dr. Fell, "I heard from Sonia, the maid. (I mentioned it to Mrs. Logan in the pub at Southend, if you recall?) A very sharp girl, Sonia. With regard to the second, you are good enough to point out in your narrative that Saturday afternoon was the first time anybody had tasted a cup of tea in that house; so there was no opportunity for her to have learned his requirements in the matter of sugar.

"However, those are merely outward instances. If you think back to the words, thoughts, deeds, and even atmospheres of those two, the love element (at least on his side) burns bright and strong. You recall that wildly out-of-character speech of his, when he accused you of not having regard for the 'spiritual' things? An echo of his overmastering love for Gwyneth Logan. Observe, too, that in the stress of excitement she once threw a glass at him: a liberty she took with nobody else. Observe also that, when he was hurt in the fall of the chandelier, it was Gwyneth Logan who went in to be with him at the nursing home. — But perhaps," added Dr. Fell, "I had better tell you the story?"

Tess spoke in a hollow voice.

"I think," she agreed, "perhaps you had."

It is difficult for Dr. Fell to look malevolent, but he managed it then.

"Clarke was the evil genius, of course," he said. "Clarke came to England with the deliberate intention of compassing Logan's death. He knew all about the house with the hidden death trap, though Herbert Longwood had not originally intended it as a death trap at all. (As you can guess, the idea was merely to startle visitors when a revolver jumped and fired a blank cartridge from the wall: without a misplaced typewriter and typewriter table, nobody would ever have been in danger.) Clarke wanted to compass Logan's death. But he would not, emphatically, kill Logan himself. No, no. He never took *any* chances.

"At this time, Andy Hunter and Gwyneth Logan had already met—"

"Just a moment," I interposed. "We're not questioning any of this; but how do you know it?"

Dr. Fell rubbed the side of his nose.

"From young Hunter himself," he explained apologetically. "When he recovered his life and his reason after that smash with the chandelier, he was (you recall?) for many months a mentally sick and chastened man. It cured him, fortunately, of his infatuation for Gwyneth Logan. But at the time of the murder he was frantic.

"Their affair had not been precisely platonic, as you've guessed; though she tried her best to make it 'spiritual' and put him into an even worse state.

Didn't you see it stamped on his forehead then? Didn't you observe his behavior all the day after he learned she had (shall we say?) granted favors to her own husband on Friday night?"

"Yes," admitted Tess. "But I thought . . . Never mind. Go on."

"Now I don't wish to say anything against the character of the attractive Gwyneth Logan," pursued Dr. Fell. "I understand she is cutting quite a dash as a merry widow on the Riviera these days. But, if you've observed her with half an eye, you'll have seen that she is a woman who has to dramatize herself or die. That little affair with Hunter was her safety valve for emotional acting. She entirely convinced him that Logan was a sadistic brute who led her a life no woman could endure. (By the way, Hunter twice incautiously let this slip to you later on.) Her poses before him were amazing. There was, he says, talk of murder. He swore he would deliver her from Logan. She never wanted anything of the sort. Logan was the sound sort of man who could provide for her. It was dreams again, exciting dreams. But, if she didn't mean it — by thunder, Andy Hunter did!

"And, at this stage of the game, enter Clarke.

"The museum enthusiast goes once to the Victoria and Albert, he goes twice, he goes three times. He always sees the lovers, one of whom (Gwyneth) he already knows. He watches. He learns much of what firework vows are being made. Thus he gets an inspiration from heaven.

"If Andy Hunter were to kill Logan . . . or if things were to be so maneuvered that Hunter got an opportunity to kill Logan without ever even suspecting Clarke had given him that opportunity . . .

"Admirable!

"For (a) Longwood House appears for sale on the market; (b) Hunter is an architect; (c) discreet questioning reveals that Hunter is a friend of one Robert Morrison, whose acquaintance Clarke already has.

"Oh, yes. He let *you* send him to Andy Hunter. He even let *you* suggest Hunter as a guest for the house party, knowing that the suggestion was obvious and certain. A rare gentleman, Mr. Clarke. Always wangling, always maneuvering, always deftly shifting pieces so that he never has to undertake the responsibility about anything. As we know, he never takes any chances.

"Now hear what happened:

"At the beginning of the last week in March, after getting the keys of Longwood House and an order-to-view from the agent, Clarke called on Andy Hunter. Professionally, that is. He asked Hunter to go down into the country and inspect the place carefully. He added that he had heard there were curious relics and papers in the attic — handing over also a key, a key to a box, which he had NOT got from the house agent.

"Hunter visited the house. As a matter of human curiosity, he opened this box stuffed with ancient papers. And in front of his eyes he found a neat little drawing: a plan showing the electromagnet trick in the study, with details of how it could be turned into a death trap with the proper placing of a typewriter table and a typewriter."

Tess intervened.

"Wait!" she cried. "That old Longwood man — the one who caused all the trouble — he was supposed to be great at drawing plans. Do you mean he left that plan there?"

Dr. Fell chuckled. But it was not his usual chuckle, and it died immediately.

"Hardly. Clarke merely made use of his knowledge of that habit. It was Clarke's plan, in printing so that it could not be identified. It was done on paper, with a pencil. It was dust-saturated. For Clarke, as you know, had added his own little twist of the typewriter-table murder.

"The next few days were the crucial time. If Hunter came back to him, and said, 'Good God, sir, look here! An electromagnet in the mantelpiece. A gadget to kill! What do you think of this?' For, if Hunter had no idea of murder, he would say that. It's sufficiently unusual an attribute to a house so that any ordinary honest architect would certainly comment on it. But Andy Hunter said nothing.

"Clarke must have hugged himself. 'You recommend the house as sound and a safe buy, Mr. Hunter?' 'Yes, sir, definitely.' 'Good! That is satisfactory. I trust you will join a little housewarming party when I do move in? Only a few — including my good friends, the Logans.'

"And the blood went into that poor young devil's head and eyes; and he says he had to hold to the back of a chair to steady himself.

"If he *had* reported the electromagnet, then that would have been that. Clarke would simply not have bought the place, and tried some other plan. For, as we know, he never takes any chances.

"Parenthetically, I may remark that Andy Hunter never did know there was more than one electromagnet in the house. He never suspected until Saturday afternoon, when I asked him to get up on a chair with his hands raised under the chandelier, and a draught from the open door (nothing more) moved the chandelier. Then, he says, he realized all of a sudden what might have killed the butler. Immediately afterwards, the grandfather clock mysteriously started in the hall—Clarke did that little bit of business, just as Elliot said—and Andy Hunter could be thundering well certain there was something fishy beyond what he knew about. He got some pins and a stepladder, and climbed up in the middle of the night to see whether the iron was magnetized. He never found, or looked for, the switch controlling the magnet; and we still don't know where it was. He simply gave the chandelier a brisk push; it clanked and rang, and started to swing with an ease that he couldn't believe; he staggered; he lost his balance on a shaky stepladder as the thing surged back at him; he grabbed for support—

"That's all. Another near tragedy.

"But I have told you the end of the story first. Let's return.

"During April, when the house was being redecorated for the housewarming, Clarke kept a close eye on the lovers at the Victoria and Albert. Once he deliberately walked into Mrs. Logan there just after she had left Hunter. Once again, apparently by chance, he met her there. He fell to meeting her in other places too, the object being outwardly a little mild flirtation and really to keep tabs on her emotional pulse."

"Is that why," demanded Tess, "she admitted Clarke was the man she'd been meeting there?"

"Yes. You understand, she thought that was safe. There really hadn't been anything in those episodes. But, as she put it, wild horses wouldn't have made her mention Hunter's name. Because that affair was not so innocent; there was a little hotel, not far from the museum itself, where, if the register were to be examined —

"Gwyneth Logan is a very modest young lady. Even with her husband dead, she was still modest.

"While keeping an eye on the lovers, Clarke furnished the house. 'I think, Mr. Hunter, I had better have a typewriter in the study. Yes, and a typewriter table. Now let me see. Where shall I put it? North wall or south wall?' And that humilated young scapegoat, burning with hatred against Bentley Logan, writhing in his soul because he is taking advantage of this good-natured employer, says: 'South wall, sir. Over there. I could have them rig you up a light above it.' Clarke considers. 'Well, Mr. Hunter, if that is your advice!' Covering himself again, you perceive. For, as we know, he never takes any chances.

"And so we come to the ghost party, and the murder on Saturday. Your own memories will fill up the gaps."

"No, they won't," I said. "For the thousandth time, who was the man in the brown suit? Somebody was standing outside the window. Who was it?"

"Julian Enderby," answered Dr. Fell affably.

"*Julian?*"

"H'mf, yes. Oh, yes. Ho! You—er—haven't seen much of him in recent months, have you?"

Tess laughed. "We never see him. He married a most distinguished gal; and I never do get on with 'em somehow. He's doing well, I hear."

Dr. Fell wheezed. The corners of his bandit's mustache were pulled down, and his lower lip outthrust.

"He'd have done much less well," growled the doctor viciously, "if he'd dared to tell the police that story he told you in the bedroom in the middle of the night. He tried it out on you; but at the last moment he couldn't screw up his courage to tell it to the police. He couldn't, even though Clarke promised him much fine legal business if he did tell it . . . "

"NOT CLARKE AGAIN?"

"What else did you expect? Do you follow the twists of that?

"Julian Enderby, walking in a strange garden for the first time, heard a strange woman's voice giving interesting speech through a partly open window. He was violently and sneakingly curious. He saw a wooden box, left there by a gardener with no sinister or ulterior purpose at all. He put the box near the window, climbed up, and looked . . . "

"Then he did see the murder after all?"

"He did. As we compelled him to admit, when he didn't want to present himself as an eavesdropper before an inquest, and at first denied it."

"But afterwards? The second story?"

"Clarke's. Clarke's mind is still at work. He conceives another scheme. Genially, and in strictest confidence, he speakes to Enderby that same evening. 'Sir, you are in an unpleasant position; your professional friends won't like it.' 'I know they won't.' 'Then why, between ourselves, admit that you looked in at all? Why not say you saw someone else there?' 'Mr. Clarke, you insult me. That would be a lie; and, anyway, it would make my position even worse.' 'Not at all, if you say you saw someone there, and that person doesn't deny it . . . meaning me.'

"That was the way it was put up to him. 'Say you saw me, or someone like me.' And much good business might come to the energetic Mr. Enderby from the wealthy Mr. Clarke?"

Again I called for an interruption.

"But why should even Clarke *want* Julian to say that?"

Dr. Fell sighed gustily.

"I fear, my lad, I very much fear that our friend Clarke took an instantaneous and violent dislike to both Inspector Elliot and your humble servant. In fine, he was laying a trap for us. He did lay a trap for us; and Elliot fell into it.

"Clarke already had his alibi. (Don't you recall the expression on his face when he came back from the pub and found Logan had been murdered, as he hoped?) He could blow our accusations sky-high whenever he liked.

"He wanted us to accuse him. He wanted us to think he was the man at the window, and to believe that the switch for the gun magnet, if we discovered it, was under the window sill. Then, when we accused him, he could make absolute chuttering fools of us. He would show us up for dunderheads, and feed that vanity which made him decide to compass Logan's death merely because the man infuriated him by doing him down in a business deal: he would do this, I say, by playing the ace of trumps in the form of his alibi.

"Hence his proposition to Julian Enderby. Now, it is doubtful whether Enderby ever really intended to tell that whopper to the police. He is too cautious; and I believe he smelled a rat. When tried out the story on you, it seems clear from your description of his behavior that he was inclined to trust Clarke even less than you did. But Clarke hoped for the best.

"And Clarke would do more. If we—Elliot and I— tumbled to the hocus-pocus with the electromagnet, Clarke would not be content with proving his own innocence. He would make more outstanding asses of us by solving the mystery himself. He would outline the case against Hunter; he would trace the flex of the magnet back to a window by which Hunter had been standing; he would, inevitably, send that young man to the gallows. And this, by thunder," said Dr. Fell, snorting so savagely that sparks flew from his pipe, "I was determined to prevent.

"I had already determined that Clarke was the scene-shifter and Hunter the actual criminal. I knew that a magnet had been used. (By the way, you now can understand why several weapons in that tier of pistols seemed to be 'disarranged,' ragged and pulled out of line, though there were no fingerprints on them. None of them had been changed in their positions, as the too-imaginative Sonia suggested and even you imagined. But they had been pulled about, because the magnet acted on them as well as on the .45 revolver; and their different positions were in ratio to their weight and their distance from the magnet.)

"But how in blazes was I to circumvent Clarke?

"The man was in an almost impregnable position. He had done nothing that could be proved against him. Once accused, he would retaliate by accusing Hunter. Even worse: I dared not tell Elliot the truth. Elliot is a scholar and a gentleman; but he is also a policeman. His duty would have been to arrest Hunter, and he would have done it. Which would have been a pity, because in actual fact . . . "

Here Dr. Fell coughed, hesitated, and did not pursue that line.

"There seemed only one way out of the impasse. You saw how sick and defeated Clarke looked when his house went up in flames. As he said, it had done him. We couldn't prove he had committed the murder, but he couldn't prove who else had. Once I made sure the switch of the magnet was actually in the billiard-room, hidden under an invisibly hinged board where Hunter had only to tread on it, I realized it was the only way out of the impasse. That . . . harrumph, ha! . . . that was why I set fire to the house."

If the garden had tilted up in our faces at that moment, I could not have had a more reeling sensation in the head and stomach. Tess let out a kind of squeak.

"You set fire—"

"Sh-h!" urged Dr. Fell, starting guiltily and peering round as though there might be a policeman lurking in the laurels. "Do not, I beg of you, shout the fact. Arson is a serious offense, though I cannot (alas) feel that any destruction of Clarke's goods and chattels is likely to weigh very heavily in my conscience.

"I set a slow fuse, after ascertaining that there was nobody in the house, and then joined you in the sunken garden. Not being an actor of outstanding merit, I feared that my expressive dial might betray me; and I had some very queasy moments at the time of those explosions. But let me assure you it was the only way. You see, there was still another reason why I didn't want Hunter arrested for the crime."

"Which was?"

"That Hunter, in fact, was not the murderer."

Things were getting worse and worse.

"But you said—"

"No," returned Dr. Fell firmly. "I said he wanted to kill Logan. I said he stole the pistol from Gwyneth's room that morning . . . she had told him about it, of course, as a warning against what Logan might do . . . and hung it up on the wall. I said he set the trap and prepared to spring it. All that was quite true. But I did not say he committed the murder."

"Then who did commmit it?"

Dr. Fell turned his head round ponderously. He blew another film of ash off the bowl of his pipe. His little eyes, with a quizzical twinkle behind the eye-glasses, fixed steadily on me.

"As a matter of fact," he said, "*you* did."

Pause.

"I fear I startled you," he resumed, as the metaphorical black specks ceased to whirl, and my breath crept back to my lungs. "But don't misunderstand me. This is not *Roger Ackroyd* all over again. I am not accusing you of being the villain who planned the murder, consummated it, and concealed any facts in your manuscript. But, d'ye see, you really did shoot Logan.

"Andy Hunter is the wrong type of man for a murderer. He couldn't have done it, and at the last moment knew he couldn't do it. He planned the trap, got ready, stood by the window — and realized he hadn't the stomach for it.

"Don't you remember, he was not even looking at Logan when the shot was fired? He had made up his mind to give it up. He was going to tell you all about it. He turned away from the window, started to fill his pipe, and began: 'It's about this haunted house' — but he got no further. You, as you say, crowded after him. You trod on the board which completed the electric circuit. The revolver jumped and struck Logan dead. Then, as you later say, Andy Hunter turned slightly green and refused to say anything more. Archons of Athens! Can you wonder?"

Birds were bickering down at the end of the garden. It was some minutes before I could fully appreciate exactly what all this meant.

"Do you mean," I said, more than a trifle queasy about the stomach, "That I've been a murderer for over two years and have never known anything about it?"

Dr. Fell chuckled.

263

"In the technical sense, yes," he replied. "Logan's death was the result of a tragic accident like Hunter's own near-death. There you have the truth. I should not let the matter worry you, since no guilt could be charged to you even if the real facts were ever to come out.

"But the real truth will never come out now. Andy Hunter, alive and prosperous, is never likely to mention it. Gwyneth Logan could never tell it, because she does not know. Don't you realize she never even suspected Hunter? To her he was the 'nice boy' with whom it was impossible to associate any crime of violence; and, indeed, she was right. She believed, and still believes, that the murderer is Clarke.

"There was only one person who might have spoken: Clarke himself. He dared not accuse Hunter without actual evidence; for, as we know, he never takes any chances. Since the evidence went up in that gigantic bonfire, he has prudently kept mum. Up to this week, however, there was always the possibility that something might make him betray the truth . . . "

"And why not now?"

Dr. Fell scowled.

"Clarke's prophecy has been fulfilled. He always said, you remember, that there was going to be a war. He loathed and feared the prospect more than most men loathe and fear it. He decided that it was not prudent to remain in England in case of air attack."

Very slowly Dr. Fell drew out the newspaper which had been folded in his pocket. He held it out for a moment, and then let it drop on the grass. We saw the headlines:

LINER ATHENIA: FULL LIST OF VICTIMS

Dr. Fell got to his feet, sighing gustily as he propelled himself up on his crutch-headed stick. He put on his shovel hat. He arranged the box-pleated cape round his shoulders. And he stared up at the silver barrage balloon clear and lonely in the pink September sky.

"For, as we know," said Dr. Fell, "he never took *any* chances."

>>> If you've enjoyed this book and would like to discover more great vintage crime and thriller titles, as well as the most exciting crime and thriller authors writing today, visit: >>>

The Murder Room
Where Criminal Minds Meet

themurderroom.com